CW01636406

SUMMIT OF ALL FEARS

J.D. WHITELAW

RED DOG
UK

Published by RED DOG PRESS 2021

First Edition

Paperback ISBN 978-1-914480-28-7
Ebook ISBN 978-1-914480-29-4

www.reddogpress.co.uk

To my darling Anne-Marie, my wonderful Henry and all the wonderful days to come.

One

"ALWAYS REMEMBER... Next time, the star crook in our spotlight could be *yours*! Goodnight!"

The rapturous applause filled the studio, rattling the heavy lights and rigging on the ceiling. The crowd rose to its feet, clapping, cheering, shouting—elated. They moved as one big entity, all eyes locked on the stage at the front, their heroes bathed in the hard, artificial light.

Murray and Roberta Steiner stood centre stage. Hand in hand, they blew kisses to their adoring fans. Smiles as bright as the beaming studio lights shone back at them, everyone lost in the trance of the glitz and glamour of Hollywood TV. The couple took a small lap of honour, stepping down from the stage and greeting their followers in the front row with handshakes. More smiles, more congratulations. Then it was time for them to leave.

Once more back on the stage, a quick bow, another round of blown kisses and the couple made their exit into the wings.

"Goddamn it," Murray wheezed. "I thought they were going to pull my goddamn arm off there at the end. Where do we dig these troglodytes up from?"

"That's your adoring audience Murray," Roberta sniffed. "They fill your pool with water."

"Yeah and my doctor's pockets with cash when I'm ripped apart by them, the hounds of hell that they are."

He snapped his fingers. A runner appeared from nowhere, towel, cigarette, lighter and gin in hand. Murray snatched the towel and dabbed the sweat from his wrinkled brow. The runner popped the cigarette in Murray's dry lips and lit it. He pawed at the drink before sinking it in one gulp, his smoke not disturbed.

"God almighty!" he wheezed, his face twisting. "What the hell is this?"

The runner, already petrified to be this close to living TV legend, Murray Steiner, mumbled nervously.

"Is there… is there something wrong, Mr Steiner?" he just about managed.

"Something wrong?" Murray screamed. "This tastes like a turd has been filtered through a hobo's sock! You call this a drink?"

He threw the glass down on the studio floor. It shattered, making the runner jump. The backstage area was busy—there were plenty of people about as the show was brought to an end—but none of them seemed to care about this little outburst. They'd all seen it hundreds of times before. Thousands even.

Only the runner was terrified beyond belief. He stood, shaking, as Murray grabbed him by the lapels of his shirt. Snarling, cigarette burning as it was flattened between his teeth, he breathed hot smoke into the young man's face.

"Let me give you a free tip kid," he growled. "If you want to make it in this business, you've got to learn to respect your elders. And that means doing what we say. You got that? I've been on TV for thirty years. I've got awards coming out of my wazoo and a million loyal fans out there ready to take a bullet for me? My face is on T-shirts, coffee mugs and mouse pads. I *own* this town. So you don't want to mess with a guy like me, you got that kid? Huh?"

He shook the runner hard. The younger man didn't dare look into Murray's eyes. He was too afraid, too embarrassed, too out of his depth.

"You listening to me?" Murray barked.

"Yes… yes, Mr Steiner. Yes, I am. Sorry sir… sorry. It won't happen again, I promise."

"Good," said Murray, releasing his grip. "But how do I know I can trust you?"

The runner looked up at him, confused.

"Trust me?" he asked. "I… I don't understand."

Murray grabbed his arm. He pushed the young man's sleeve up past his elbow. Then, taking his cigarette, he put it out on his forearm.

The runner made a horrible howl, loud enough to bring the whole studio down. And still nobody took notice. Everyone else was too busy with something else to worry about the assault taking place in the wings of one of America's most popular reality shows.

"There," Murray smiled. "Now you'll always remember when you messed up."

The runner pulled himself free. He took off, disappearing into the bowels of the backstage area, whimpering in pain as he held his injured arm. Murray watched him go, his self-satisfaction growing by the second.

"Let it never be said that you're still classy, Steiner," said Roberta, lazily.

This was hardly Murray's first offence. And it wasn't going to be his last. Being married to one of Hollywood's biggest television personalities had shown her that the world could be a very strange, very brutal place. And that was even before they'd made it big with their reality criminal investigations show.

"The kid has to learn," said Murray. "The way I learned from my dad."

"Oh come on, Murray. Not the old school of hard knocks routine again. That's as old as the ark."

"You're as old as the goddamn ark!" he screamed.

Roberta laughed. Not his best insult. And certainly not his most pointed. Four decades of marriage could have that effect on the insults and barbs, she supposed, as it had on everything else. The creativity wasn't what it used to be.

Murray stormed off towards the dressing room. Roberta followed quietly behind, checking her phone. One thing she had managed to salvage was a career of her own. Invitations from magazines, websites, blogs and press agents were never far from the door. While Murray had painted himself as the friendly next door neighbour who could help you out in a jam, Roberta

Steiner had become a fashion icon and prominent public speaker. 'America's Conscience 'was how Time magazine had once described her. It was a moniker she would take to her grave.

They reached a long corridor lined with private rooms and offices. A gaggle of network executives and other faceless drones from the studio were waiting to greet them. She didn't have the time or the energy. Making her polite excuses, she reached the door of her dressing room and prepared to sit down in the peace and quiet.

"We've got dinner at the Governor's mansion tonight!" she called out to Murray, heading for his own dressing room down the hall. "We've to be there for eight."

Murray dismissed her with an ignorant wave. He was already transfixed on a young executive half his age. Pert, tall and blonde, just his type. Roberta sneered in disgust as she thumped open the door of her room. By the time it had closed, Murray was kissing the young woman's hand—the sour taste of his gin now clearly long forgotten.

Two

MILK, BREAD, GRAPES, apples, cereal, juice, butter, yoghurts and toilet roll. Martha had committed that list to her memory. And it was going around and around in there as she walked up and down the aisles.

She used to write her shopping down. A scrap bit of paper, the back of an envelope, anywhere she could. Then Geri introduced her to social media and its weird and wonderful sub cultures. There were communities on there, whole groups of people, who liked to share lists they'd found at supermarkets or on the street. Picture after picture of crumpled and torn bits of paper with all kinds of goods written down.

There was no way of identifying who's lists they were of course. They were just a random collection of items needed by somebody who had carelessly thrown it away. But something about having that intimate information plastered all over the internet made Martha uncomfortable. So uncomfortable, in fact, she'd stopped writing down her shopping straight away.

Now she was wandering the aisles, trying her best to remember what she needed. It wasn't easy, not as easy as it should have been anyway. Her rampant paranoia aside, she thought improving her memory would probably be a good thing professionally. She was, after all, a private investigator now. It paid to be able to recall even the smallest detail.

"Milk, bread, grapes, apples, cereal, juice, butter, yoghurts and toilet roll," she whispered to herself. "Milk, bread, grapes, apples, cereal, juice, butter, yoghurts and toilet roll. Come on Parker, you know what you're in here for. Hold it together."

She rounded the trolley, wonky wheel and all, into the next aisle. Thankfully the milk, butter and yogurts were here. That was three off the list. She'd never been happier to feel the icy chill of the fridges. Pulling her cardigan about her, she hurried away, trolley squeaking as she went.

As she rounded the corner, the trolley came to a juddering halt. It stopped Martha dead, and she was lucky not to end up head over heels in the milk fridge. As the ringing of the metal faded in her ears, she looked up to see another trolley ahead of her with two elderly women huddled around it, dusting each other off like they'd been in a car crash.

"Sorry," Martha said, assuming it was her fault. "I wasn't concentrating. Sorry."

The pensioners finished their fussing. They looked alike—sisters by Martha's reckoning—both with identical haircuts and dyed black hair. She thought about just sliding her trolley away while they composed themselves, but the two women caught her eye. Then their faces lifted, wrinkles retreating.

"Oh," said one of them.

"Is it?" said the other, their voices identical.

"It is, you know, Rose," said the first.

"You know I think it is, Pat," answered the second.

Martha stood politely quiet. While she hadn't been in this position for very long, she had very quickly learned that she didn't care for fame and attention. Since the Coulthard affair had gone national, occurrences like this were becoming part of everyday life. It seemed that Martha's notoriety had now extended to the dairy aisle.

"You're that Martha Parker girl," said Rose.

"That's right, Martha Parker," agreed Pat.

"You're the girl that caught that murderer."

"She is! Oh wow! A real life celebrity. Isn't this a treat, Rose?"

"It certainly is Pat!"

Martha could feel her cheeks flushing. The two old women, dear as they were, were practically shouting. Two fans, if she could call them that, were bad enough. She didn't want a whole throng of them mobbing her when she was out for her shopping.

"Yes, it's me, hello," she said, trying to sound as humble as possible. "Sorry again about your trolley. I didn't mean to—"

"The trolley, oh don't worry about that!" babbled Rose. "We're sorry for bumping into a big, famous detective like *you*."

"Oh please," said Martha. "I'm not famous."

"Yes, indeed. This is a great treat, isn't it, Rose?" said Pat. "I mean, I didn't even know she shopped in here. Did you know that she shopped here Rose?"

"Eh?"

A high-pitched whistle sounded out from the old woman's ear. She started fumbling about with the settings on her hearing aid.

"Your hearing aid Rose!" Pat screamed. "Fix your hearing aid."

"Hold on a minute Pat," said Rose. "I'm fixing my hearing aid."

Other people were looking now, making Martha feel a little hot and dizzy. The cooling comfort of the dairy fridges was a distant memory. She was up to her neck in fandom. And she didn't feel comfortable.

"Excuse me ladies, I really would love to stay and chat," she said, pulling her trolley away. "But I'm actually in a bit of a rush and—"

"Could we get a picture with you Martha?" asked Pat.

"A what?" Martha was shocked.

"A picture. Yes, a picture," Rose agreed. "Wait until we tell the girls down at the bingo that we bumped into you when we were out at the shops. They'll die of jealousy."

"I… I don't really want anybody to die," Martha said, feebly. "And I'm hardly dressed for a picture."

"Nonsense!" Rose, hurried around their trolley. "Please, it would be really very special, wouldn't it, Pat?"

"Oh yes, very special," Pat agreed.

Rose took Martha by the arm. She squeezed it tightly, making escape impossible. Pat began rummaging around in her handbag.

"Where did I put that bloody phone?" she mumbled to herself.

"Where did you put your bloody phone Pat?" Rose shouted.

Martha really wasn't feeling very well. She tapped her foot, trying to distract herself as her legs turning to jelly. She wanted to be polite, seem patient, but this was really very taxing. In the six months since the Coulthard affair, she'd had her run-ins with moments like this. And none of them were getting any easier.

"Found it!" Pat exclaimed, waving her phone in the air, before flagging down a shop attendant—a young woman with long, blonde hair that reached all the way down her back. She was chewing gum and looked thoroughly uninterested.

"Excuse me, dear," said Pat. "Would you be able to take a picture of me and my sister with Martha Parker here."

"Who's Martha Parker?" asked the shop assistant.

Martha wasn't sure how she should feel about that slight. On the one hand, she was relieved that at least somebody here didn't know who she was. On the other, it was a little disappointing—risking her life the way she had should attract at least a glimmer of recognition. She'd been in all the papers and magazines, after all. Even on TV—although she tried to forget that bit as much as possible.

"*This* is Martha Parker, dear," said Pat, incredulously. "She's a detective."

"Private… Private Investigator," Martha said, feeling foolish at the correction.

"She's the one who caught that awful banker who murdered his friend," said Rose. "She's a hero."

"Well, hero's a bit of a strong word," said Martha. "And it wasn't just me of course. My sisters were pretty involved too, you know."

"You're a hero alright, no point arguing about that," Rose patted her arm.

The surly shop assistant had lost interest a long while ago. She took Pat's phone and nodded towards Martha and Rose. The three of them stood together in front of a special offer of square sausage and rashers of bacon—two-for-one on selected lines.

Martha tried her best to smile. The scene had attracted the attention of the other shoppers now. A small crowd had gathered around the four of them, all huddled at the top of the aisle. Martha could see them all talking amongst themselves, whispering, laughing, pointing at her and the pensioners. With every passing second the shop assistant didn't take the picture, her blood pressure cranked up a notch.

"Say cheese!" the young girl instructed.

"Cheese," said the trio.

And with that it was over. The pensioners hurried as fast as their little legs would take them to collect the phone. When they snatched it from the shop worker they began to laugh and cheer, congratulating themselves and each other.

The small crowd began to disperse and the shop assistant went back to work. Martha saw her chance and backed away slowly. When she was far enough away from the pensioners, knowing they wouldn't be able to give chase, she turned and jogged away. Martha didn't stop running until she was clear of the supermarket and bounding across the car park to her trusty motor. She climbed in, pulled away and sped up the road—her shopping list long forgotten.

Three

"THANK YOU FOR coming in today Helen, I know you were supposed to have the day off."

Professor McCauley sat behind his desk, flanked by an insurmountable number of books. As faculty Dean, he had an image to uphold. While the world continued to move to a paperless environment, he was stubborn enough to insist that his office was a haven to dusty old textbooks and unmanaged files. The very definition of the 'old school'.

"That's quite alright Professor," said Helen, sat on her hands. "What is it you wanted to speak to me about anyway? I was a little surprised to get your voicemail message."

"Voicemail message?" the academic half-sneered.

Helen didn't particularly enjoy Dean McCauley's company. She found him a little too insincere and savage. She also knew, as did most of her fellow tenured Grad students and teaching assistants, that he wasn't half as technophobic as he liked to make out he was. One look inside his rather nifty, brand new Range Rover would attest to that.

"Your message," she said again. "On my phone."

"Oh yes, that," McCauley sneered fully this time. "Ghastly devices though. I've got no idea how anyone can manage with those blasted things, I really don't."

Right on cue. Not that Helen needed to justify her thoughts on the stuffy old man across the desk from her, but again, she knew for a fact that he was the proud owner of the most expensive smartphone on the market. Feeling reassured by the benign familiarity of his technophobe schtick, her nerves began to ease.

She'd always enjoyed working here at the university. It was her haven, her sanctuary. Helping young undergraduates with their studies, marking, taking tutorials. They all felt a little bit like a big, extended family. And when she had to get away from her *real* family, her work was always there. A constant presence in what had been a rather tumultuous few months, if not years. The whole ordeal of being kidnapped, tied up and shot at had rather jangled her nerves. Helen was glad to still have somewhere she could go and effectively hide.

"I'm afraid we're letting you go," said the professor.

"You're what?" Her voice was much louder than she had expected.

"We're having to let you go Helen. You and a handful of the other Grads. The budget just won't stretch to keeping you all on, I'm afraid."

He leaned back in his chair and steepled his fingers. His thin, lizard-like lips pursed as tight as they could. Looking at her over the top of his spectacles, Helen thought he might even be enjoying this.

"But… But I don't understand, professor," she said. "I mean, you've never expressed any displeasure in my work before. I always turn in my marking on time and to the highest of my abilities. And I've always loved working with the students, watching them grow from snotty-faced kids into actual functioning members of society. I don't get it."

McCauley took a long, drawn out breath of the stagnant office air in through his nose. Then he blew it out again. His nostrils whistled, freeing a long, white hair that made Helen feel just a little sick.

"I'm sorry Helen, it's just about the pounds and pence." He leaned forward and picked up a folder. "I've just had the department's latest budget through and I'm afraid we're not going to be able to keep you and some others on for the coming term. Belts are being tightened all over the university. There's increased scrutiny on how we're spending our money. And we all have to do what we can."

Helen couldn't explain it. She just suddenly felt very angry. A flash of red mist came down over her.

"And just what are you going to be doing Professor McCauley? What are *you* going to be doing to help out?"

McCauley was unshaken. Here was a man very much accustomed to being in control. From Helen's first day, she had been reminded of that fact. The Dean had *total* control over his dominion. He was well versed in making sure things stayed that way.

"Please Helen, let's not get into a mud-slinging competition here," he said, with all the warmth of a sharp knife. "I'm simply laying out the facts as they are presented to me. The numbers don't add up any more and we're having to make adjustments. Unfortunately that means the department, and by extension, the university, cannot continue to offer you employment."

A sudden panic struck Helen as she sat across from her boss. She pushed her chair back and stood up. McCauley's concentrated glare followed her as her imagination began to run away with itself.

"Well, I'm not going to sleep with you, if that's what you think!" she blurted out.

The Dean's face went from pallid grey to purple almost instantaneously. He let out a sudden cough that was half-burp, half-yelp of panic. He slammed his hands down on his desk with a clap, steadying himself.

"I beg your pardon?" he wheezed.

"If you think I'm going to sleep with you to keep my job, professor, you're wrong! That's absolutely *not* going to happen!"

McCauley tried to gather himself. His head looked like it was about to explode. He gulped at the air and tried to speak. Helen watched on, still not quite sure if this was all some sort of horrible dream.

"Miss Parker," said the Dean, finally able to speak. "I can assure you, I am *not* wanting to solicit *anything* of a sexual nature with you."

"Are you sure?" Helen asked. "I mean, you hear about these things all the time, don't you? Young women like me being coerced into all kinds of things just to get along in life. It's happening *everywhere*. Well we don't have to stand for it any longer, McCauley. I don't know what you think you're trying to pull here but I can assure you, I won't be *pulling* anything. And I won't be quiet about it either. I've got friends in the media, I've made them very quickly. I'll sing like a… like a… like a songbird. Yeah! Wait until my sisters hear about this. They'll have your guts for garters… whatever garters are. I always meant to look up the origin of that phrase actually, thank you for reminding me and—"

"Helen!"

McCauley's voice made the bookshelves shake. Silence ensued between the two of them, Helen nearing the office door, the Dean clinging on to his desk. She stood watching him as some semblance of normal colour returned to his face.

"I can assure you that I am not trying any funny business with you," he said, calm and measured once again. "And I have absolutely every sympathy for people who find themselves in the kinds of situations you have implied. I agree with you, it's incorrect and has gone on too long and we all must do what we can to flush it out."

Helen nodded in agreement.

"In that spirit of honesty, then, I feel I should probably tell you that the decision to let you go hasn't wholly been because of our budget constraints," he said.

Her ears pricked up. The giddy fear retreated. She stepped forward, her sleuth's hat now firmly on her head.

"Oh?" she said. "If it's not just about the numbers, what *is* it all about then?" she asked.

McCauley hesitated. He looked down at scattered files on his desk and then back to Helen. For the first time in their working relationship, Helen thought she saw a sliver of sympathy creep into his dull features. His eyebrows arched upwards and his eyes seemed to soften.

"Your friends in the media Helen, the ones you just mentioned, they've certainly been doing a very good job over the past few months, haven't they?" he asked.

"I don't understand," she said. "The media? Good job?"

"Your profile, well, not just *your* profile—you and your sisters. How do you young people say it? It's gone through the roof."

"I don't think young people say that, professor, but yes, it has. Go on."

McCauley slumped back down into his chair. He rubbed his forehead.

"The department, and university, has come under a lot of scrutiny over the past few months," he said. "And yes, our budgets are being cut back, but it's been felt that having someone of your… extracurricular experience, shall we say, in and around the students could be seen as something of a distraction."

"Distraction?"

"Yes," he clicked his tongue. "I've been inundated with requests from undergrads who want to be a part of your classes and tutorials. They're desperate to just be in your learning groups, to the point where the admin staff can't keep up! It seems your brush with fame, Miss Parker, has given you a degree of celebrity that the department can't handle."

"So you're letting me go?" Helen could hear her voice beginning to crack.

McCauley took his spectacles off. He pinched the bridge of his nose.

"You'll be reimbursed for the whole of the first semester," he said. "And for what it's worth, Helen, I am sorry that we are losing you."

"Sorry? But I… I…"

She was about to start crying. Then she heard her sisters' voices in her head. Martha would be urging her, willing her to stay dignified in defeat, play the long game, keep a cool head and pick up the pieces when the conflict was over. Geri, on the other hand, would want her to thump him.

Helen settled on something in between. She nodded again and pushed back her shoulders, standing as straight as her wiry frame would go.

"I understand," she said.

"You do?" McCauley couldn't conceal his surprise, his guard was down.

"Yes, I think I do," she said. "I understand that I'm being sacked because I foiled the machinations of a murderer and his mistress. I understand that I'm being shown the door because I did some good in a world that's intent on eating itself. I understand that this university, one of the oldest and best in the country, isn't standing by me, despite all of the above. I understand Dean McCauley. I understand perfectly."

"Helen. Please!"

She turned quickly and hurried out of the door. Slamming it behind her, she didn't stop for pleasantries with the admin staff who had clearly been listening in. Instead, Helen Parker walked straight out of the building, down the street and headed for the student union. Be damned with the time, she was going to treat herself to a drink.

Four

"OH COME ON, stop sitting there with a face like a depressed camel," said Geri, handing over the money. "You'll get over it. And besides, you have all the joys and wonders of unemployment to look forward to now."

"Oh god," said Helen, sinking her head into her arms.

The barman returned with Geri's change. She winked at him as he headed off to serve someone else. Shrugging, she nudged her sister in the shoulder, the shot of bright pink alcohol swishing in its glass.

"Here, get this down your neck," she said.

Helen looked up. She blindly grabbed the drink and sank it back. Geri timed the pause, counting it down in her head. Then Helen began to cough.

"Oh god!" she spluttered again. "What the hell *was* that? It tasted like kerosene!"

"Steady on, Granny," said Geri, drinking her own. "Just a little livener to bring you back to life."

Helen coughed a little more, before twisting on her bar stool. She hiccoughed loudly, her whole body shaking. Then waved an accusatory finger out at the rest of the bar.

"Why don't they put on some halfway decent music in here for a change?" she asked, although it felt more like a telling off. "Where's the Vivaldi, the Corelli, the Georg Philipp Telemann for God's sake."

"Firstly, it's a student union. Secondly it's only four in the afternoon. Thirdly, you're drunk."

"I am not," Helen said lazily. "And besides, even if I *was*, I lost my job today. I have every right to be dunk."

"Drunk."

"Drunk. What did I say?"

She blinked her eyes, one after the other. Then spun back around to the bar and grabbed the pint glass that still had some flat beer left in it.

Geri smiled at her sister. She took Helen's arm and squeezed it tightly.

"You'll be okay, sis," she said. "You always land on your feet. You're smart, resourceful and a total fox. The world is your oyster."

"Pffft," Helen batted her away. "I'm a thirty-year-old Grad student, who has no experience of the outside world beyond the four walls of this place. I stand about as much chance of getting a proper job as you do of getting your leg over with that barman."

"What?" Geri laughed.

"He's gay," Helen whispered to her sister.

Geri looked back down at the barman. He was busy pouring another pint. She drummed her fingers on the rim of her gin and tonic and tutted.

"You win some and you lose some, eh?"

"Ha," Helen laughed.

The sisters sat for a while listening to the jukebox. A steady flow of pale students were happy to keep it going. When the clock hit five the place started to get busy.

"Right, that's our signal," she said, standing up.

"What signal? Where are you going?" Helen said, slurring a little.

"I'm not hanging about here as the great unwashed of this place start to arrive. It's bad enough during term time. I don't want to get sucked down the rabbit hole of people with nothing better to do with their summers than get drunk and listen to the Arctic Monkeys and Ed Sheeran in public."

"The who monkeys?"

"Come on, Hel," she said.

Geri dragged Helen out of the bar. They had to battle the oncoming surge of bodies as they trotted down the stairs of the union. When they reached the front door, a wave of fresh air hit them both and brought them around. Geri fished a cigarette out of the pocket of her denim jacket and lit it. Before she could take a puff, Helen had it in her mouth and sucked it hard.

"Glad I could be of some help," she said.

Helen continued to puff away, unsteady on her feet. Geri put out an arm and held her up.

"You know what, you're right Geri. You're absolutely right," said Helen. "I don't need this place. There are plenty, plenty of universities and colleges that would jump at the chance to have me on their staff. When word gets out that I'm on the market, I'll be batting them off like flies around… around…"

"A poo?"

"Yeah, one of those!" she tugged on the smoke again. "And then I'll show this place. I'll show them all that it *pays* to be a celebrity!"

That made Geri laugh. Her fingers tapped and danced across the screen of her phone. Multitasking had always been her strong point. It was only when she finished did she realise what Helen had said.

"Hold on. Celebrity?" she asked.

Helen looked blankly at her.

"Eh?

"Celebrity," said Geri. "You said celebrity. That you're a celebrity. What's that got to do with anything?"

"The uni," said Helen. "That's why they let me go. The Dean, that stupid old fart, he said that the department couldn't cope with all the new requests from students for me to be their tutor. Apparently I'm too famous to be able to do my job."

"But that's ridiculous!" Geri shouted.

Her voice echoed about the tall, misshapen buildings of the university. A few stragglers who weren't so keen to get inside and get drunk, threw her dirty looks.

"Why didn't you tell me when you called me to come down here?" she asked her sister.

"Didn't I tell you? Oops," Helen laughed, the only one amused.

"Right, that's it, we're going to see your boss!" Geri had the bit between her teeth now.

"What? No!"

"Yes! We are. This is discrimination Helen, outright discrimination. You shouldn't be punished for having a life outside of this dump. If anything they should be *thankful* that you're doing so well with us at the agency. We're doing them a favour, putting this place on the bloody map."

"Language…" Helen said, sternly, mimicking Martha. "What would your mother think, young lady."

"What's his name?"

"Who?"

"This Dean that's given you your P45. What's he called?"

"Why?"

"Why?" yelped Geri. "Because I'm going to hang around his car and wait for him to come out of his office."

"Why would you do that?"

"Because, when he's not looking, I'm going to hit him over the head with a baseball bat."

"But… but you don't have a baseball bat, Geri?" Helen hiccoughed again.

"My shoe then! These Doc Martens can give a good whack, if applied correctly."

Helen laughed. She did a big, wide loop as she tried to steady herself again and then sucked on her cigarette that had gone out.

Geri was fuming. She hated injustice and she hated bullies. It was bad enough when it was happening all around her. But to involve her sister was the ultimate insult. She knew that Helen had worked just as hard as any of the Parker Sisters on the Coulthard case. More so after the kidnapping. Now she was being punished for doing a good job. It wouldn't stand.

"Right, come on, pull yourself together, we're going," she said.

"Going where?" Helen said absently.

"To beat up the Dean."

Before they could go anywhere, a car pulled up at the edge of the kerb in front of them. Geri recognised it straight away. Only one woman in the known universe could still be kicking around in something that out of date. The window rolled down and Martha smiled from within.

"You two need a lift?" she asked.

"How does she do that?" asked Helen, staggering slightly. "How does she have such impeccable timing?"

"I texted her about twenty minutes ago when you were passed out on the bar," said Geri, rolling her eyes.

She leaned down into the window and waved.

"Hi Mart, you can take Helen home," she said. "Just as soon as she tells me the name of the Dean who has given her the sack."

"The sack?" Martha bleated. "What has she done?"

"Nothing, absolutely nothing. That's why, as soon as she tells me his name, I'm going to bash his face in!"

"Helen?" Martha questioned, leaning across to see her sister. "Is this true? Have you lost your job?"

"It's fine, honestly," said Helen, with a mellow smile on her face. "It's totally cool, Martha. Seriously. It's just the universe's way of telling me that I'm destined to be… destined to be… destined… oh god what's happened!" She burst into tears.

"That's it!" Martha said, throwing open the door. "Get her in, we're going home."

"Aww, Martha!"

"Don't aww, Martha me. Geri, you too."

"But I was wanting to crack some skulls," said the youngest Parker sister. "There's nothing I like more than to cause a bit of mischief at a uni where I'm not a student. It feels so naughty."

"I'll pretend I didn't hear that," said Martha.

Geri helped Helen into the front seat and then climbed into the back. When the doors were closed, Martha drove them away from the union. They passed the huge, ominous spire of the university as they headed for the motorway.

"Aren't you going to ask what happened?" asked Helen, bobbing about in the front passenger seat.

"I don't have to," said Martha. "I can smell the brewery coming out of your pores."

"Ouch," said Geri. "An old one but a good one there Martha. Nice."

Martha was about to chastise her youngest sister for encouraging it, when the familiar tinkle of her phone interrupted her. To her surprise, similar noises came from both Helen and Geri.

"What's that?" she asked, swerving a little.

"I think we all got a message at the same time," said Geri.

"All of us?" Martha squeaked. She reached for her phone mounted beside the steering wheel. Pressing the message that had just dropped, she scanned it quickly while still trying to drive.

"No. Way!" Geri exclaimed from the back. "Are you reading this, Martha?"

"I'm trying to drive here, Geri."

"You're going to flip when you do, then. This is unbelievable."

"What is it? What's happened? Is it Mum?"

She looked at Geri in the rear-view mirror. Martha felt her stomach contract a little as her sister shook her head.

"Geri," she said. "Whenever you get a look like that on your face, my teeth begin to itch."

"I'll bet they do," said the youngest of the Parker sisters. "I'll bet they do."

Five

"OH GOD, MY head feels like it's going to implode," moaned Helen. "I can actually feel the weight of my hair lying on top of my skull."

She clamped her hands onto her ears, eyes bloodshot and tongue furry. Even the comfort of her chair in the office couldn't help. The agency's profile might be high but the Parker sisters were still holed up in Martha's draughty garage. In the height of summer it was fine. But in the winter it could be hell.

Not quite the same hell that Helen was going through though. Her hangover had kicked in very early this time. So early that she hadn't even gone to sleep yet.

"Please make it stop," she moaned, pulling her whole face down two inches.

"Could you *please* stop your moaning, Helen!" Geri called over at her. "You only had one shot. And it took you three hours to have your *only* pint!"

Martha smiled. Some things never changed. Helen being a notorious lightweight drinker would remain forever.

"Besides, we should be celebrating the fantastic news!" Geri shouted.

"Too loud," Helen whimpered. "You're *far* too loud."

Martha sat in her comfy chair near the door. Toby the cat was lying flat on his back at her feet, trying to cool down as best he could. She nudged him now and then to make sure he was still alive.

Her phone was in her hand. The message that had arrived while she was carting about her sisters still on the screen. It was short, only a few lines. But it was weighing heavy on her shoulders.

"I'm going to have to pack," said Geri. "Do you think there'll be like a gala ball or something? I should probably scrub up a bit, shouldn't I? I don't think they'd like me scuffing the floor with my boots. Helen, you should buy a new pair of sandals, and a pair of socks to wear with them!"

"Please stop talking," Helen moaned.

"Do we honestly think this is real?" asked Martha.

The garage fell silent. Geri stopped her hopping around. She looked across the untidy desks and boxes of weed killer at her oldest sister.

"What do you mean, real?" she asked.

Martha shifted uncomfortably. She waved her phone in the air.

"This. The message. Do you think it's real?"

"What?" Geri spluttered. "Why wouldn't it be real? You know what it is, right? You know what we're being invited to here? This is SteinerCon, Martha. *The* SteinerCon. And *we're* the guests of honour!"

SteinerCon. Even the name made Martha shudder. She looked back down at the message, her paranoia dialled all the way up to eleven.

"It's the biggest convention in the world for Private Eyes like us!" Geri continued, her excitement growing. "This is like us winning the World Cup or the Eurovision Song Contest. I don't know why you're not more excited!"

Geri skipped around the desks, almost knocking over a strimmer. She took Martha's phone from her and read out the message.

"Dear Martha Parker. You have been invited to the twelfth annual SteinerCon at the Imperial Hotel, Park Lane in London. For your outstanding contributions to the world of private investigations and amateur detective work, you have been chosen to be among the guests of honour of SteinerCon founders Murray and Roberta Steiner at this year's event. More details to follow blah, blah, blah. Martha! This is amazing! We all got the same message, why aren't you jumping for joy?"

"I don't know," Martha lied.

She knew *exactly* why she wasn't jumping for joy. Ever since the Coulthard case had exploded, everyone knew who she was. At first she hadn't minded all the attention, it had felt like free advertising for the agency. And that was very welcome, especially considering the business they had pulled in as a result. While the cases hadn't been on the scale of murder most horrid again, they'd kept a steady flow of income coming through the garage door.

Fame, however, had come at a price. The experience in the supermarket was just the most recent in a long line of similar, embarrassing incidents. Now the invitation to SteinerCon had arrived, it felt like the universe was mocking her.

"I wonder how they got our personal numbers?" Geri tapped her chin. "Still, the way data is bought and sold these days, I don't imagine it's all that hard to find. We're talking about Murray and Roberta Steiner here, after all, not some pimple-faced gumshoe operating out of his mum's attic."

"Who, or what, are Murray and Roberta Steiner?" Helen croaked.

Geri rolled her eyes. Helen placed two Post-it notes over her eyes and lifted her feet up on her desk.

"And before you start having a go at me for not knowing anything or being hugely out of touch from the rest of society, I'd like to remind you that I'm currently suffering from the worst hangover in the history of the world."

"For somebody so clever, you really don't know a lot, do you, Hel?" Geri laughed. "Not that the Steiners need any introduction, but for your benefit, they're American TV royalty."

"American," Helen sniffed.

"Yes, American. They host a show called Double Trouble and it's been on for a hundred years. They've got books, films, podcasts, lunch boxes, action figures and commemorative plates with their faces on it. When it comes to Private Investigation, these two are *the* biggest names in the business. And now they want us—*us*, the Parker sisters—to be guests of honour at their biggest event of the year!"

"Alright, we get it, you're a fangirl," said Helen.

"Damn right I'm a fangirl! Geri fired back. "Roberta Steiner was one of the few women in the 1970s who could command a higher daily rate for her investigations than most men in the industry. She's a pioneer, not to mention being a total babe even though she's in her seventies. This is the woman who paved the way for us to even *have* a business let alone charge what we charge and get the chance to do what we do."

"And what about Murray?"

"Yeah he's pretty good too. C'mon Martha, back me up here."

"They're a pretty big deal," said Martha with a sigh. "I remember watching them on Parkinson and Wogan with Mum when they were doing tours over here. That must have been thirty-odd years ago. They're proper Hollywood like, all white teeth and good wigs."

"But that's just an image," said Geri. "You've got to look the part when you're on TV over there. It's like a uniform isn't it."

"They seem like nice enough people," said Martha. "I just don't know if we should, you know, be mixing with these types of people is all."

Geri looked dumbfounded. She turned to try to salvage some support from Helen, but their middle sister had started gently snoring, her head tilted back in her chair. Martha could sense the disappointment growing in her sister. And she felt bad.

"Look, I don't know, Geri," she said, getting up. "I just… I don't know. I sort of feel a bit uncomfortable with the whole high profile thing we've become recently, you know? It just feels like things are running away from us. And I don't want to expose you and Keith Richards over there to something that might cause us problems."

Geri smirked. It was that little, playful smile that Martha had seen her do ever since she was a toddler. Her youngest sister was smart, savvy and ready to take on the world, no matter what it threw at her. She began to laugh.

"What?" Geri asked. "What's so funny?"

"Nothing," said Martha. "Nothing. I just… saying it out loud while you and Helen are here. Looking at you, knowing what you're both like. It just sounds silly, that's all."

Martha felt a little better. She always did when she was around her sisters. She only wished they had been with her in the supermarket earlier. Or any other time she felt alone, frightened and overwhelmed.

"So…" said Geri, still smiling.

"So what?" Martha smiled back.

"So… does this mean we're going to London?"

"We don't even know when it is, Geri, all we have is a mysterious text," said Martha, already caving.

"And that's what makes it so cool!"

"Fine," she said. "If it's genuine, we'll go."

Geri whooped loudly as she punched the air. She started playing air guitar and kicked over a wastepaper basket. All the noise made Helen wake with the most unladylike of snorts. The middle Parker sister peeled the Post-it notes off her eyes and blinked over at the others.

"What's going on?" she said with a yawn. "Have we won the lottery?"

"No," said Martha. "We're going to London."

Six

"BAH! YOU CALL this a hamburger? It tastes like something I'd feed my cat."

Murray pulled the half-chewed meat out of his mouth with his hand. He slopped it down on the plate and made a gagging sound in his throat. He pushed the plate across the table and sneered at the waitress who looked thoroughly shocked.

"Is this what stands for food here in England?" he bawled. "Seriously? We bring all this business to the hotel, pack it out for three nights, spend hundreds of thousands on advertising and this is the crap you serve me? I want your manager up here, right now, so he can fire you on the spot!"

"I'm… I'm sorry," said the waitress, gathering up the plate. "It's… it's usually very highly thought of sir and… and your wife approved of—"

"What did you say?"

Murray's eyes went wide. They stood out like golf balls, white on the darkened, weather-beaten leather of his Californian face.

"What did you say to me?" he stomped around the table to be in her face. "Say it again. Say it *again*!"

The waitress was close to tears. She shook her head apologetically and skulked away from the TV legend.

"You see this!" he shouted after her. "This watch cost more than your goddamn house! Get the manager up here! Right now!"

Nobody else bothered to look up. The penthouse of the Imperial looked more like a Turkish bazaar. Staff were buzzing in and out of the various rooms delivering gifts, bouquets of flowers, welcome gestures and luggage. Murray was still in a foul mood from the flight. And the British summer time, if you could call it that, was wreaking havoc on his sinuses.

"Get them up here right now!" he barked again.

The waitress was long gone, hurrying out of the room as fast as she could go. She didn't even warn him of the stray bit of lettuce dangling from the corner of his mouth. Roberta thought the same and stifled a laugh as he sat down on the far end of the same sofa.

"Goddamn Limeys," he said, fishing out his phone. "They think because they have a Royal family they can treat us like peasants. Even though we saved their asses twice in the wars. We're spending a goddamn fortune here and they try and feed me some half-assed bit of undercooked ham and pass it off for a burger."

"Why must you insist on playing the pantomime villain, Murray?" said Roberta, not even looking up from her magazine. "You catch more bears with honey."

"Are we only talking in cliches now, Roberta?" he said, vindictively.

"I'm surprised we're even talking at all." She darted him an unpleasant look. "You spent the majority of the flight staring down the tops of the stewardesses. And the rest of the time, your snoring kept that nice Saudi Prince in front of us awake."

Murray snorted something inaudible and went back to his phone. Roberta's mood was pretty sour, too. Her husband's antics had a way of somehow making everything that little bit worse. She slammed down her magazine and folded her arms—watching the chaos unfold all about her.

"Do you remember when we first started out, Murray?" she said, wistfully. "All those years ago. When it was just the two of us, staking out laundromats and suburban houses at all hours of the day and night. We used to have so much fun. Everything was brand new and exciting. When we got our first book-deal, when we did our first interview. Even the TV stuff, that first show, everything that came along with it. It made us feel like we were alive. Do you remember?"

Murray was silent, engrossed with his phone screen. Roberta stood up and walked to the windows. From the penthouse she could see the whole of London's skyline. In the far distance was Big Ben, the London Eye, all the famous sites of the British capital. If she squinted she could just about make out the outline of Buckingham Palace, nestled neatly among the trees of Green Park.

The scenery had changed a lot in forty years together. The seedy, filthy back alleys of Detroit, then Los Angeles couldn't have been further from this place. Sure, London had its own crime problem, Roberta wasn't so detached to think that was a myth. Up here, though, among the clouds, everything seemed that bit more special. Deep down, she knew it was false— a fabrication, put together for rich tourists like her and her husband. They'd spend a fortune on this weekend, like they always did. But the books would always add up in the end. SteinerCon had been a neat little earner for them both over the years. Just another success to add onto their pile of accolades.

"I wonder if we still have it?" she mused, watching the light rain spray the window. "I wonder if we've still got the touch."

"What?" Murray answered her this time.

"I wonder if we'd still be able to crack a case," she said. "A real one. An actual crime. Not the fabricated bullshit that we put on the air. An actual, proper case."

She turned slowly to face him. A jolt of excitement ran through her. It was something she hadn't felt in a very long time. Everything around her melted away. The room, the dozens of staff, everything but Murray, sat there on the sofa. She was even able to forget how horrible he had been—to her and everyone else. For a brief, all too fleeting moment, he was the young, headstrong, clever man she had fallen in love with at college.

"What do you say Murray?" she asked, smiling. "You think we could maybe get our hands dirty while we're here? A little side project that we can do, just the two of us? Like the old days."

Murray's face was empty of emotion. He stared back at her across the penthouse. Roberta thought that she had him. She thought she saw a twinkle of that same excitement now in her husband's eyes. All the money, fame and power could be forgotten about, put on hold, just for a little while. She wanted to spend time with Murray, like they always used to do. And this felt like the right moment.

Then Murray ruined it all. He threw his head back, laughing with an ugly arrogance that only he could muster. The world came back sharply into focus all around Roberta. She felt like she'd been hit by a runaway lorry, her whole core gutted.

Murray refused to stop. He kept laughing. He slapped the arm of the sofa, thumping it hard every time he tried to catch a breath. Eventually, when he bored of the act, he stopped. He leaned forward and took a gulp of over-priced water, before belching loudly.

"Oh I knew there was a reason I kept you around for so long, Roberta," he said, giggling a little more. "You make me laugh so goddamn hard at times."

Roberta stood firm, mulling over what he'd just said, and then nodded curtly. She made her way towards the door, lifting her coat.

"Where are you going now?" Murray barked at her. "Going to stop a crime from happening, eh? Maybe an unhappy housewife and her cheating husband? Or perhaps a couple of teenagers have pinched a Butterfinger from a local shop!"

He started laughing again. Roberta ignored him. She cursed herself for letting her guard down. She cursed herself for thinking she might actually get through to him. But most of all she cursed herself for still loving him—even after all of these years of abuse. It was the hope that killed you. Never had a truer word been said about loving Murray Steiner.

As she headed out the door, the young waitress was coming back up the hallway—slinking behind a stern looking woman in a manager's uniform. They stopped and clicked their heels to attention when they saw Roberta coming.

"Mrs Steiner," said the manager, as efficient and cold as her demeanour. "Julie here tells me that Mr Steiner is unhappy with the cuisine. I can assure you and him that our chefs are among the very best in the world and we'll endeavour to make sure that he—"

"Just give him what he wants," Roberta said, with a sad sigh. "He always gets what he wants in the end. It makes your life and mine easier if you just nod and say yes."

The manager briefly let her guard down. She quickly recovered, her severity chasing away the lingering surprise. Roberta, on the other hand, was too tired to continue. She turned and marched down the hallway in the opposite direction before any more questions could be asked.

Maybe she would find some fans to speak with, pose for some pictures, press the flesh a little. If Murray wasn't going to pay attention to her or take her seriously, then there were plenty of people that would. She was, after all, Roberta Steiner.

Seven

"ARE YOU SURE this is all paid for?" Helen asked, lugging her suitcase behind. "I mean, this doesn't look like the normal crumbling guesthouse we're used to. I don't want to be hit with a massive bill for a room in a place I don't particularly want to be staying in. I just lost my job, remember?"

"How could we forget?" asked Geri. "It's all you've been talking about."

"And what's *that* supposed to mean?"

"You know exactly what it means."

"No I don't think I do."

"Ladies, please," said Martha, steady as always. "Could we keep the fighting until we're safely locked up in the room, and we don't have the staff looking at us like we're toothless yokels from the back end of nowhere's back end."

Helen and Geri quickly bit their tongues. The lobby of the hotel was brightly lit and well-polished. The only thing more impressive than the decor was the turnout of the staff. Immaculate uniforms, immaculate haircuts, immaculate jawlines and figures. Martha wasn't entirely convinced they weren't all models in their spare time.

"London," she said under her breath. "It's a different world."

The hotel was busy—busier than Martha had been expecting it. A place with such prestige—and prices to match—would always be teeming with activity. Standing in the lobby, however, the atmosphere of the whole place was electric. The air felt like it was alive. People from every corner of the world were here, sat about on the comfortable chairs, talking on phones, eating, drinking, living. Martha and her sisters were right in the centre of it.

"I suppose we had better check in," she said. "Before security throws us out for loitering."

She spied the main reception desk running along the far wall and pulled her suitcase behind her, wincing with every squeaking wheel, fighting the urge not to cry or run.

"Hi," she said to a friendly looking concierge. "Martha Parker here to check in. I understand there are three rooms booked for myself and my two sisters."

"Hold on one moment," said the concierge, checking his computer. "Parker did you say?"

"That's right."

A sudden, icy feeling made Martha's heart race. She'd been dreading this moment the whole journey down. What if this was a scam, after all? What if there were no rooms, no conference, no keynote speech? What if this was all part of some elaborate ruse to get her out of Glasgow for a few days, at her own expense, only to show up online in some candid camera prank show? What if she had been a complete and total idiot this whole time? Could she handle that sort of rejection?

"Ah yes, here we are," said the concierge. "Three suites, overlooking Hyde Park. All courtesy of a Mr and Mrs Steiner, I believe."

Martha just about heard Helen and Geri high-fiving each other over the thumping of her heartbeat in her ears. She let out a long, slow breath, relieved beyond all imagination.

"And it's all paid for, yeah?" asked Helen, nudging up to the desk. "We don't have to cough up a penny? There are no hidden costs, no extra add-ons like paying for the electricity in the place or anything?"

"Helen!" Geri barked. "Would you give over please, you're making us sound like we're skint."

"Speak for yourself Geri, I *am* skint!"

The concierge gave them a warm, friendly laugh. He nodded politely with a big smile as he handed over the key cards.

"Your bills have been settled in advance," he said. "Mr and Mrs Steiner are among our more revered guests here. They've already seen to your expenses during your stay. Please, enjoy."

Helen snatched her key away before it could be taken away. Martha and Geri were a little more laid back.

"Honestly Hel, you need to stop being so paranoid," said Geri. "We're here as guests of honour. Guests of *honour*. That means we won't have to pay for squat and we'll have all these beautiful people running around after us offering to wipe our backsides."

"What you get up to in your own time is totally up to you, Geri," sniffed Helen. "I'm just trying to be financially prudent is all. What is it Mum always says—if something looks too good to be true, it usually is."

Martha laughed a little to herself. She thought about telling the others about her own anxiety. Then kept quiet. Maybe Geri was right, maybe she *was* panicking a little too much. The whole Coulthard affair had shaken her, moved her life on in a direction she never thought it could go. Her fame, as little as it was, could be a good thing. Especially when she and the others had earned it the way they did.

She was about to congratulate her sisters for the millionth time, when her breath was taken from her. Martha stopped dead at the bottom of a huge, sprawling staircase that led to the conference area of the hotel's lobby. Only the loud thump of her bag hitting the floor behind her shook her from her trance.

"No way!" Geri said. "You've got to be kidding me."

High above the entranceway to the conference wing was a massive poster for SteinerCon. On one side of the convention's logo were Roberta and Murray Steiner—all smiles and side-on poses, looking very professional. On the other side were the Parker Sisters.

Their faces must have been ten feet high, at Martha's rough estimate. Broad smiles just as big as the Steiners'. They all looked much cleaner, leaner and more Hollywood than they ever had. Below the SteinerCon logo was a message of welcome from

Murray and Roberta to all attendees. And beneath that were Martha, Helen and Geri's names—surrounded by gold stars and exclamation marks.

"I… I… Is that… is that us?" Helen gasped.

"This is unbelievable," said Geri. "I've got to get a picture of this."

"I don't remember posing for those photos," Helen continued.

"That's because we didn't," said Martha, squinting at the giant banner. "Although I've never seen us all look so good. Look how clear my skin is. And I'm pretty sure you've got green eyes up there Geri, not, you know, your actual blue ones."

"The PR machine must be in overdrive," said Geri. "Although I'm pretty sure they have to ask our permission to use our likenesses. Maybe we should be getting paid or something."

"Do I have… do I have eyeliner on?" Helen asked. "I don't think I've ever worn eye liner in my entire life."

"You have to give it to them though," said Geri. "Roberta and Murray Steiner know how to put on a show."

Martha stood looking up at the huge banner. Suddenly the incident in the supermarket didn't seem so bad after all. That had only been a couple of old dears looking for a photo. This, on the other hand, was a whole other level of weird. Having to stand by the frozen chickens and cold meats for a pic was one thing. Your face blown up to the size of a house in a conference centre was something completely different.

Martha spotted Geri laughing. It was a welcome distraction from the banner.

"What's so funny?" she asked.

"Nothing," said Geri. "I'm just putting this on our Twitter account."

"Our what?" Helen and Martha said at the same time.

Geri looked up at them and shrugged. "Social media guys, it's how the world talks to each other nowadays. If you're not on it, you're nowhere. And what better way to launch our account than on the back of this conference? Check this out, I'm captioning it Mount Blushmore."

Martha couldn't stop Geri, not when she was in full flight. And she knew, deep down, that her sister wouldn't do anything to harm their reputation. Instead she sighed loudly and picked up her bag, marching off towards the lifts, keeping her head firmly down.

"Where are you going?" Helen called after her. "Shouldn't we, you know, speak to somebody about this thing?"

"I'm going to the room to sit down," said Martha. "Then maybe I'll think about getting some plastic surgery—if my embarrassment ever goes away enough to leave the hotel again."

"Excuse me?"

A short, bespectacled woman with an American accent stepped in front of Martha. She was holding a large tablet in one hand and a smartphone in the other.

"Yes?" said Martha, surprised.

"You're Martha Parker, aren't you?" asked the woman.

"I am," Martha thought about lying, but she couldn't think of a different name fast enough.

"Eleanor David," she said. "I'm the director SteinerCon. I'm so glad to finally meet you in person Ms Parker, I've read and seen so much about you in the past few months. Roberta and Murray are just delighted to have you and your sisters as the main guests at this year's summit."

Eleanor took Martha's hand with a firm grip, expertly juggling her devices to make room. She shook her hand vigorously before letting go. Martha was still catching her breath as the others joined them.

"Ah, and there they are," said Eleanor. "The second and third parts of the world famous Parker Sisters. I'm Eleanor David, director of SteinerCon and I was just saying to Martha here how absolutely delighted we all are to have you guys among the guests."

"Guests of *honour*," said Helen.

"Absolutely that," Eleanor beamed. "Now I understand from the hotel staff that you've just checked in, so please don't let me hold you back from getting settled. I just wanted to give you a very quick run-down of how things are going to pan out over the weekend."

Eleanor David spoke at machine gun tempo. Martha couldn't get a word in at all. Helen and Geri were left equally bewildered and impressed.

"The rough plan, which is subject to change of course, would be to have you all deliver your keynote speech tomorrow afternoon around three," said Eleanor. "That gives you all of the morning to take in the summit, speak at various fringe events and explore any marketing and commercial work that you might want to undertake. I don't need to tell you all that your stock has never been higher."

Geri waved her phone at Martha. Martha ignored her youngest sister.

"Then after the speech you'll be ushered into one of the smaller conference halls for the meet and greet session. I don't mind telling you all that we've been absolutely inundated with requests for this."

"Meet and greet?" asked Martha. "Who exactly are we going to be meeting and greeting?"

"Fans," smiled Eleanor. "Other private investigators, the media, loyal customers of SteinerCon over the years who never miss a convention. It's a chance for you to meet your public and again explore any commercial opportunities that might come your way."

It all sounded dreadful. But Martha kept quiet as they arrived at the lifts.

"Then tomorrow night is the gala dinner, you'll all be seated at the top table of course," Eleanor scanned her tablet. "We can arrange for hair and makeup to be at your suites first thing in the morning and again later in the evening. We want you to be looking your best for the TV special."

"TV special," Helen blurted out. "Nobody said anything about television."

"Don't worry," said Eleanor, rubbing her shoulder. "It's a pre-recorded taping that will air in the States next month. Nothing to worry about, you can have as many takes as you like. It's great publicity, trust me."

Helen clamped her mouth shut. Martha's heart was racing again. The only one enjoying all of this was Geri. She had that look in her eyes of someone already cashing in cheques that hadn't even been posted. Martha was worried.

"And what about tonight?" she asked, desperately searching for some vague normality in all of this. "Can we explore the city? Maybe go for something to eat or catch a show?"

For the first time, Eleanor's smile dropped. She sucked her teeth as she prepared her bad news.

"Tonight I have you down for dinner with Roberta and Murray," she said. "So we'd really need you all ready to be picked up and escorted from your rooms by around six if that's okay."

"That's like two hours from now," said Helen.

"A little under," corrected Eleanor.

She pressed the button for the lift. The doors opened right away and she stood to one side.

"Like I said before ladies, it's an absolute honour to have you all at this year's event. You've made Murray and Roberta so, so happy just being here. And I'm sure you're going to have the most wonderful time here at SteinerCon with us."

Eleanor's phone began to ring. She feigned her apologies as she answered it, and hurried back towards the main lobby. Martha looked at Helen and Geri, blank and a little breathless.

"Well," she said. "At least we don't have to worry about dinner."

"Brilliant," said Geri, distracted by her phone. "Mount Blushmore has gone viral."

Martha didn't want to know. Not until she'd had a lie down.

Eight

MARTHA LOOKED AT herself in the full-length mirror. The huge, opulent suite she'd been given by the Steiners stretched out behind her. She'd never stayed in a room like this before. The furnishings, the wallpaper, even the carpets felt more expensive than her own family home back in Glasgow. Not to mention the size of the place. The biggest hotel they'd ever stayed in was in Florida when the kids were younger. That room had barely had enough space for four of them. This one, on the other hand, could have comfortably housed the whole SteinerCon summit.

Despite all of the space, Martha had kept her stuff neatly in the corner by the door. She didn't want to make a mess, after all. Everything seemed so expensive and gaudy here, like she was living in a music video. She felt guilty when she dirtied a glass at the minibar by leaving fingerprints on the crystal. It had taken her almost five minutes of rubbing and obsessing to clean it again.

Not for the first time that afternoon she asked herself what she was doing. The humble garage and petty misdemeanours of a few randy husbands or wives seemed a long, long way away. The people here at the convention were clearly professionals, they knew what they were doing. She'd simply stumbled upon a terrible murder and risked it all to get to the bottom of it. Imposter syndrome didn't quite cover it all.

As was often the case, her mind refused to let it go. Martha had to keep reminding herself that she was proud of the agency and of her sisters. They had every right to be there, and just as much right to call themselves private detectives. She pinched the bridge of her nose and tried to stop thinking. It was hurting her brain.

A knock came from the door. She'd never been happier to be distracted.

"Come in, it's open!" she shouted.

Helen was the first to arrive. She was still wearing the same clothes from earlier, only now she'd tied up her frizzy hair into an untidy knot.

"You're not changing?" Martha asked, foolishly.

"No," said Helen, rocking back and forth on the heels of her sandals. "No, I thought I'd just go like this. It's not a black tie thing or anything is it?"

"I have no idea," said Martha, packing away her make-up. "I have as much information as you do Helen."

"Oh," said her sister, wandering over to the balcony door. "Your room has a much better view than mine."

"I thought they were all looking out onto the park."

"Yeah, they are. Except you can actually *see* the park from here. Mine has a little wedge of green if you crane your neck all the way around. Still, not to worry, I've pocketed all the peanuts and crisps, will do us for the train back home."

She winked. Martha rolled her eyes. Her sister wasn't just the scruffy, university educated intellectual she appeared to be. She was a savvy saver too apparently.

"Are you all set then?" she asked, meandering to the minibar.

"All set for what?" Martha could feel her shoulders and chest tightening.

"The great meeting tonight," said Helen. "A chance to pick the minds of our great American benefactors. You know I was reading all about them in the brochure for the convention in my room. They're quite a big deal Mart, like 'rich list 'big deal."

"There's a brochure?"

Martha's panic rose again. She always liked to do her homework, especially heading into meetings. She hurried over to the huge coffee table in the reception room of the suite and dug through the magazines scattered about the marble surface. She found the brochure Helen was talking about, and began flicking through its glossy pages.

"Yeah, it seems that they're self-made millionaires," Helen continued. "They had a small agency in Detroit in the seventies before packing up their bags and moving west to LA. And ever since then it's been a non-stop thrill-ride all the way to the top."

Martha flicked through the brochure. There were pictures of extravagant mansions and supercars with unpronounceable names. Every other image showed Murray and Roberta Steiner in the company of actors and actresses, politicians and dignitaries, even a meeting with a Pope.

"Seems their big break came when they foiled a multi-million dollar telemarketing scam that had links to the Mafia back in 1981. That made them national news and they were signed up to a book deal about their lives. It was on the New York Times Bestseller List for like a year or something crazy. And from there they moved into TV. That's where it went super crazy for them. But yeah, self-made people. Pretty cool I suppose, you know, if you're into that sort of thing."

Martha put the brochure down. There were undeniable echoes of the Steiners' story and what was happening to her and her sisters. It gave her chills.

"Did you pick up on what that Eleanor woman was saying earlier Helen?" she asked.

"She said a *lot* Martha, and very quickly, too. You'll have to be more specific."

"*Commercial opportunities*, those were her exact words. She said it a couple of times. Commercial opportunities. Are we expected to be trying to sell ourselves here or something?"

Helen looked a little concerned. She ran a hand through her unwashed frizzy hair.

"I can't say I noticed," she said. "But now that I'm unemployed, maybe I *should* be thinking that way. I mean, I'm hardly the biggest champion of commercialism. Or capitalism for that matter. That said, would I be entirely unreceptive to endorsing some dodgy product for the sake of a quick buck? I'm not so sure."

"Bells," Martha smiled.

"What?"

"Bells, it's made for you. You could call them Hel's Bells."

"Very good," Helen winked. "Why didn't I think of that?"

Another knock at the door. This time it opened without permission. Geri stood brightly to attention, a tall, handsome member of staff standing beside her. Her arm was looped into his elbow and he didn't seem to mind.

"Ladies, I'd like to introduce you to Ahmer," said Geri loudly. "And he's going to be making sure that we get to our dinner appointment on time and in one piece. I caught him lingering about outside the door and bless him, I think he was a little embarrassed when I pinched his bum to let him know I was behind him."

Ahmer smiled weakly. Martha fetched her handbag and sucked in the air.

"You're in over your head with this one, Ahmer," she said, Helen joining them. "So please, before my sister causes you anymore embarrassment, lead on. We don't want to keep our hosts waiting."

The group wandered through the top levels of the hotel. Ahmer did his best to remain professional as Geri still clung tightly on to his arm while Helen and Martha followed closely behind.

"The hotel opened in April 1963," he said, trying to divert the conversation away from himself and his bottom. "It's one of the most revered resorts in the world and is famous for its fine dining, luxury rooms and impeccable service. It stands at 101 metres tall, has 28 storeys and 453 rooms including 56 suites. In 1967 the Beatles met Maharishi Mahesh Yogi here. They subsequently went to Uttar Pradesh with him in order to meditate."

They headed into a lift and climbed a single floor. The doors opened to reveal a long, rectangular room that stretched out in front of them. At the far side were tall panoramic windows. The dying sun flooded in through the immaculately polished glass, giving everything a rich, homely, warm glow. Soft piano music drifted through the air, mingling with the diners who were enjoying an early dinner. Martha did all she could not to let her chin hit the floor.

"Please, if you'd like to follow me ladies," said Ahmer, taking the lead.

He strolled up the central aisle of the restaurant, tables lined up on either side. Martha, Helen and Geri kept close to him, drinking everything in as they went.

"Bloody hell," said Geri, quietly.

"I was just about to say the same thing," agreed Helen, dazzled by the chandeliers that seemed to float in mid-air above their heads.

"Is that… is that him?" Geri whispered, tapping Martha on the shoulder. "Is that him out of that thing?"

She pointed at a handsome looking man in a tight-fitting grey suit standing at the end of the bar. He was deep in conversation with a woman who looked far too beautiful to be a real person.

"Yes," said Martha. "Yes I imagine it probably is."

Geri stifled an immature snort. They continued on through the restaurant, edging closer to the huge windows at the far side.

A long table had been set up just in front of the view. There, sitting amongst the blazing glow of the early evening, were Murray and Roberta Steiner. Martha had to remind herself that they weren't ghosts. The light seemed to bend around them, giving them an unearthly glow.

"Ladies, your hosts, Mr and Mrs Murray Steiner," said Ahmer, standing to one side.

Martha tried to swallow, but found her mouth was dry. Helen and Geri shuffled up beside her, the three Parker sisters presented, ready for inspection.

"Ah!" Murray boomed, his voice almost rattling the windows. "There's my three favourite Brits in the whole wide world!"

He stood up and offered his hand. Martha stepped forward, unsure if she was supposed to kiss the huge, ornate class ring on his middle finger. Thankfully Murray knew what he was doing.

He took her hand, shook it gently and then kissed the back of it. It made her a little giddy.

"Martha Parker," he said, all teeth and eyes. "I've read *so* much about you. And to finally get the chance to meet you, it's such an honour. *Such* an honour."

"Oh no, please Mr Steiner," said Martha. "It's us who are honoured, really. And grateful too, you've been a very gracious and generous host."

"Nonsense," he bellowed. "Nothing but the best deserves nothing but the best. Please, my wife Roberta has been dying to meet you all too."

He let go of Martha's hand. She was startled to find that she was a little disappointed to not still be being held by him. Roberta Steiner reared up from her chair beside him and gave a generous smile equal to her husband's.

"You are a true inspiration Martha," she said. "Really you are. You *all* are."

She welcomed the others up to the table. Murray kissed Helen's hand and then did the same to Geri.

"Blimey," said the youngest Parker sister, batting the air around her face. "I knew you were good looking Murray but I didn't think you were *this* good looking."

There was an awkward, split-second pause. Geri froze, as did Helen. Martha was mid-way to saying something when Murray Steiner let out a deafening, gut busting laugh. He slapped the table and looked around for approval.

"We've got a real livewire here," he said. "I like you kid, you're gonna go far in this world."

Roberta ushered the sisters to their seats. An army of waiters and waitresses were on hand, everyone with a specific role to fulfil. Martha was still overawed at the beauty of the place. She didn't even notice a napkin had been placed on her lap, her wine glass filled and a menu opened and put right under her nose.

"You've got to try the salmon," said Roberta. "Murray and I had the salmon the very first time we stayed at this hotel. And it hasn't changed a bit. You know the chef is—"

"Yack, yack, yack," said Murray to the table, although he was focussed on Geri. "You'll have to excuse my wife girls, she just *loves* to talk about the old days."

Roberta quietened at that, her mouth a thin, razor sharp line across her face. Martha curled her toes with embarrassment. It took a few moments for her to release them.

The waiting staff arrived with the entrees. They took away the menus before Martha had a chance to choose. She figured that the Steiners would probably be ordering anyway. And they didn't seem the types to get something like food wrong.

"So tell me, girls," said Murray, cracking open a prawn the size of a tennis ball. "Are you all single?"

"Murray, please," said Roberta, nervously rubbing the back of her neck. "You want to try and tone things down a little with our guests huh?"

"What?" he said, sauce ringing his lips. "I'm curious. I've read their files, I want to know about the real people behind the headlines."

"Well I most certainly *am* single Murray," said Geri, reaching over and touching his hand.

"Helen over there is *painfully* available and has been for a very, *very* long time."

Helen was mid-way to swallowing a gulp of water. It stopped somewhere in her gullet and came back up. She excused herself politely and fled to the toilet.

"And what about you Martha?" said Murray, locking his sights on her. "Are you footloose and fancy free?"

"Erm… no," she said. "I'm married, Murray, happily, for twenty years. I've got a grown-up daughter who is doing well and I live to work at the agency. I'm very happy, very happy indeed."

"There, you see Murray," said Roberta, spitefully. "Not everybody is as interested in having such an exotic personal life as you, it would seem."

"Hey, I'm just trying to liven things up, babe. You don't have to be such a downer all the time," he snorted and laughed, thumbing at his wife to Geri.

"Yeah, well, one of us has to be realistic. That's how we got where we are now."

"Eh… no," he said. "We got where we are now because of goddamn hard work and a few lucky breaks."

"Lucky breaks and hard work," hissed Roberta. "Is that what you call what I've done for us?"

"Yeah it is. What *we've* done."

"We, yeah, that funny little word you use when you want to get something."

"Hey!" he barked. "I always get what I want."

He winked at Geri who batted her eyelashes. Martha noticed her top had slipped off her shoulder—deliberately of course. She was going to say something, but the sparring match between the Steiners had taken over the conversation.

"What must you think of us?" said Roberta, although there was no shame or embarrassment there. "Here we are, bickering like the old, married couple we are, when we should be congratulating you on everything you guys have achieved."

"That's… that's very kind of you," said Martha. "And it means a lot, really it does, coming from you Roberta."

"So are you guys going to earn off of this, huh?" said Murray, licking his fingers.

"Excuse me?" asked Martha.

"Earn. You know? Money?" he rubbed his greasy fingers together. "What? You think you have to go through all of the crap for nothing? C'mon Martha, you're a smart lady."

"Well… I mean, we were paid well for the Coulthard case, yeah."

"And we've had a steady stream of business since," said Geri.

"Please," said Murray. "You think deadbeats and lowlifes are going to make you rich? Get a grip of yourselves. You three… hey, where's the other one?"

"Bathroom," said Martha, weakly.

"You three are a hot ticket, you've got an angle, you're sisters for Christ's sake!" he gargled a laugh that sounded like it came from his backside. "You should be bleeding the people who come to this summit dry. I'm talking corporate sponsors, TV networks, the goddamn tourist board, they should all be paying just to have a sniff of you. Am I right Roberta? Tell them!"

Martha looked over to Roberta Steiner. Her eyes were a little glassy. For a moment the fight appeared to be gone. She nodded and took a deep breath.

"You've got something a lot of people want ladies," she said. "Integrity and talent. Don't sell yourselves short. You should grasp this opportunity with both hands. We can give you the platform but you are the ones who have to take it."

"Like I said," Murray picked up another huge prawn and dunked it into some sauce. "People are desperate for a sniff of you. Charge them. Especially you young lady, you shouldn't ever, *ever* let anyone smell you for free."

He grasped Geri's hand and squeezed it. She let out a laugh Martha had never heard before—a squeak and a giggle all in one. Murray finished eating his prawn and wiped his saucy hands on the tablecloth. Roberta, it seemed, had long given up pretending to not be disgusted. She sneered at him, as she offered another large bowl ringed with prawns to her husband. He snatched at them greedily, stuffing his face as he laughed and flirted with Geri.

All Martha could do was watch. She had been to some awkward dinner parties in the past. Friends, friends of friends, even people she didn't like. None of them had been like this. Across from her were two of the most powerful people in the media world. They had success and riches that she could only imagine. But none of that mattered. It was clear as the end of her nose, as her mum used to say, that they absolutely despised each other with a passion.

"What did I miss?" said Helen, thumping down beside her.

Martha didn't have the heart to tell her. She didn't have time.

Nine

"I NEED A stiff drink and a shower," said Geri, her boots slung about her shoulders. "And if I don't hear that laugh of his before the end of the universe, it will still be too soon."

Martha smiled at that notion. She couldn't agree more. The three sisters walked down the wide corridor that led to their rooms. All was quiet on the upper floors of the hotel. At the far end, a small window let in the twinkling lights of the London night sky. Martha had no idea what time it was, only that she should probably have been in bed a long while ago.

"I mean, that was weird, right? Tell me I'm not the only one who found that whole dinner weird," said Geri.

"Yeah, it was weird," agreed Martha. "I don't think there was a part of it that *didn't* seem weird. The whole dynamic between those two is a bit… well, messed up, for want of a better expression."

"Totally," said Geri. "Like, there's being hostile and there's being a jerk. And I think Murray Steiner might be a jerk. Or an arse. It's difficult to tell which one is worse."

"Depends on what side of the Atlantic you come from, I suppose," offered Martha.

"I thought they were alright actually," said Helen, picking her teeth.

Martha and Geri stopped dead. Helen wandered on a little bit before she realised the others weren't beside her anymore. She stopped too and turned back to look at them.

"What?" she shrugged. "I thought they came across as a perfectly normal couple."

"Helen?" Geri started. "I sometimes wonder what planet you live on. Seriously? You didn't think there was anything off with Murray and Roberta Steiner?"

"Come on Helen," said Martha. "Geri's right. None of what happened just there struck you as being a bit odd?"

Helen shrugged again.

"What about the constant one-upmanship?" asked Geri.

"And the flirting?" asked Martha.

"Not to mention the incessant bragging about how rich he was and how it was all his doing?"

"Oh, did you notice the name checking from Murray?"

"I *did*," laughed Geri. "I think if he mentioned another baseball player or some singer that's not made it over here yet one more time I would have thrown him out of those big windows they have up there."

"I would have helped you," Martha laughed too. "You didn't pick up on *any* of that Helen?"

Helen finished picking her teeth. She shrugged for a third time and scratched her chin.

"I just thought that's what married couples did," she said. "How many people do we know have been together as long as Murray and Roberta Steiner eh? Hardly anybody, right? In fact, we spend most of our time with folk whose marriages are in the gutter. Let's face it, that's why we're brought in, that's where our business comes from. Goes with the territory. I just figured that was what everyone descended into when they'd hung around with each other for far too long. Resentment and jibes."

Martha, strangely, could see a logic in her sister's thinking.

"Although I don't know how much longer that marriage would have lasted if we hadn't finished our puddings when we did," said Helen, giving Geri a dirty look.

"And just what are you getting at there, sister of mine?" asked Geri.

"Oh, you're so clever, Murray. How can I be a big shot like you, Murray? Can I flush the toilet for you, Murray? Maybe give you a goodnight kiss, Murray?" said Helen, batting her eyelids.

Martha laughed at that. Even Geri let herself smile.

"Yeah, well, he's a dirty old bugger isn't he?" said the youngest Parker. "A bit of flirting doesn't hurt. Besides, he *has* paid for all of this for us. We're his guests of honour."

"We've already earned that accolade Geri," said Martha, reaching her room. "And he knows it."

"Yeah, I know," she said. "But where's the fun in not living dangerously, eh?"

"Just so long as you *do* know that Ger," she reached out and hugged her sister. "You earned your right to be here on your own merit, *both* of you did. And you don't have to go about currying favour from rich old men for *anything*. Nobody does. Got that?"

She let Geri go.

"That all goes for you too, Helen," she said.

"Gotcha," said the middle Parker. "Loud and clear."

"Okay then. I'm going to bed. Would you two *please* promise me to have an early night. And to at least try to work on something to say at this conference tomorrow."

"We promise," said Helen.

"Scout's honour," said Geri, with a salute.

"You weren't in the Scouts," said Martha.

"Yeah I know… but I knew a lot of them."

"I bet you did," smiled Martha.

She bid her sisters goodnight again and retired to her room. The air conditioning clicked on as she closed the door, the whole suite lighting up as if by magic. Martha even had to stop herself from being startled when the curtains drew themselves back to reveal a glorious view of the city.

"Fancy," said Martha, pulling off her shoes.

She wandered through the suite. It was still far too big for her. There was just too much room. One thing Martha had learned this evening was that money, lots of it, clearly didn't buy happiness. Her eye caught the SteinerCon brochure on the coffee table and she picked it up.

She carelessly flicked through the pages again, seeing the Steiners smiling back at her. Now that she'd met them in real life the images took on a different light. Martha focussed more on Roberta Steiner—the more palatable of the couple. Geri had been right before, she was a strong, independent woman who had, in her own right, become an international style and business icon. There were interviews and spreads in the brochure that saw her rubbing shoulders with the biggest, brightest and best minds from all over the world.

Yet every time she was pictured with her husband, she appeared weak and secondary—almost like an afterthought. Martha stopped on a two-page spread in the brochure. Murray and Roberta were at some huge rally somewhere—bathed in red, white and blue ticker tape. They were smiling out to the crowds, on a stage with some politician she vaguely recognised.

Martha peered closer at the picture. Roberta and Murray were holding hands and celebrating. But there was a sadness to Mrs Steiner. It was a veneer, a mask, her eyes told a different story. Coupled with what she had seen of the pair at dinner, it was clear to Martha that this was something of a toxic relationship.

"Huh," she said aloud. "1997. A long while ago."

Decades had passed since that picture was taken. Martha had no idea what a lifetime of that sort of struggle could do psychologically to a person. She flicked a few more pages and another huge, glossy spread stared back at her, this time a more recent image.

The Steiners were posing in front of a huge mansion that looked vaguely like The White House—all colonnades and pristine lawns. They were dressed in matching white weekend wear, like they were going for a spot of sailing. Murray's hands were tucked firmly in his pockets, expensive gold watch glistening in the sunlight. Roberta's head was resting lovingly on his shoulder as they both stared and smiled at the camera.

The headline above the picture was *At Home with the Steiners*. There was no warmth there, no soul. Martha couldn't help but feel unconvinced that this puff piece was doing its job properly. Clearly there was an image the Steiners wanted to portray to their fans and followers. But it was lightyears from the reality Martha had just witnessed.

She wasn't surprised, not really. In her line of work this was fairly common practice, run-of-the-mill even. The Coulthards had proven it could be done, to a fatal level. Only they hadn't been together for as long as Murray and Roberta. Decades of punishment and indiscretion had passed between these two. Yet here they were, still together, still successful.

It was all making her head hurt. Not for the first time in her life, Martha felt like she was overthinking things. The private lives of the rich and famous were none of her business. And the Steiners were treating her and her family very well. She dropped the brochure and yawned.

"Too much thinking for one day," she said, as she wandered towards the bedroom. "Far too much thinking."

Ten

THERE WERE FEW worse sounds Martha could hear than a banging door. The furious thumping echoed through the suite. She opened her eyes and sat up, suddenly breathless. For a moment, Martha was perfectly still. She wondered if she was imagining things, the remnants of a deep sleep still hanging over her. Was it just a bad dream, lingering in her mind? Her sudden motion set off the automated curtains. They drew back smoothly to reveal the very early morning light, long shadows stretching out across the park and beyond. The sky was a milky blue, soft and comforting. Then the banging started again.

Martha gathered the sheet about her neck, as if it would protect her from whatever was on the other side of the door. The hammering grew louder and louder, getting faster all the time. Whoever it was, they *really* wanted her attention.

She quickly got out of bed. Running to the door, she skidded to a halt, remembering she was only in her pants and faded Rolling Stones Voodoo Lounge world tour 1995 T-shirt. Ducking into the ensuite she pulled out a hotel robe and fastened it around her waist as she hurried back to the door.

She pulled it open to see Geri on the other side. Her sister was white as a sheet. She was gasping for air.

"Geri," Martha said. "What the hell's wrong with you? Why are you banging on the door? What time is it?"

"He's dead!" Geri gulped.

If Martha thought the banging on the door had been bad, she had another think coming.

"What?" she said, her voice barely louder than a whisper. "Who?"

Even before Geri had said who it was, Martha knew. Somehow she just knew. It was an awful feeling that was becoming an altogether too frequent occurrence these days. Just as it had in the Coulthard case, the creeping discomfort of her being correct—morbidly so—was starting to take hold.

"Murray Steiner," said Geri.

There would be plenty of time for questions later. And Martha's head was full of them. Right now, her youngest sister was clearly devastated. Shaking, shivering, her skin an unhealthy shade of grey. Martha grabbed her by the hands and squeezed them tightly in hers.

"Come here!" she said, pulling Geri in close.

She slid her hand around the back of Geri's head and held her tight to her shoulder, hushing her, rocking gently from side to side. "It's okay, it's okay," she whispered. "Just take a long, deep breath and try to calm down."

Geri was sobbing now. Martha could feel the little breaths she was taking.

"What's going on Geri?" she said quietly. "Murray Steiner is dead. Start from the very top and work your way down."

Geri sniffed loudly. She stood back up. Colour was starting to flush back into her cheeks. Martha was worried. Out of all of them, the youngest Parker was normally the toughest. Yet here she was, in bits.

"You better come up to their penthouse," she said. "Roberta..."

Roberta Steiner. Martha's blood suddenly turned cold. The questions that had been dancing in her periphery were now very much in the forefront of her mind. She took Geri by the shoulders and stared into her eyes.

"Geri," she said. "Tell me you haven't done something you shouldn't have."

Geri's bottom lip wobbled. She bowed her head, rubbing more tears on her arm.

"I was with Murray last night," she said. "All night, in fact."

"Oh Geri," Martha groaned, slapping her forehead. "What did I tell you?"

"Nothing happened, I swear," Geri pleaded. "I swear nothing happened Martha, although God knows he tried to make it happen. But nothing, I promise you, I promise on your and Helen's lives that I didn't sleep with him."

"Then what the hell were you two doing?" Martha snapped. "Playing Monopoly?"

Geri looked hurt. She cowered away from her sister. Martha instantly regretted her harsh words.

"I'm sorry," she said. "I'm just… I'm just trying to get my head around all of this. It's not what you expect to wake up to on a Saturday morning."

"I didn't do anything Martha," said Geri, her voice hard now. "I swear to you I didn't. We just talked. That's all. I only went up there to try and get hints and tips to take us to the big time. I was there for business Martha, and that's all."

The steely resolve had returned to Geri. She wiped her cheeks and took a deep breath, just as Martha had told her. There was no doubt in her mind now that Geri was telling the truth.

"Okay," she said. "I believe you."

"Thank you," she smiled.

"So what happened?"

Geri rubbed her arms. She shivered and shook her head.

"When you went to bed last night I headed back to my room," she said. "I got in, and my phone went. It was Murray."

"He called you?"

"He did," said Geri. "He invited me up to the penthouse. He said he was impressed with my business acumen and he was happy to share some of his extensive knowledge with me… with *us*."

It was Martha's turn to shiver. The thought that Murray Steiner had been soliciting her sister made her sick to her back teeth. How people like him could get away with it all, in the twenty-first century, was as baffling as it was terrifying.

"And you went up," she said.

"I did," Geri said. "I knew what I was doing Martha, I knew what his angle was. Come on, I hope you'd expect me to know that. Remember the whole lecture you gave me before you went to bed."

Martha smiled at that.

"So I went up there and he was trying his very best to, you know, make it a more physical relationship," said Geri. "But I wasn't going to do that, Martha. You know I wouldn't."

"What happened then?"

"I fell asleep," said Geri, shrugging. "He'd drank a bottle of whisky in the time that I'd been with him. I went to sleep on the bed, must have been about three this morning. Then I woke up and he was… he was… dead."

Her voice cracked. She blinked, fighting back more tears.

"He was on the chair across from the bed, just sitting there," she said. "His head tipped back, mouth wide open. He was dead Martha, just dead. Sitting there like a big dead guy. I… I don't know what else to say. I called down to the reception, they sent somebody up..."

"And what about Roberta?" asked Martha.

Geri's sadness evaporated. It was replaced with fear

"She… she knows, yeah," she said.

"About Murray? Or the fact you were in his room all night?"

"Both," said Geri, biting her nails. "She knows the lot, she was there when the staff arrived. She wanted to talk to me but I… I couldn't, not alone. I said I'd have to get you first. I… I don't want to face her on my own Martha. Not after what's happened."

"Okay, okay," said Martha. "That's alright Geri, you don't have to do anything you don't want to. We'll sort this out, it's going to be fine. Just remember what I always say—the easiest thing in the world is to tell the truth. You've done absolutely nothing wrong here. Okay?"

Geri nodded. Martha hurried back into her room and pulled on her jeans and trainers. She threw her robe on an empty couch and rushed back out to Geri who was waiting in the corridor, staring into space. She was worried about her sister. How would this impact her? Going to sleep and waking up to find a corpse staring back at you—hardly what you want on a family trip away.

They walked quickly along to the stairwell at the end of the hallway. Geri led the way and they were soon at the front door of the penthouse suite. It was open, the sound of voices filtering through from one of the rooms in the rear. Martha walked carefully, taking in everything about the Steiners' suite She didn't know why. She just had that gut feeling again. Something about all of this didn't seem right.

Geri took her hand as they followed the voices. As they got closer they realised it was Roberta Steiner speaking. The Parkers eased in through the door that led to the main living room of the huge penthouse. There were a dozen people gathered there, all standing to stiff attention. At the front, by the huge windows, Roberta was holding court.

Eleanor David stood to her right, head bowed, face flushed with tears. The rest of the people in the room, Martha assumed, were private staff and part of the Steiner entourage. They all wore headsets and carried far too much tech to be anything else.

"I can only plead with you, from the bottom of my heart, for confidentiality at this time," said Roberta. Martha and Geri lingered at the back.

The TV queen looked immaculate. Her hair was done, makeup pristine. She wore a dark suit that oozed power and grief all at once. Designer of course, the only sign of colour was the blood red lining of her heels.

"We will, of course, be alerting the media, just as soon as I can bring myself to do so. My plan is to carry on with the convention. We have five thousand people downstairs that have travelled from all over the world to be here. Not to mention sponsorships and TV commitments. Murray, as you all know, would have wanted the show to go on. He loved his work and he lived for it. And I can think of no better tribute than to make this the very best SteinerCon we've ever had."

Sounds of gentle sobbing drifted between the gathered crowd. Some of the staff were being consoled by others, others stood like statues, eyes locked on their fearless leader, Roberta.

"Eleanor will be handing out revised schedules as soon as we have them," she said. "From the bottom of my heart I thank you—both for your continued professionalism and for the dedication and love you've shown me in these last few hours. Murray was my husband for over forty years. I spent every day of those decades in his company. And not much has happened in my life without him. What happens from here on in is anyone's guess. But you all mean the absolute world to me."

Roberta caught Martha's eye. She lingered there before finishing her speech. "And we… *I*… couldn't do any of it without you. Every one of you. Thank you."

She clasped her hands to her heart. There was a moment of respectful silence before Eleanor David stepped forward. She started to disperse the crowd, flipping between her phones and tablet.

As the well-oiled machine of the Steiner operation began to crank back into gear, Roberta moved through the thinning crowd. She had locked her sights firmly on Martha and Geri. Moving through the ensuing chaos like a shark on the hunt for prey, she reached them in no time. Beckoning with her finger, she was serious and gruff.

"You two. With me. Now," she said.

Martha and Geri did as they were told, following the TV icon back through the penthouse to a small office near the front door. Roberta clicked the doors closed behind them and turned the lock. Martha felt her heart thumping on the inside of her chest. She wasn't sure why. Roberta Steiner suddenly seemed very intimidating. If a raging bull had broken through those locked doors, Martha wouldn't have bet against the seventy-year-old putting it on its backside.

"Roberta look, I told you—"

"Don't," said Roberta, cutting Geri short.

She breezed past them again and over to a large desk. Opening a drawer, she pulled out a bottle of vodka and one small shot glass. Filling it, she sank the drink in one well-practised gulp. There was no flicker of emotion on her face, nothing to indicate the shot had had any effect. She turned the cap back onto the bottle and leaned forward on the desk, staring at the Parkers.

"Now then," she said. "It looks like we're in a bit of a pickle here, ladies. My husband is dead, found in his room by you, young lady. I've got staff all over my penthouse, asking questions that a grieving widow shouldn't have to answer just hours after her other half has passed away. And to top it all off I have five thousand eager fans downstairs, not to mention the millions at home who are going to be heartbroken when they find out that their precious Murray Steiner has shuffled off this mortal realm without so much as a please or thank you.

"In short ladies, I want you to think long and hard about what you're going to tell me in the next few seconds. It could make the difference between you remaining free women of the world or spending a very, *very* long time in jail."

She sat down on the chair behind the desk. Opening up her hands to Martha and Geri, she smiled.

"Please," she said. "The floor is yours. I'm *all* ears."

Eleven

MARTHA DIDN'T KNOW what to say. What *could* you say at a time like this? She was certain she'd never been in quite as intimidating a room before. For an office in a plush hotel penthouse, it had all the comfort and welcome of an interrogation room.

She suspected that it was a deliberate room choice on Roberta's part. Everything was dark—the walls covered in a fine, black and charcoal wallpaper. The furniture was just as dark—polished glass and marble for a desk and bookshelves. Mrs Steiner sat in the middle of it all like some looming queen of the underworld.

Martha moved to speak first. She cleared her throat. It was enough to raise a perfectly plucked eyebrow from Roberta.

"Mrs Steiner," she started, unsure where formalities lay all things considered. "I can assure you that nothing untoward has gone on between your late husband and my sister here. As you can probably tell, she, both of us, are just as shocked by Murray's passing as you are."

"Martha is right," said Geri, growing in confidence. "I couldn't believe it when I saw him just… just sitting there. I mean, he was so full of *life*. You should know, you were married to him for long enough."

Martha stifled a wince at that. Roberta remained ice cold across the desk from them, listening to every word. While she may now be a fashion icon, and a champion of global women's rights and all her other titles, she was a detective at heart. Martha could see that cold, steeliness that only comes through hard sleuthing and investigation. Roberta Steiner was on the case. And the Parkers were the suspects.

"I think what Geri is trying to say," she continued. "Is that this has been a terrible, terrible tragedy. Murray was, in the short hours I knew him, a very generous, almost larger than life character. The thought that he's not with us here, for his own convention, is as appalling as it is sad. Am I right Geri?"

"Absolutely," Geri nodded. "And I can't stress enough that nothing happened between us Roberta. Absolutely nothing."

The air seemed to chill ever so slightly. Martha could feel her stomach knotting. But Geri continued.

"He invited me to his room last night," said the youngest Parker. "He said he wanted to tell me how to further my career, *our* careers and how this summit could be a fantastic launching pad for bigger and better things. So I followed him. I'm not stupid Roberta, I could tell he was angling for more than a bit of company. But nothing happened, I swear to you and to my sister here. I wouldn't have dared do something like that to you. Or myself for that matter."

Martha shifted uncomfortably in the upright chairs near the desk. She fidgeted, suddenly itchy with sweat and nerves. She knew it wasn't doing her any favours—restlessness usually a sign of guilt—but she couldn't help it. Having Roberta Steiner staring her down, mulling every syllable over and over in order to process what was going on, was incredibly off-putting.

"You believe her?" said Mrs Steiner, turning to Martha.

The question was straight and hard, like a sword slicing through the air. Martha blinked and then nodded.

"I trust Geri implicitly Mrs Steiner," she said, some of her own confidence returning. "If she says she didn't do anything with your husband, then I absolutely believe her. One hundred per cent."

Roberta tapped her long nails on the marble desktop. She chewed the answer over for a moment before nodding too.

"Okay," she said. "Okay. I believe you. I believe *both* of you. You're green behind the ears. Nothing more than country hicks who have lucked out on a big case. No offence. I can spot a liar at ten paces, a hundred if it's a man. And you two don't strike me as being the type who would harm a fly, let alone cause somebody like me a whole heap of aggravation."

Geri let out a long breath of relief. Martha swallowed, her throat completely dry.

"Thank you," she just about managed.

"What for?" asked Roberta. "You haven't done anything and I'm not doing anything in return. What we have here, ladies, is an impasse. A moment in time that's as unfortunate as it is unavoidable."

She got up from the executive chair. Striding over to a small couch at the far side of the room, she picked up a bag. Rifling through it, she pulled a beaten-up, battered purse from its depths. Roberta handed it over to Martha and nodded to Geri.

"Open that up," she said.

Martha looked at her sister. Geri was wide eyed, staring at the purse.

"Go on," said Roberta.

Martha unclipped the purse. Inside was a stack of small, old photographs. The corners were dog-eared and the edges frayed. Martha carefully fished them out and started looking through them.

"Is that? Is that you and Murray?" asked Geri, peering at the pictures.

Martha stared down at the images in front of her. Roberta and Murray, smiling and laughing. Only they were different from those in the brochure and on TV. Here was a young couple decked out in flares, complete with perms and sideburns. They were in bars, with friends, enjoying drinks in gardens and at the beach. Martha flicked through the pictures and stopped at the last one—the pair on their wedding day. She held it up to Roberta.

"You were a beautiful bride," she said.

Roberta smiled back. The coldness was gone from her, her eyes glassy and wet. All the glamour and hardened exterior seemed to melt away, revealing the tender seventy-year-old beneath.

"Do you know what these are ladies?" she asked them.

"They're your history," said Geri. "Memories, happy memories, from a long, long time ago."

"They are," said Roberta. "But they're much more than that. They're the last time I was happy with my husband."

She took the wedding day photo from Martha. Sitting down on the edge of the desk, she waved the old picture in front of her.

"We got married at Woodstock," she said, laughing.

"That was a music festival," said Martha to Geri.

"Thanks Martha," Geri answered sarcastically. "Next you'll be telling me The Beatles broke up."

"They had a little tent that was serving as a recovery station for people who were too out of their minds," Roberta continued. "And there was this little old padre there. I don't know if he'd gotten off the bus at the wrong stop or something. But it was just so weird and so right, you know? Murray asked if he would marry us, right there and then. And he agreed. My parents were *so* angry when they found out. They were working class teachers, they didn't approve of Murray's long hair and moustache. He wasn't store-bought enough for them."

She touched the picture, her fingers caressing Murray's face. Martha could feel the sting of tears biting behind her nose.

"All of these pictures were taken around about that time," said Roberta, nodding down at the collection. "No later than about 1971, maybe 1972. By the time the decade was over we were already on our way to becoming the TV royalty you see before you now. And it was never the same, never the same."

Her words lingered hauntingly between them. Her sadness was already retreating. She was putting her armour back on.

"Murray was a difficult man to live with, ladies. And God knows I tried. His drinking and his insatiable appetite were one thing. But he loved women, absolutely loved women. The amount of times I found him in bed with somebody, hah. I'd be a millionaire in my own right if I had five bucks for every time that happened."

"And you stayed with him?" asked Martha. "Why?"

"Because I loved him," sniffed Roberta. "I loved him more than anything else in this world. That's why I keep these pictures. Nobody, and I mean nobody, has ever seen them before. I keep them in this old purse and carry them around with me for safe keeping. And when I'm feeling low or I think about divorcing him, I dig them out and they remind me of the times when we used to be happy. When we used to be free."

"And that kept you with him?" asked Geri. "That was enough?"

Roberta paused for a moment. She looked at the wedding photo and then handed it back to Martha. She clapped her hands on her thighs and pushed herself up from the desk.

"You were the latest in a very long line of women who were drawn in by Murray's light," she said to Geri. "And I believe you when you say you didn't sleep with him. You're a clever girl Geri, very clever from what I've been told. That would have only driven the old son of a bitch over the edge even quicker. What age are you again?"

"I'm twenty-one," said Geri.

Roberta rolled her eyes. She collected her photographs and stuffed them back into her old purse. She clipped it closed and waved it at both Martha and Geri.

"I assume I can trust you both not to mention this to anyone," she said.

"Of course," said Geri.

"You have our word Mrs Steiner," said Martha obediently.

"Good. Now, I know this is highly unconventional, pun intended there of course. But I'm going to have to ask you both and your sister, Helen isn't it?"

"Yes," said the Parkers.

"I'm going to have to ask the three of you to continue with your keynote speech this afternoon. And there might be a little more press duties for you than you were perhaps expecting. I'm hoping that I can rely on you both to keep the details of how you found Murray to yourself. I wouldn't want any further unnecessary scrutiny put on your personal lives. When those vultures in the press get a sniff of scandal, they're all over you like flies around a turd. Believe me, I know."

Martha felt a surge of reassurance. Roberta was taking charge. She was a woman who knew what she wanted and how to get it. Her personal life, clearly, was much more fractured and delicate than anyone could ever know. Yet she had confided in Martha and Geri, here in this terrible place, just a few short hours after her husband had died.

Martha didn't need much more convincing that Roberta Steiner was a good role model for the likes of Geri and millions of other women around the world. Even she was in awe of her control and determination.

"Thank you, again," said Geri. "For everything Roberta. You've already been so kind and generous to us all, and I feel so awful that it's all turned out like this."

"You're a good woman Geri Parker," said Roberta, winking. "And you've got a very bright future ahead of you. But I want you to promise me one thing."

"Anything," said Geri, eagerly.

"The next time a dirty old man invites you to his hotel room. Give him a kick in the nuts from me. Understand?"

The three women laughed. Roberta guided them towards the door of the oppressive office. She bid them goodbye and ushered them out. The penthouse was an even greater hive of activity now—phones ringing and raised voices making a terrible din.

Martha grabbed Geri by the arm.

"You okay?" she asked.

"Yeah, strangely," said Geri. "I don't think I knew what to expect in there. I mean, it could have gone very differently. I was the last person to see Murray Steiner alive. And the first to see him, you know, dead. I thought at least she would have given us a good rollicking. But no, far from it. I'm still a little shocked actually."

"She's a lovely woman," said Martha. "Very clever, very sincere. She could have done a lot better than Murray as far as husbands go, by the sounds of things."

"Definitely," Geri agreed. "The path of love never did run smooth though, did it? And we should know, we get enough clients that way."

Martha laughed in agreement.

"What do we do now?" asked Geri, staring out at the chaos.

"Nothing. Not yet," said Martha. "We do what we're told and that's all. But first, before anything else, we're going to find our sister and fill her in on recent events. Then, maybe, when my nerves have finally settled and my stomach has untwisted itself, we'll get some breakfast."

"That's the best idea I've heard all morning."

The Parkers weaved their way through the maelstrom of staff and workers and let themselves out. Meanwhile the world was waking up to the news that Murray Steiner had passed away silently and peacefully in his sleep. He was survived by his adoring wife Roberta and his legions of fans all around the globe. SteinerCon would be continuing, just as Murray would have wanted it. He was seventy-one.

Twelve

THE MOOD OF the convention was noticeably different. Martha and Geri stepped out of the lifts and felt it straight away. Where there had been excitement and anticipation before, now there was grief and mourning.

The main lobby was littered with delegates, huddled together in small groups. Some were in tears, being consoled by their friends. Others looked dazed, walking around aimlessly, decked out in their Steiner caps and T-shirts, tote bags full of merchandise never to be signed.

"They already know then?" said Geri, quietly.

"It would seem that way, yes," said Martha.

The Parker sisters headed out into the main thoroughfare. Martha couldn't help but feel like she was walking through a battlefield after a terrible skirmish. The uneasy sense of peace and calm after waves of violence made for a strange atmosphere.

They headed for the restaurant near the entrance to the convention centre. On their way they passed a middle-aged woman, her face flushed red as tears streamed down her puffy cheeks. Two friends, equal in age and upset, were trying to calm her down. She looked up as Martha and Geri walked by, howling even more as she recognised them. A distorted, washed-out picture of Murray Steiner was on her T-shirt, his faded face smiling back at them.

"Man, I wasn't expecting this," said Geri. "I mean, I know he's a global superstar and all that. But this is like the death of a Royal or a popstar."

"Or a head of state," Martha nodded at a TV screen mounted on the wall beside the mourners.

Murray's death was breaking news. The screen flipped between clips of him in action and various tributes and messages of condolence on social media. Martha was just as surprised as Geri, if not more so. She hadn't quite expected this level of global recognition.

Even after spending time in his company, there was something Martha didn't believe about Murray's fame. She thought he had perhaps exaggerated it all, for bravado and for his ego. Yet here was the world all coming together to celebrate his life and mark his passing. The scale of the whole ordeal suddenly came very sharply into focus for her.

"Where's Helen?" she asked hurriedly, panic looming.

"I've texted her," said Geri. "Not like her to be up and away from her room before noon is it? Maybe she pulled last night after I left her."

"Too soon Geri. Too soon."

"I'll text her again."

Martha and Geri had headed to Helen's room before they went downstairs. There had been no answer. Ordinarily Martha wouldn't have minded. Only now, with everything escalating again, she wanted to know her sister was safe and well. And, most importantly, by her side.

"Anything?" she asked.

"Steady on Mart, I can touch type on these things but I'm not *instant*!" Geri waved her phone about.

"Okay, as soon as she answers, let me know."

Martha and Geri headed into the restaurant. It was busy with guests and convention goers, the mood just as gloomy in here as it was in the main lobby. The screens dotted about the walls all carried the same grim news. Murray Steiner, private investigator, author, TV personality, philanthropist, dead.

"Hold on a minute," said Geri. "Is that… is that Helen?"

She pointed across the busy restaurant. In the far corner was a woman with long frizzy hair laughing and hitting the table. Martha squinted, wishing she had her glasses. The harder she peered the more she recognised her younger sister.

"She's with someone!" said Geri. "It's a man!"

"A man? Helen? No, it can't be," said Martha.

"I *told* you Martha. Didn't I tell you? She pulled last night. Look! They're having breakfast together. How cute."

"Geri, please, take a hold of your senses. If there are two things on this earth that Helen Parker doesn't get on with, it's breakfast and men. She's not very well going to combine the two is she?"

"Let's go find out then!"

Geri marched off through the tables. She was too quick for Martha who trailed after her, apologising to the other guests as they weaved between them.

"Helen!" Geri shouted. "Oh Helen! Sister dearest. Where *have* you been?"

As they got closer, Helen looked up to see her sisters approaching. Her face turned pale. Then it flushed with colour. The laughing, smiling woman they had seen from the entranceway had been swallowed up by the usual Helen Parker.

"Oh," she managed, as Martha and Geri reached the table. "This isn't what it looks like."

"*What* isn't what it looks like?" Geri beamed.

"It's not anything we're just… we're just friends, I mean, we're not even that. We're just having breakfast."

Helen was getting herself in a muddle. It was a sure-fire sign that she had been caught out. Martha smiled. She offered her hand to the man sitting across from her sister.

"Hi, I'm Martha," she said. "I'm Helen's older sister."

The man gave her a friendly smile. He stood up and bowed a little as he took Martha's hand. He was tall and tanned, his shirt open enough to show a broad, muscular chest. His jeans were weather-beaten, as were the scuffed toes of his boots. His hair was tied untidily back into a short, stubby ponytail and his eyes twinkled with a knowing kindness.

"Tom Hopgood," he said. "The pleasure is all mine, Martha."

"You're Australian," said Geri, butting in. "Perth maybe?"

"You've got a very good ear," he said.

"Geri," she said. "Geri Parker, I'm the youngest of our little trio of troublemakers."

"Geri," Helen hissed. "Can you give Tom his hand back please, you're going to shake it off."

"Oh sorry," she said, letting him go.

"No, please, no harm done," he said. "I couldn't find a table, and your sister Helen here very kindly said I could share."

"I'll bet she did," said Geri.

"Geri," warned Helen, a little too loudly.

A few of the other guests looked around this time. Helen mouthed her apologies. Tom laughed again. He flashed them his beaming, easy smile and sat back down.

"She was just telling me about you guys," he said. "Sounds like you've been through the mill a bit recently. And now you're headlining SteinerCon. Not too bad for three women from Glasgow is it?"

"That's right," said Geri, pulling up two chairs. "So what's a good looking Australian doing at a private investigators 'summit in London? Looking for a wife?"

Helen kicked Geri under the table. No one else noticed.

"I'm a private dick too," said Tom, taking a bite from a thick slice of watermelon. "If you've got trouble in Trigg, Tom Hopgood is your man."

"Trigg?" asked Martha.

"It's my hometown, born and raised there. Right on the beach, lovely part of the world. You're all welcome to swing by my place if you ever find yourselves Down Under."

"And the wife?" Geri asked.

Helen went to kick her again. This time she missed and banged her knee on the table leg. It made the cutlery rattle and she did her best not to scream in agony.

"I'm not married, Geri," he said bashfully. "There's something about the late night stakeouts and the ungodly hours I keep when tracking down small-time crooks that, somehow, doesn't seem all that appealing to the good ladies of Trigg. Or anywhere else really."

"Oh I wouldn't say *anywhere* Tom," Helen snorted.

Geri drew her a look of total embarrassment. Helen turned back to her cereal, loading her mouth with cornflakes.

"You're very kind, all of you," he said. "I try to come to SteinerCon every year actually. Gives me a chance to catch up with some family who live here in London. The ones that weren't shipped out to Oz, am I right?"

He winked. Helen snorted again, still chewing.

"But it's a good opportunity to meet people like yourselves, other detectives. I don't need to tell you guys that it can be a lonely business. And you have to make mates wherever and whenever you can. You never know when it'll come in handy. Still, I wasn't expecting the terrible news though, eh?" said Tom.

"News?" asked Helen, dribbling milk.

"Murray Steiner," said Tom. "He's dead. It's all over the news. Turns out he died in his sleep."

"A real shame," said Geri.

Martha could feel her sister tensing up. Her shoulders were square and her head dropped.

"Murray Steiner?" asked Helen, eyes like golf balls poking out of her head. "*The* Murray Steiner? The dirty old ba… bugger who bought us dinner last night? He's dead?"

"Yes," said Martha. "Please Helen, eat with your mouth closed, we've got company."

"He's dead though?"

She turned around quickly to look at the screens around the restaurant, as though noticing them for the first time.

"Bloody hell," she said, loudly. "That's awful. And I was going to ask him for some career advice too. Bloody hell."

Martha didn't need to look at Geri to know that one stung. She grabbed her hand beneath the table and squeezed it.

"I think we should probably get going Helen," she said. "I understand that we're still going to be making our keynote speech later at the conference, despite everything that's happened."

"But you haven't had anything to eat yet," Helen said.

"That's okay, we can get something upstairs. We need to talk."

Martha stood up. She shook Tom's hand again, as Helen, reluctantly, did the same.

"Lovely to meet you Tom," Martha said. "And you're absolutely right. It really is great to make new friends and people you can connect with. Maybe after our speech we can all get together for a drink or something."

"I would love that Martha," he said, getting up.

"It's a date," said Helen.

She paused, waiting for a sarcastic comment from Geri. But her younger sister was silent. Sensing there was something wrong, she slid out from the table and joined the others.

"What the hell is going on with you two?" she said, as they hurried out of the restaurant. "I was having a very lovely breakfast with a gorgeous Australian who didn't find me repulsive, crass or too feminist for my own good. And you had to ruin it."

"Just drop it Helen," said Geri. "Please."

"Drop it? What would *you* have done if I'd come blundering into one of your dates, Geri? You'd have me skinned alive in front of everyone."

"Would you two keep your voices down," said Martha, guiding them back through the tables.

They left the restaurant and headed back across the main lobby. Helen was still fuming, stomping behind Martha and Geri. She was about to start off on another tirade, when Martha bundled her into a quiet corner where nobody was looking.

"Geri was with him last night when he died," she said, her voice low and serious.

"With who?" asked Helen.

"Murray Steiner."

It took a moment for Helen to work out what was going on. Then the penny dropped and she began to shake her head.

"Oh no," she said. "Oh no, no, no. Geri, you didn't… you didn't *do* anything did you?"

"No," said Geri, her head still bowed.

"She didn't do anything, Helen," said Martha. "But it didn't help you talking about career advice and all of that. That's what Geri was after, when Mr Steiner tried on a few of his old tricks."

"Yuck," said Helen wrinkling her nose. "How awful. What about Mrs Steiner? Does she know?"

"She knows everything," said Geri. "And she's fine with it all. I didn't do anything with him, Helen. I fell asleep, and when I woke up, he was there, dead, just staring through me. It wasn't nice."

Helen could sense her sister's hurt now. She reached out and touched her shoulder.

"You okay?" she asked.

"I'll be fine," said Geri. "I don't know. It's all a bit much. I thought I would get over it. But it's all just a bit too raw for me at the moment. I don't know how I'm going to get through this speech."

"Don't worry about the speech," said Martha. "Helen and I can handle that."

"We can?" asked Helen.

"I can handle it then," Martha rolled her eyes. "What's important is that you don't tell anybody about this Helen. Not a soul. Roberta swore us to secrecy. And I'm in no mind to start messing with one of the world's most powerful women."

"Yeah, of course. Sure," said Helen. "Blimey. This is getting serious girls. I mean, we're right in the thick of it with this one aren't we. Bloody hell."

"We wouldn't be us if we weren't," said Geri, with a sad smile.

"No, that's true," said Martha. "At least there's no foul play on this one."

Something about what she said made the others fall silent. Martha hadn't really thought about the cause of Murray's death until that point. She'd been so caught up in Geri's involvement that it hadn't even occurred to her to wonder what had killed him.

"Do we know what the cause of death was?" asked Helen, as though reading her mind.

"No," said Martha curtly. "No. I think it's still too early."

More silence. Martha didn't like it. She looked at her sisters in turn, but neither of them said anything.

"What?" she asked. "What's wrong?"

"Nothing," said Helen, her mouth a tight, thin line across her face. "Nothing at all."

"Geri?"

The youngest Parker looked at the floor. She kicked around a ball of lint rolled up on the carpet.

"I don't know," she said. "Murray Steiner, he was old, right? But he wasn't *that* old."

"What are you getting at?" asked Martha, guessing where this was going.

"It's just something that's bugging me."

She looked at the others.

"Like, we didn't do anything, you both trust me on that one. He was drinking heavily and he'd been eating all night, even when we got into his room. It's like, why now, when then, why last night? Sure, the old geezer was excited and all that, who wouldn't be having me for company?"

She smiled weakly again.

"It's just, I don't know, it seemed like such an odd thing to happen when it did. Just passing away like that. You'd think I'd have heard something, *anything*, during the night. But I slept all the way through. Nothing, zilch. I don't know guys. Maybe I'm just paranoid. Or in shock. Or both. Maybe it's just my imagination running away with me because we're at a convention full of private investigators. I don't know."

Geri took a deep breath. She shrugged. Martha was about to tell her to stop worrying, to keep her head up, to stay positive, when she was distracted by raised voices. The Parker sisters all peered around from their little hidey-hole and saw a huge pack of journalists crowding the lift area. Flashes went off as cameramen and photographers jockeyed each other for the best view of Roberta Steiner.

The grieving widow was flanked by security guards who shoved a clear path through the rampant pack. Roberta headed straight for the convention area and vanished, leaving behind a wake of media hacks.

"We've got to work on our speech," said Martha.

The others agreed. They headed for the lifts in silence, none of them wanting to talk any more. Suspicion hung in the air now, joining the morose sense of mourning that had enveloped the summit. Martha didn't know what to think. There was no foul play with Murray's death. He was an over-sexed, overweight, overly stimulated pensioner who had enjoyed years of an excessive lifestyle. Time caught up with everyone in the end. And last night it had been Murray Steiner's turn.

That had to be it. Didn't it?

Thirteen

"UNLUCKY FOR SOME," said Helen, flicking through the channels.

The TV screen in the green room behind the main stage still flashed images of Murray Steiner. Helen's button bashing was beginning to irritate her sisters.

"I mean come on, *National Treasure*? They clearly never met the guy," she said with venom.

Geri snatched the remote and threw it across the room. It dropped down behind a sofa, two stagehands watching it vanish before going back to their conversations.

"Enough," she said.

Helen folded her arms and huffed. Martha was doing her very best to ignore them both. She was staring down at the speech she'd written, rewritten, binned, salvaged and redone around a million times already. The words all seemed to be jumbled up, letters dancing around on the page beneath her scribbles, lines and circles. It was a mess, much like her mind. And there wasn't long left until she had to deliver the goods.

She sighed loudly and put the papers down with a flounce. Rubbing her eyes, she leaned forward, elbows on her knees and stared aimlessly at the carpet.

"What's the matter with you?" asked Helen. "Are you as heartbroken about the passing of the late, great, incredibly rude Murray Steiner as the rest of the world?"

"I told you to drop it Helen," Geri interrupted.

"Oh come on, don't give me all that, Geri," she fired back. "You were at dinner last night. In fact, *you* should know more than any of us how repugnant a human being he was. All of this outpouring of grief from Z-list celebrities and orange-faced politicians is just a sham."

Geri shook her head in disbelief. She got up with a grunt and went over to the small table littered with various soft drinks, tea and coffee. One of the stage hands tried to help but she batted them away.

"I'm not heartbroken, as it happens, Helen," said Martha. "I'm nervous as hell."

"Why?"

"Why?" Martha gulped. "Why? Because there are hundreds of people just a few feet outside that door and they're expecting us to go out and tell them how wonderful we are. That's why."

"Oh, it'll be fine," Helen said, reclining on the sofa. "Roberta is going to be there. She's a professional, that woman. She knows what she's doing. We're just the dressing."

"The what?"

"The eye candy," she said. "We're only there to make Roberta look good. It's a well-known tactic for these celeb types and famous people. They like to appear to be taking no-hopers like us under their wings in public. Makes them look generous and giving."

"Roberta *has* been generous and giving," said Geri, returning with her tea. "You're only here because she's footing the bill. Or had that escaped your unemployed mind, sister dearest?"

Helen stuck out her tongue. Martha took in a big breath of air. Maybe Helen was right. Maybe this wasn't going to be a total disaster. Maybe her anxiety, worry and general nausea would all be for nothing. Maybe, just maybe, this was all part of the celebrity sham she knew nothing about.

Her speech stared back at her from the coffee table. She felt sick again.

The door opened, and another stagehand appeared. He was wearing a headset with a mic that swooped down in front of his mouth. He knocked on the open door and nodded at the Parker sisters.

"Two minutes ladies," he said. "Mrs Steiner is just finishing her introduction and then we'll get you on. Okay?"

"Okay," said Martha, although she had no idea where it had come from. She was not okay.

The nausea had ramped up a few notches. Her legs had turned to jelly and a cold sweat was making her shirt stick to the back of her neck. She picked up the speech and held on to it in a shaking hand. Helen and Geri stood up and waited for her.

"Oh God," she said. "Are we really going to do this?"

"Yeah I guess we are," said Geri.

"It'll be a breeze, trust me," said Helen.

"You know, you're remarkably calm about all of this," said Martha, just about finding the energy to stand up straight. "I was half expecting, actually, scrap that... I was *hoping* you'd be a nervous wreck and I'd have to be coaxing you to go on to the stage. You know, pulling you kicking and screaming. In fact, I'd sort of banked on it, to try and distract me from the sheer bloody terror I'm feeling just now."

"Nope," said Helen. "I'm perfectly calm."

They headed for the door. The two stagehands gave them a thumbs up as they went. It didn't help Martha. A small corridor lined with thick, black curtains snaked its way from the green room towards the stage. The sound of Roberta Steiner's voice was getting louder and louder as they approached. Martha felt like a Christian being led through the bowels of the Colosseum, ready to be fed to the lions in front of thousands of Romans thirsty for her blood.

A rapturous applause made her stop dead. It sounded huge, ominous even, like there were a million people crammed into the conference centre. Helen and Geri bumped into her back and the spell was broken.

"You know why Helen isn't nervous don't you," said Geri.

"What? Who? No, why?" said Martha, unscrambling her brain.

"It's because her Australian boyfriend will be outside and she wants to make a good impression."

"Geri," Helen shouted.

"Is that not the case?" Geri asked her.

"It absolutely is *not* the case," said Helen adamantly. "Honestly. You can share a breakfast table with a complete stranger without your next step being up the aisle you know, Geri."

"Pull the other one Hel," said Geri, gulping her tea. "I saw you two at breakfast. Sure my head feels like it's been screwed on backwards. But I couldn't miss the puddle of drool that had formed around you as you stared into Crocodile Dundee's eyes."

"His name is Tom," said Helen. "And we are just friends. That's all. I don't care how deep, dark or mysterious his eyes are. Or how tight his bottom looked in those jeans he was wearing. It is purely a friendly, professional relationship. If he spots me on the stage today and wishes to pay me a compliment about my performance, then that would be most welcome. If not, it's hardly the end of the world now is it?"

Geri gave a snigger. They came to the end of the dark corridor and the stagehand with the headset was waiting for them. The bright lights of the stage were dead ahead now. Martha could make out Roberta standing amongst the illumination. She looked wonderful, strong and defiant, like a woman who could take on the whole world and emerge from battle somehow even more brilliant.

She thought about the pictures Roberta had shown her, the happy couple at the beginning of their lives together. She thought of the pain and suffering she must have endured for so long. And Martha wondered if, now that Murray was dead, Roberta would feel a little relief. Love was a very strange business, she saw that every day at work. Roberta must have loved her husband dearly to have endured him for so long.

"Okay ladies, here we go," said the stagehand.

"Ladies and Gentlemen, it gives me great honour to present to you our very special guests at SteinerCon this year," said

Roberta, her voice booming like a giant's. "Martha, Helen and Geri—the Parker sisters!"

Another roar of applause seemed to make the whole building shake. The stagehand gave them a thumbs up and then ushered them on to the stage. Martha didn't really know what she was doing. Her legs moved of their own accord, back and forth, back and forth, carrying her out of the shadows and into the blazing light. She knew Helen and Martha were behind her, but they felt a million miles away as the sound of adulation washed over her.

She winced as she stared out at the crowd. Everyone was on their feet, clapping and cheering, at least a thousand strong, all there to see her and her sisters. Camera flashes twinkled like stars in the huge auditorium and Martha felt like she was floating through the vast expanse of space. Only when Roberta grabbed her by the hand did she feel safe again.

The grieving Mrs Steiner raised their hands up together in unison. There was a roar of approval as all four women basked in the limelight.

"Bloody hell," said Geri below the noise.

"Bloody hell is right," said Helen. "Oh god, what are we doing? What the hell are we doing here, on stage, in front of all these people. They're going to find out we're frauds, or worse still, that I'm unemployed, a disgrace to the grad student name. I don't think… I don't think…"

"Martha Parker ladies and gentlemen," said Roberta.

She stepped to one side and offered the stage to Martha. Expertly taking her leave, she guided Geri and the panicking Helen over to a set of seats waiting beneath a giant screen. Martha stepped up to the lectern and placed her speech down in front of her. The applause slowly died down.

Martha looked down at the pages in front of her. Despite everything that was going on she'd managed to rehearse at least of some of what she had wanted to say. It wasn't very good and she hated public speaking, always had done, even when she was in school. How she longed for the sweaty, stale air of Mrs

Calder's primary five classroom now, the smell of chalk and sawdust lingering all about her.

She could make out the opening lines of the speech. But something was stopping her. It wasn't fear or worry, not any more. It was something else. She looked up at the crowd stretching out expectantly in front of her. They were silent, eyes staring out from row after row, all eager to hear what she had to say. Then she started.

"I had a speech prepared," she said, her voice sounding strangely small after Roberta's eardrum bursting performance. "In fact I've got it written down here."

She raised it up to show the crowd. Placing it back down on the lectern, she smiled out at her audience.

"But I'm not going to read from it."

That drew a few murmurs from the crowd. Martha was almost certain she could hear Helen squeaking with panic from behind her.

"It was written before everything that happened overnight," she said, finding her voice. "It was written during a time when I was nervous and frightened and overawed by the sheer luck that had befallen my sisters and I. We received a mysterious text inviting us to be guests of honour here at SteinerCon. It was like something from a dream. Then, when everything had been worked out, we were introduced to Roberta and Murray Steiner. And let me tell you something, that was probably the most nervous I've ever been in my life. Maybe second to right now actually."

The crowd laughed at that. It made Martha feel a little better.

"Tragedy, however, has struck, and now we're all here, together, joined in mourning, when we should all be celebrating the fantastic work that we all do on a day-to-day basis," she continued. "Instead I'm standing here, in front of you all, to the backdrop of great sadness at the passing of Murray Steiner."

The hairs on the back of her neck stood on end. She felt a sudden urge to turn around. As she did so, she saw the huge face of Murray staring down at her from the screen at the back of the stage. Another round of applause went up as the crowd joined together in saluting their dead hero. As they settled, Martha took another long, deep breath.

"I only knew Murray briefly, which in itself is a small miracle. He was a larger than life character, exactly as he appeared on our TVs and in interviews. A hugely generous man, it was clear to me from the moment I first laid eyes on him that he was always going to be the life and the soul of the party. And I'm still reeling in shock about what's happened. But that brings me back to my speech. In short, it was going to thank Murray and Roberta for inviting myself and my sisters here to their summit to talk to you all. We're humble people who try to do as much good as we can. And, despite what you might have read in the newspapers, we're not these great, big, famous detectives. Not like the Steiners, who are the real deal, so to speak.

"Being real is tough in the modern world, Lord knows I don't get it. Geri is the tech whizz of our operation, I don't know a tweet from a twit. What I do know, however, is that you can't hide how genuine and loving a person is. No filters, no makeup, no digital profile can ever mask a person's true self and personality. And with that in mind, I know, for certain, that Roberta Steiner is one of the most genuinely wonderful people that I've ever had the fortune of meeting."

Martha looked over at Roberta sitting with her sisters. The crowd applauded again, only this time it was much more sedate. They sounded less like football supporters and much more dignified and genuine.

"Again, in the short time I've been in her company, Roberta has been nothing short of caring, generous and giving," said Martha. "And the fact that she is standing here, in front of you all, at this convention, merely hours after the death of her husband, the love of her life, is nothing short of remarkable. If that doesn't give you some idea as to how great this woman is, even before you take in her success and her trailblazing career, then I don't know what will.

"So in closing ladies and gentlemen, I want you to join me in toasting Roberta Steiner. Without her none of this would have happened. And if there's anyone who deserves our love and hope right now it's her. To Roberta!"

The audience echoed Martha's words. Roberta rose from her seat. She blew kisses out at the crowd as she strolled confidently up to the lectern. When she got there she hugged Martha tightly.

"Thank you," she whispered into her ear.

Roberta took up her place and waved out at the crowd. She clapped her chest and mouthed more thanks to them all. Martha could only watch on in admiration. Roberta seemed to radiate energy. She was glowing. The more the applause came, the brighter she appeared to shine.

"Thank you, Martha. Thank you so much," she said into the microphone. "I am truly humbled by your words. Really I am. It's people like you that kept me and Murray working all of these years. And it's detectives and investigators like you and your sisters who keep that spirit alive to this very day. Thank you."

Martha felt lightheaded. The adulation, the noise, even being so close to Roberta was infectious. The widow urged Helen and Geri over to join them. The other Parkers smiled and waved to the crowd and the four women embraced. The audience showered them with applause, every person in the auditorium now standing up and clapping.

"This is amazing," said Geri to the others. "I'm speechless Roberta. Truly I am. Thank you."

"No, thank you Geri," she smiled back. "This is all because of you and your sisters. You're the guests of honour, these people are here to see you."

"She's right," said Helen, reaching out and grabbed the mic from the lectern. Martha had a sudden fear. Only a few moments ago Helen Parker had been rooted to the spot in fear—bowled over by the sudden adulation. Now it seemed she was thriving in the spotlight.

"Hello London," she shouted, the mic screaming.

"Helen!" Martha shouted.

"You know it's so kind of you, really it is. We love you. We actually love you all, every single one of you."

"What's she doing?" asked Roberta.

"She's babbling," said Geri. "You'll have to excuse our sister, Roberta. She tends to get a bit carried away. She's an emotional car crash."

"We're the Parker sisters, I'm Helen, you've heard from my older sister, Martha, of course," Helen snorted.

The crowd were still cheering. Martha stood, a terrible feeling of dread consuming her. Then it happened.

"And of course the youngest of the Parker sisters—Geri," said Helen. "You know, she was the last person to see Murray Steiner alive? Can you believe that? She was with him, last night, in his room. She's a part of history now. My sister, a part of history?"

In an instant the clapping stopped. It felt like the air had been sucked out of the auditorium. All Martha, Geri and Roberta could do was stand and watch on as Helen kept smiling, laughing and waving, oblivious to what she had just done.

"Oh no," said Martha.

"What did she just say?" hissed Roberta.

"Oh no is right," said Geri.

The silence quickly turned to a low rumble of voices. Martha wasn't used to big crowds. But she knew when people were confused. As Helen's announcement swept through the auditorium, the voices grew louder. A thousand different conversations made for a sudden souring of the mood.

Roberta snatched the mic from Helen and threw her a bitter look.

"That's all for this session now, folks. If you want to consult the main timetable you'll be able to see what other events are happening here on the first day of SteinerCon. Thank you and god bless."

She threw the mic down on the lectern and grabbed Helen by the arm. Shoving her towards the side of the stage and out of the limelight, Martha and Geri followed at a safe distance.

"You ever get the feeling you've just blown something?" Geri asked quietly.

"Yeah," said Martha. "It's like a sinking feeling, like you're going down with the ship and there's no chance of escape."

"Yeah," agreed her sister. "That's exactly the feeling I've got right now."

They picked up their pace as Roberta and Helen vanished down the corridor towards the green room. A chorus of boos had started from the very back of the auditorium. And it didn't sound like it was going to stop any time soon.

Fourteen

"WE'RE IN FOR it now guys," said Geri. "I mean, *really* in for it. We can forget about any endorsements or cushy TV deals. This is it."

"We don't know that," said Helen. "This could all be for effect."

"All for effect? You mean like when you blurted out to a room full of die-hard Murray Steiner fans that I had spent the night with him in his hotel room. In front of his wife, just hours after he's died. You mean just like that Helen?"

"Quiet you two," said Martha.

They found themselves back in the green room. The mood, much like in the auditorium, was much frostier than it had been before. The stagehands didn't seem quite so welcoming now. And the noise of disgruntled fans and conference goers could be heard penetrating the wafer thin walls.

The Parker sisters sat in a row on a couch across from the door. They were all straight-backed and tense. Roberta had told them to wait there and not move. None of them wanted to upset her any more than they already had.

"I just don't understand *why*," said Geri. "I keep going over and over it in my head, Helen. Why the hell would you think that was an appropriate thing to say?"

Martha had to agree. She'd been trying to come up with an excuse for her sister. Nothing was coming to the fore.

"I don't know," said Helen, shrugging. "I guess I got swept up in the moment. I think I was so relaxed and then so frightened, it must have turned my brain to scrambled eggs."

"So what's your excuse for the rest of your life then?" Geri spat.

"Well maybe if you hadn't spent the night with Murray Steiner we wouldn't be in this mess in the first place, would we, Geri?"

"I told you—"

The door swung open, clattering against the wall with a thud as Roberta came storming into the green room, Eleanor David in tow. Martha didn't know why but she stood up. It was like a superior officer had come into the room and she felt she had to do something.

"Sit down," Roberta barked.

Martha did as she was told. The grieving Mrs Steiner paced back and forth in front of the sisters. She was rubbing her forehead, pinching the bridge of her nose, massaging her temples.

"What the *hell* were you thinking?"

Roberta stopped pacing. She was staring down at Helen, her hands like daggers, pointing straight at her throat. Martha thought, for a brief moment, that she might lunge forward and strangle her sister there and then. She wouldn't have blamed Roberta if that's what she wanted to do. In the whirlwind twenty minutes since her almighty gaffe, she had thought about murdering Helen too. That would have been too easy though. At least from Roberta Steiner's point of view. She wanted her revenge, Martha could see that particular fire in her eyes. And she wasn't going to stand in her way.

"Well?" Roberta asked.

"Well what?" Helen fired back, defiantly.

"What were you thinking?"

"I've been asking that same question since it happened," said Geri, sliding forward onto the edge of the sofa.

"Thank you, sister dearest," said Helen. "Stabbed in the front."

"You still haven't answered me," said Roberta. "And I'm not a patient woman. In fact I'm pretty impatient at the best of times. And unless you haven't noticed, this *isn't* the best of times."

The room fell silent. The throbbing noise of the crowd was a dull heartbeat in the background.

"Look, I'm sorry, okay?" said Helen, a distinct lack of empathy in her voice. "I was a bit of an emotional wreck up there. I just got caught up in it is all. I mean, I didn't exactly tell any lies, did I?"

She shrugged and looked about for support. There was none forthcoming.

"Helen," said Martha, sinking her face into her hands.

"Well did I? Geri was in Murray's room last night. She was the last person to see him alive. It's just facts. I can't help it if all I've done is tell the truth."

"Listen to me Helen Parker," said Roberta.

She stepped forward, expensive stilettos squeaking on the carpet. She bowed down so that her nose was almost touching Helen's. Like a hawk sizing up its breakfast, she stared long and hard into Helen's eyes.

"Your little revelation has just set off a ticking time bomb out there," she said, her voice measured, calm and collected. "Right now you've got eight, maybe ten thousand people all Googling your name, your sisters 'names, trying to find out just who in the hell you are. They'll be Tweeting, Skyping, Facebook live broadcasting, YouTubing, Twitching, every goddamn thing to get in a piece of the action. Your truth-telling stands a very good chance of being picked up by the bigger media outlets. And the journalists out there, the rabid dogs that they are, have now got a story where there wasn't one before. So yes, you're right, you've told nothing but the truth. But that's handed them plenty of scandal on a plate. And it's a triple-decker crap sandwich that I've got to clear up. All before lunchtime and long before Murray is cold in the ground. Do you understand what you've done?"

Martha ground her teeth. She was waiting for Helen to make some sort of sarcastic comeback. Only she was silent. Slowly, Martha pulled her face from her hands. Her sister was sitting, eyelids heavy, mouth curled in one side into a sort of smile.

"If you like," said Helen.

Roberta blinked once. Martha reckoned it was the first time she had done since she'd stormed into the green room.

"Do any of you other Parker sisters have something to share?" she asked. "Any other home truths you want to get off your chests. Or do you think my husband's reputation has been tarnished enough for one morning?"

Geri was silent. Martha knew she should be too.

"Roberta, really, Helen might not sound like it, but I'm sure she's sorry, as we all are," she said. "I think the sense of occasion and everything that's happened has all just become a little too much."

Roberta was stoic, standing over them like a huge, inanimate colossus. None of the warmth she had shown Martha and Geri was there anymore. The mask was up, covering that fragile, endearing woman from the private office of the penthouse. Looking at her now, Martha wouldn't believe that she existed at all. This was the price of wronging her it would seem.

"And I think I speak for all three of us when I say that we're all completely happy to do whatever it is you need us to do to make this whole unsavoury mess run as smoothly as possible for you."

Again silence from Roberta. She was thinking. Martha could tell from the flexing tendons in her temples. This was one of the most intelligent women they'd ever met. Had they just made a very powerful enemy?

"I think it's only fair," she said, hoping for a response. "Especially given how generous you've been to us all. We're not up-to-speed with this lifestyle I'm afraid. We don't have your experience. And it looks like we've shown that at the worst possible time. But I'm appealing to your better nature, as a friend, to let us at least help as best we can."

Roberta nodded her head ever so slightly. She clicked her fingers and Eleanor David hopped into action. She produced a sheet of paper and handed it over to Martha.

"What's this?" she asked.

"A waiver," said Eleanor. "We'll need you to sign it, swearing you to secrecy on what's happened here. You won't be able to discuss any of what transpired at SteinerCon or Mr Murray's untimely death, including details of his last few hours. If you do you'll face some very harsh legal ramifications."

"Wow, hold on a moment," said Geri. "This sounds an awful lot like a gagging order to me."

"Yes, it is," said Roberta spitefully. "That's exactly what it is. My empire turns over more money than you can count young lady. I can't risk any of that on your blabbermouth sister here spilling her guts to the first reporter who waves a Dictaphone under her nose. I need some protection, and this is it. Of course, if you think you'd be able to match wits with me in court then you're very welcome to try."

Something about her tone, her words, stung Martha. She felt like she'd been punched right in the chest. She looked down at the contract and saw their three names at the bottom.

"If we sign this," she said, her voice trembling. "Will that be the end of it? Will this all be handled by your people? I have to have some assurance that my family will be protected as much as they can be, Roberta. Helen made a mistake. Geri too. I'm their older sister and I'll protect them until the end of time itself. But I need to know that you'll take care of all of this."

Roberta's frosty look eased a little. Eleanor moved furtively from one foot to another.

"The contract is what it is," Eleanor said. "All the details are in there and—"

"You have my word Martha," Roberta said, interrupting her. "You have my word that, if you all sign the gagging order, then I'll make sure none of this comes back on you."

Martha did her best to hide her jangling nerves. She took a dignified breath and looked at Helen and Geri. Her sisters seemed confused, and angry. This was the cost of leadership. She had to make snap decisions that would protect them both, no matter what the cost.

"Do you have a pen?" she asked.

Eleanor was halfway to clicking one before the question was finished. She shoved it into Martha's hand.

"On the dotted line please," she said.

"Oh, is that where it goes?" asked Geri, sarcastically.

Martha signed her name. Helen was next and then Geri last. She handed the contract back to Eleanor who filed it away amongst a stack of papers in a big folder under her arm.

"So," said Helen, sitting forward. "Now what? Do we get lines or something? Have to run around the sports field a hundred, million times. I know you Americans love everything mind-numbingly athletic."

"Shut up Helen," said Martha.

"I'm glad you said that before I did," said Roberta, the faintest hint of a smile on her thin lips. "The three of you are booked on a private jet back up to Scotland. It leaves in three hours and I want you all on it, buckled up and in the air. When you land, you'll be taken back to your homes and that is where I suggest you stay for the next week or so while my media machine does its best to tackle the herculean nightmare that you've created. Is that all perfectly clear?"

"Crystal," said Martha.

"Excellent," Roberta turned to leave them. "Now I suggest you all go and pack your bags. My people will collect you from your rooms and take you to the airport. Don't speak to anyone, don't look at anyone, don't even *think* about anyone. Understood?"

"Yes," said Martha again. "Completely understood."

Roberta marched quickly to the door. Eleanor opened it for her and another wave of noise, angry noise, angry people, flooded into the green room.

"Roberta," Martha called after their former host.

The grieving Mrs Steiner stopped. She straightened her shoulders before looking back at the Parker sisters still sitting on the couch.

"For what it's worth, thank you," Martha said.

Roberta didn't smile this time. She vanished out of the door, Eleanor trailing behind her. When they were gone, Martha started to breathe again.

Fifteen

MARTHA COULDN'T HELP but feel a little sad. She was packing away her things much earlier than she had anticipated. The circumstances were horrible, and nothing had gone the way she had hoped. Death, it seemed, always complicated matters.

There was, however, relief too. She didn't like this world of fame and fortune. It came with far too much pressure. The expectations were far too high and it required a gumption and dedication she knew she was never going to be capable of. It was better, she decided, that the limelight was given to others. Not her. And certainly not her sisters.

She didn't dare turn on the TV. The last thing she needed was to see even more coverage of Murray Steiner's death. Or, indeed, any mention of the scandal and rumours that would be flying around after Helen's little speech. Martha might not have known a whole lot about public relations but she knew when to keep her head firmly in the sand. And this was very much one of those moments. Hear no evil, see no evil, speak no evil.

She zipped up her suitcase and let it sit on the bed. It looked back at her, blank and silent. She almost wished she could climb inside and never come out. Sitting down beside it she stared blankly into the distance.

She'd made the right decision. Hadn't she? Signing the gagging order, keeping quiet about everything they knew. That had been the correct thing to do, the proper thing. Roberta Steiner was a powerful woman, more powerful than Martha probably knew. You didn't go after someone like her. You didn't even *think* about going after her.

What would it achieve anyway? Martha had read all about these so-called scandal exclusives in the Sunday newspapers and online. Nobody came out of those things smelling of roses.

Private conversations, deepest, darkest secrets, it was all sensationalist rubbish. She wanted better for Geri and Helen than that. They both *deserved* better.

Yes, she had done the right thing. They would return home, lock the doors and wait for Roberta Steiner's people to work their magic. In a week it would be old news. In a month barely spoken about. And in a year nobody would know who Helen, Geri and Martha Parker were.

"Bliss," she said aloud.

Her phone buzzed. She pulled it out of her pocket and looked at the message. It was Helen. She was asking when they were being collected. Martha clicked on the number and it began to ring.

"Hello?" Helen answered.

She was out of breath. Martha's heart rate picked up a little.

"Helen, where are you?" she asked.

"I'm in my room," she said, curtly.

Martha didn't believe her. There was a lot of background noise, raised voices.

"Are you actually?" she asked.

"Yes, of course I am."

"What's all that noise in the background then?"

"What noise?" Helen laughed nervously. "What are you talking about Mart? I'm in my room, there is no background noise."

"There is. I can hear it," she said. "I can hear raised voices. It sounds like you're outside."

"Oh…" Helen tailed off. "Oh that! No, no that's not voices, it's… it's the TV. Yeah, I've got the TV on. There's a really interesting program on about… about… crowds."

Martha's blood turned to ice. She shot up from the bed.

"Helen, please, don't lie to me. Not after everything we've been through this morning," she said. "Please, please, *please* tell me that you're not doing anything stupid."

"I'm in my room Martha," said Helen again, laughing this time.

"You heard Roberta, she told us to stay in our rooms until we were collected," she said.

"I know, that's why I'm asking, that's why I texted you. When are we getting picked up? So… so I know when to be ready."

Martha's heart began to thump harder. She wasn't feeling well, her dizziness returning.

"Helen, please, I'm begging you," she said, her voice cracking. "I don't know what you're doing or what you even *think* you're doing. But please, for your own good, not to mention my sanity, please, *please*, just go back to your room."

Helen didn't say anything. Martha could definitely hear voices in the background now. They were much clearer, louder. She thought she heard someone say SteinerCon and mention Murray Steiner. Then it dawned on her.

"Tom Hopgood!" she blurted out.

"What?" Helen chirped.

"Tom Hopgood. Tom Hopgood. Tom Hopgood! You're trying to find that Australian you met at breakfast!"

"Don't be absurd!" Helen laughed nervously again. "How desperate do you think I am anyway? That I would risk even more wrath from that dried up old prune Roberta Steiner, just to be in the company of the rugged, no-nonsense, immaculately polite Australian private dick?"

"Helen," Martha drew out her sister's name.

There was a pause, a moment's hesitation. Then Helen came clean.

"I won't be long," she said. "I just wanted to say goodbye and exchange email addresses. That's all".

"Helen Parker! You've been told!"

"I promise I'll be back before they come to pick us up. I won't take long. He's bound to be around here somewhere."

"There are thousands of people at this summit, Helen!" Martha yelled. "And they'll probably all be baying for your blood. How the hell do you think you'll find him when you don't even know where to begin!"

"Instinct, my dear Martha. Instinct."

Helen hung up.

"Helen? Helen!"

Martha growled at her phone. She paced around her room looking for something to kick. It all looked far too expensive to damage, so she clenched her fists tightly into balls to try and relieve some of her frustration. It didn't work.

"That bloody sister of mine," she said out loud, hoping that if she talked to herself, a solution would be forthcoming. It wasn't of course. She knew there was only one thing to do.

She caught sight of herself in the long mirror by the bedroom door. She looked awful—gaunt and pale, tired physically and drained emotionally. This really was the last thing she needed.

"Don't look at me like that," she said to her reflection. "You've done nothing wrong here. In fact, you're the only Parker sister that has any semblance of dignity and standing left at this bloody conference."

Martha had half hoped for her reflection to talk back to her—to offer some sort of sage advice and wisdom. The worst part was, she wouldn't have been surprised if it did. It had been that kind of trip.

She quickly pulled up Geri's name on her phone and called the number.

"What?" Geri shouted at her phone.

"Geri, it's me," said Martha.

"I know it's you, Martha."

"What?"

"I know it's you. It's called caller ID, I can see who's calling me. You know, mobile phones, the twenty-first century."

"Yeah, I know, I know. Sorry, my head's up my backside."

"Could you make this quick please," said Geri. "I'm currently trying to cram as much free stuff into my stupid little bag as possible. So far I've got slippers, bath salts, shampoo, conditioner, two robes and one of those cool little sewing kits you only get at decent hotels."

"Geri, listen."

"I'll probably never use it, right enough."

"Geri!"

"Imagine me doing needlework."

"Geri! It's Helen, she's gone AWOL."

"What?"

Martha clapped her hand against her forehead.

"Helen, she's downstairs, out of her room. She's wandering around the conference looking for Tom Hopgood."

"That hunky Australian guy at breakfast?"

"The very same."

"But Roberta said we had to stay in our rooms."

"I know."

"So what are we going to do?"

Martha looked at her reflection. Still no wisdom. But sometimes silence was the most telling advice anyone could ever receive. It usually meant that everyone was in agreement.

"We're going to have to go after her," she said.

"Of course we are," said Geri. "Of course we bloody are. And what if Roberta's people come to collect us and we're not here."

"It's a risk we're going to have to take," she said. "All for one."

"And none for all I think is more appropriate here, Mart."

That made Martha smile. She needed that smile. It had been an awful morning.

"I'll be there in thirty seconds," said Geri. "Best get a move on, though. I doubt Roberta wants us hanging around any longer than we need to."

"You think we've outstayed our welcome?" asked Martha.

"I think we've outstayed our welcome Mart. I think we've *more* than outstayed our welcome."

Sixteen

THE MAIN CONCOURSE of the exhibition centre was heaving with people. Despite the morbid news and unthinkable stupidity of the early talk, there seemed to be a good mood about the conference. There were smiles at least, people hugging, enjoying each other's company. It made Martha nervous.

In a vain attempt to hide her identity, she'd put on a pair of Geri's sunglasses. They were far too big for her face. And she suspected they actually drew attention *to* her. It was too late now. They were down among the people with the clock ticking.

"I'm going to kill her," she said to Geri, shuffling along beside her. "Your sister, my sister, she's going to be a *dead* sister when I get my hands on her."

"If you get your hands on her," said Geri.

"What do you mean?"

"Well, she's probably in the arms of that rather attractive, rugged, man's man Australian detective by now. For all we know, he's whisked Helen off her feet and is taking her back home to Oz to live as free spirits in the golden sunshine."

"Does that sound like something Helen Parker would do to you?"

Geri thought on that for a moment. Then she shook her head. "No, you're right," she said. "Helen gets airsick in the taxi to the airport. I can't see her on the plane for that long."

That made Martha smile. They pressed on through the crowd, keeping their eyes peeled for their sister. Long queues were forming outside rooms and small auditoriums. The SteinerCon schedule was in full swing. Everywhere Martha looked there were reminders of their now not-so-friendly benefactors. They reached the middle of the exhibition centre.

A small shrine had been hastily erected in memory of Murray Steiner. Another long queue of people snaked out from a table with several books of remembrance and a picture of the TV legend on top. Candles had been lit alongside floral tributes and memorabilia left by fans. There were a few tears and sniffs as people left their messages, all under the watchful eye of a steward in a SteinerCon T-Shirt.

"This is quite extraordinary," said Martha.

"He was loved all over the world," said Geri, a hint of sadness in her voice. "It's like the death of a rock star or an actor. Although even they probably wouldn't have as much of an outpouring as this. Murray Steiner, man, he had it all."

"That's what worries me."

Martha bit her tongue. She hoped Geri hadn't heard what she said.

"What's that supposed to mean?" asked her younger sister.

Martha wanted to swear. She'd been stupid, hadn't been thinking. The last thing Geri needed to hear was her paranoia and imagination having a party.

"Nothing, forget it," she said. "Come on, we need to find Helen."

"No, Martha. Stop," said Geri, grabbing her arm. "What do you mean, you're worried? Worried about what?"

Martha wasn't sure what to say. She wasn't sure, because she couldn't be certain that what she was thinking made any sense. She sighed, taking off her massive sunglasses.

"It's nothing, Geri. Nothing at all," she said. "You know me, I over-analyse everything. I look at it from every possible angle, every possibility even. I pull things apart and then put them together again, even when they're not broken. I just overthink things."

"Yeah, you do," said Geri. "But it's usually because you're onto something.

Martha couldn't deny that. She also felt a great deal of pride at hearing her sister backing her up. After all they'd gone through that morning. It was a nice little confidence booster.

"Murray Steiner," she said, keeping her voice down. "I've been thinking about him, a lot, obviously. And there's something that just… doesn't smell right."

"What do you mean 'smell right'?" asked Geri.

"About his death."

"I don't follow you. He was a dirty old man. He drank too much, smoked too much, ate too much rich food. And, without blowing my own trumpet, died after getting all excited at having a hot young woman in his bedroom."

"Yeah, you're right, I know you're right," Martha agreed. "Except, well, I don't think guys like him just die in their sleep."

"But he did Martha, that's what happened. I was there. I saw him. I saw his dead body sat at the end of the bed. Believe me. I saw it."

"I know you did. I know," she said, sensing Geri's discomfort. "Like I said, it's probably just me being paranoid. I just… I don't know. I just think that there's something missing, some part of the picture we're not seeing. Like Roberta, for example, she's not seemed suspicious of his death at all, has she? She's not accused you of doing anything, not asked for the cops to be called, not requested an autopsy. That doesn't seem strange to you? After his sudden and unexpected death?"

"Was it unexpected, though?" asked Geri. "You saw him for yourself. He was putting back those vodkas and whiskies at dinner. And that's before you even take his reputation into account. He's lived like a rockstar for twice as long as I've been alive. That sort of stuff catches up with you. And believe me, I wish it had caught up with him any other night than it did."

Martha nodded in agreement. She waved herself away.

"You're right, you're right," she said. "I'm being silly. I'm being paranoid. My nerves are shot. Geri, I'm sorry. With everything that's gone on and with Helen now running off, I feel like I'm at my wit's end."

"I know how you feel, Mart. Believe me, I know," said Geri.

Martha rubbed the back of her head. Her hair felt greasy and matted. She hadn't had a shower now in what felt like a long time. She longed to be back in Glasgow, at home, with the door firmly locked and the curtains drawn. Suburban drudgery felt like a very welcome alternative to what had been happening to her recently. She wanted to leave it all behind.

"Where could she be?" asked Geri. "I never thought I'd find myself saying this, but where would our sister go if she had the company of a good looking man?"

"I can't think, is that awful of me?" asked Martha. "The thought of Helen with *any* man just frazzles my brain. I don't mean it in a bad way of course. She's just, well, so independent, isn't she?"

"I agree," Geri smiled. "But we don't have a lot of time. Roberta's stormtroopers will be knocking at our door any minute and—"

A crackle sounded over the public address system, cutting Geri short.

"Ladies and gentlemen of SteinerCon," came Eleanor David's voice. "We have reason to believe that three guests are missing and have gone unaccounted for. If anyone sights Martha, Helen and Geri Parker, could you please notify the nearest summit steward. Thank you."

The speakers clicked. Martha felt her stomach churning and her chest tightening. This was a disaster.

"This is a disaster," said Geri. "That bloody Helen. She's really done it this time. We're finished."

"No, we just… we just… we just need to think. Quick. Where would she be?"

Martha trailed off. The world was spinning, the whole room whizzing past her in a giddy daze. Faces in the crowd all appeared to turn towards her. Dozens, then hundreds, and finally thousands. She felt like she was at the centre of the universe and everything was converging on her.

Out of the myriad shone one face in particular. It was a face she knew like her own, a face she had watched grow up from a babe in arms to the frizzy-haired, opinionated, slightly-lovable woman that was her younger sister.

"Helen," said Martha. "Over there, I can see her."

The room came to a shuddering halt. She realised she was holding on to Geri.

"There," she said. "I saw her, I saw Helen."

"Where? Martha are you alright? You sort of zoned out there for a moment. Maybe we should get you a glass of water and a pill of some kind. You look a bit spaced."

Martha grabbed Geri's hand and pulled her through the crowd. They ran as quickly as they could, charging towards the entrance of the conference centre.

"You're going to pull my arm out of its socket, Mart. Slow down," the youngest Parker squealed.

But Martha forged on, weaving in and out of the delegates. She hoped, prayed even, that nobody recognised them. She was waiting, waiting, waiting for somebody to grab her by the shoulder. With their luck it would be Roberta, come to bring them in herself.

Only nothing happened. The crowd cleared and there was Helen. Martha, Geri in tow, almost knocked her over as they clattered into her.

"Bloody hell," Helen said.

"Bloody hell is right," said Geri, freeing her arm. "How in the bloody hell did you spot Helen all the way over here Martha?"

Martha wasn't sure she knew the answer to that one. What would she say—that time slowed down to a near standstill and she was able to focus all of her mental powers like some tinpot psychic?

"I don't know," was all she managed, gasping for breath.

"I told you I wasn't going to be long," said Helen, getting her excuses in before she was accused of something.

"Didn't you hear that announcement?" Martha gasped. "They're looking for us."

"We're fugitives, on the run from the all-knowing, all-seeing law of Roberta Steiner," Geri smirked.

"Oh they only say something like that for dramatic effect," Helen dismissed the warning.

"Dramatic effect?" Martha coughed. "Are you serious, Helen?"

"You know what these Yanks are like Mart, they'll do anything to make it sound worse than it is."

"What are you doing down here anyway?" Geri asked, a hint of sarcasm in her voice.

"Nothing."

"Nothing?" she cocked an eyebrow. "See, I think you're down here to try and sneak a goodbye snog out of Waltzing Matilda before we go."

Helen's face flushed purple. "That's a ridiculous thing to say. I don't even know what you're talking about."

Geri laughed. Martha's blood pressure was rising. And she'd long crossed the threshold of a panic attack.

"This is no laughing matter," said Martha. "We're in trouble here, *big* trouble. I gave Roberta my word that we would go quietly. We've already caused more than enough trouble at this bloomin' conference that I wish I'd never heard of. And now we're pushing our luck *way* beyond its means. So come on."

"Come on where?" asked Helen.

"We're turning ourselves in and that'll be that," she said. "No more running around. No more causing bother. We're heading home and we're locking the door, drawing the curtains and there'll be no more said about this bloody weekend ever again!"

"Oh, hey guys." The easy voice of Tom Hopgood interrupted them. The chiselled Australian PI came wandering in from the main doors of the exhibition hall, his phone in his hand. He smiled at the three Parker sisters in turn.

"Uh huh," said Geri, poking her tongue firmly into her cheek as she levelled a look at Helen. "Don't know what I'm talking about eh? I suppose it's just a massive coincidence that Tom Hopgood comes breezing in through the door looking like he's stepped straight out of a Mills and Boon novel then?"

"You what?" he asked.

"Nothing," Geri rocked back and forth on her heels.

"Nice to see you ladies again," he said. "Especially after your little performance on the mainstage earlier."

"Not our finest hour," said Martha. "I'm sorry, I don't want to appear rude Tom, you seem like a really lovely bloke and all. But we have to be getting Helen back upstairs and out of here as soon as possible."

"We've outstayed our welcome you see," said Geri. "Helen's ill-timed outburst put a few noses out of joint with the top brass."

"Geri," Helen hissed, trying to remain collected in front of Tom.

"Yeah I can imagine," he said, whistling. "Are you alright though? Don't imagine what you've been through can be very nice."

"I'll live," Geri shrugged. "I've seen worse. Not a lot mind you. But worse."

"Struth," he whistled again.

"Anyway, yes, like I said Tom, lovely chatting," Martha reached out and took Helen by the hand. "But we really must be going. Maybe you two could exchange phone numbers or email addresses or whatever it is young folk do nowadays."

Geri let a snigger escape. She snorted and bowed her head, trying to suck it back in.

"Martha," Helen's indignation almost deafened them all. "That's *way* off the mark. Tom and I are just… just…"

"Just…?" Geri raised an eyebrow.

"Mates," Tom smiled, his teeth dazzling white in his sun-kissed, bristly face.

"Mates, exactly," Helen said with a slightly disappointed sigh.

"And speaking of mates," he waved his phone at them. "My mate in the Met just got back to me."

"Met?" Martha felt her chest tighten into a tiny little knot. "You mean the Metropolitan Police?"

"That's the gang," said Tom. "I've got a mate who works in their forensics department. Well, she's a mate of a mate, of a mate, actually, now I think about it. She's a photographer—bloody good one too. How she ended up taking pictures of dead bodies in horrible London alleyways is beyond me. Anyway, she says that the cops are already sniffing around Murray Steiner's passing. Can you believe it?"

Somehow, the knot in Martha's chest tightened. All of her worst paranoid worries felt like they were being dug out from the back of the closet and given daylight.

"I don't understand," she said. "Why are the police involved? And the forensics team. And why did you ask your friend about it?"

"Helen suggested it at breakfast," said Tom.

"I did?" Helen asked him, surprised.

"Yeah," he said with his easy smile. "You suggested it between mouthfuls of those corn flakes or whatever they were. Remember? When you said that Murray had died? You told me remember?"

Martha and Geri turned to face their sister. The look of bewilderment quickly changed to that of unabridged, satisfied smugness. It almost made them shudder. She pointed her nose high in the air and looked down at both of them with playful contempt.

"What do you think of that then?" she said, pursing her lips. "Not just some sex-starved blabbermouth am I? I've been thinking and, in complete contrast to you two knuckleheads, I've been working too."

Martha suddenly felt very lightheaded. This was all moving too fast.

"I need to get my head around this," she said, clamping her hand to her forehead. "Just what exactly are you implying Helen?"

Helen was about to answer. But she stopped mid syllable. She stared out beyond Martha and then swallowed.

"I think we might have been rumbled," she said, nodding her head in the direction.

Martha looked over her shoulder. The crowd of SteinerCon parted like the Red Sea. As delegates shuffled out of the way, the formidable frame of Eleanor David came barrelling through them. In her wake was a small army of SteinerCon stewards and mean looking security personnel.

Before Martha could react, somebody had grabbed her by the arm. She was yanked forward, almost tripping over her own feet.

"After them!" came the battle cry from Ms David as everyone started to run.

All Martha could do was go along for the ride.

Seventeen

MARTHA WASN'T USED to all this running. It was quite unbefitting of a woman of her complete lack of athletic prowess or inclination. It wasn't that she didn't enjoy exercise. She just preferred to leave it to the professionals, the able, the willing or the young.

Now she was thundering down Park Lane, boat shoes slapping against the warm concrete, as groups of tourists fled for cover in her wake. She wasn't alone of course. She couldn't remember if anyone had shouted 'run 'or not. The need to get out of the conference hall had been too pressing. All Martha *did* know, was her sisters were rushing ahead of her, with poor Tom Hopgood caught up in a sea of Parkers.

"Quick!" Helen shouted. "Into the park!"

The wagon train cut sharply out onto the road. A rather lovely Rolls Royce screeched to a halt. Martha remembered reading somewhere the loudest part of those cars was the ticking clock. Somebody must have forgotten to tell the driver who was honking the horn wildly and berating them with expletives out the window.

The colossal trees of Hyde Park welcomed them with sprawling, open arms. They rustled with the light summer's breeze, leaves a rich, deep green that seemed to go on forever. Running through the gates, the four companions broke out into an open field, the sun beating down hard from the clear blue sky above them. On and on they went, running and running.

Another row of tall trees loomed ahead. As they passed beneath the cool shade of the canopy, Martha realised she could run no more.

"Stop," she pleaded. "Stop. I can't go on."

She sunk to her knees on the scorched grass. The others stopped a little further away. Martha closed her eyes, sweat dripping off her nose. She tried to swallow as much air as she could, but it wasn't enough. She thought about falling flat on her face and dying there and then. But there was too much on her mind. Eventually she settled on a compromise. She rolled onto her side and wrapped her arms around her knees.

"Bloody hell," said Geri, out of breath too. "I should probably give up smoking or something, eh?"

"I'll pretend I didn't hear that," said Helen. "Disgusting habit. Am I right Tom?"

Martha looked up at that. So that's how it was going to be now? Looking to Tom for his opinion and not her. She would have said something but her body was in too much pain.

"I don't know Hel," said Tom, hunched over. "My grandad lived to the ripe old age of fifty-two. Which is convenient as that's the amount of ciggies he smoked every day."

Helen was silent for a moment and then burst out laughing. She gave Tom a playful slap on the arm as she pushed her long, frizzy, and now sweaty hair out of her face.

"Is… anyone… following us?" Martha asked between gasps.

"No, we lost them," said Geri. "Just as well, I reckon. That David woman looked quite capable of strangling us all on sight."

"I always knew there was something wrong with her," chimed Helen. "Something about that vacant look of hers. I bet she went through dozens of small, furry animals when she was a girl. And they all wound up with mysteriously broken necks."

"Struth," said Tom. "That's quite dark, eh, Hel?"

Geri rolled her eyes. She sat down next to Martha and stretched out her legs.

"We could catch some rays here guys, what do you reckon?" she asked. "Much better than being stuck in a stuffy old conference centre, anyway. A nice little tucked away part of Hyde Park. We could set up a camp and nobody would care."

"We should go back," said Martha. "Running only makes us look more guilty than we already are. We gave Roberta our word we'd go quietly. Now look at us."

"We haven't done anything wrong Martha," said Helen. "I didn't say anything that hadn't already happened. The truth must out."

"No it mustn't," she fired back. "We agreed to leave quietly, without fuss. And in return she wouldn't turn her Rottweilers on us and ruin everything we've worked so hard to build. That's a fair deal Helen."

Helen sat down too. She folded her arms, always the petulant child.

"Just smacks of bullying if you ask me," she said.

"Well nobody did ask you," said Martha. "In fact, it's because of you and your wild imagination that we're in this mess."

"Wild imagination?" Helen shot back up to her feet. "It's my so called wild imagination that usually gets to the bottom of things, Martha. And I don't recall you ever having a problem with it before."

"We weren't dealing with a flipping media mogul before!"

Helen said something unintelligible. Geri watched the pair of them. She obviously knew better than to chip in when they were in this mood. Best to just leave them to it.

Martha immediately regretted fighting with Helen. She was tired, emotional and pumped full of adrenaline. It was making her edgy and sharp. And she didn't like feeling that way.

"I'm sorry Helen," she said. "It's just been… a stressful few days is all. It feels like we've been cursed from the moment we set foot in London. Nothing has gone right. In fact, the opposite of right. It's been a complete shambles. And now here we are, in the middle of the park, baking in the afternoon sun with nowhere to go. A shambles."

A ping broke the nervous tension between the sisters. Tom pulled out his phone from his pocket. He scrolled through the screen and raised his eyebrows.

"Interesting," he said.

Nobody answered him. He looked at the Parker sisters and shrugged.

"Nobody interested?" he said. "My mate at the Met. She says there's a toxicology report being performed on Murray's body."

"Isn't that standard procedure?" asked Geri, the only one to speak up.

"Yeah true," said Tom. "I mean all sudden deaths have to be investigated right? Just to make sure there's no foul play. But my mate says there's a bit of a buzz around the morgue. Says it's all been locked down, security top priority."

"He was a celebrity," said Martha, drawn back into the conversation. "The police won't want any leaks from the likes of your friend getting to the media. Newspapers would pay a pretty penny for what you've just told us. In fact, your friend could probably cash in if she had the right contacts."

"That's not what Tom is saying, Mart," said Helen.

The draw of the mystery was pulling them all together again.

"No?"

"No," she said. "Or at least, it's not what I think you're saying Tom. I think you're saying that the morgue is being locked down because they don't know what they're going to find from the post mortem."

Tom flipped her a thumbs up.

"Bingo," he said. "Got it in one, Hel."

The suspicions that Martha had harboured all day resurfaced again. She could feel the tingle of excitement, the thrill of something to solve shaking off the cobwebs. But there were still too many questions.

"You don't know that's true," said Martha. "It could be for any number of reasons. The man was a famous celebrity. He's died overnight, found in a hotel room."

"Don't remind me," said Geri.

"You know what these journalists can be like. One sniff of a story and they're all over it. Especially when it's somebody famous. And Murray Steiner was as famous as they come."

"She has a point guys," said Geri, getting up and dusting off the grass from her skirt. "We could be letting our imaginations run away with us. I mean, it's not like you can just wander into any old morgue and take a look at a body at the best of times."

"You did it before," said Helen pointedly.

"That was… different," said Martha.

"It doesn't matter though," Helen went on. "I have all the proof I need already."

"What do you mean by that?"

Helen looked at Tom. They both smiled at each other. A giddy excitement seemed to come over them. And with it, Martha felt her stomach sink again.

"What are you two smiling about?"

"Nothing," said Helen.

"Nothing at all," said Tom.

Martha looked up at Geri. The youngest Parker sister rolled her eyes again.

"It's like being back at school, isn't it Mart?" she droned

"Nothing," said Helen. "It's just, well, you two."

"What about us?" asked Martha.

"You two. You were the acid test."

"Acid test for what?" Geri asked.

"The acid test to see if we were right or wrong about Murray Steiner," said Tom.

"This is like getting blood from a stone," said Martha, getting up to her wobbling feet. "Could you two stop messing us around and spit it out."

Helen and Tom exchanged another giddy look. He puffed out his chest and gestured to Helen.

"They're your sisters," he said. "You should tell them."

"You think?" she asked.

"Yeah, why not. It's a joint effort, but you'll do a better job than I will telling it."

"Would one of you just tell us," Geri shouted.

"We got chatting at breakfast," said Helen. "About how it would be totally weird if somebody were to be murdered at SteinerCon."

"Oh yes, classic breakfast first date chat, that is," said Geri. "Murder and Corn Flakes. Very romantic."

Martha hushed her sister down.

"Like I was saying," Helen continued. "We got talking, about how ironic it would be. If some juicy murder happened at a summit filled with detectives and private investigators. And how it would absolutely set everybody off and they'd lose their minds."

"And wouldn't it be a great place for an alibi for a killer," Tom agreed. "How could you get away with murder, with the world's biggest collection of amateur sleuths all under the same roof."

"And that got us talking about Murray Steiner," Helen went on. "We thought, wouldn't it be something if in fact it was him, *the* Murray Steiner, the organiser of SteinerCon, who was murdered. It would be like the *ultimate* crime, don't you think?"

"That's dubious," said Geri, scratching her chin. "What about stealing the Mona Lisa? Or the Crown Jewels or something like that."

"That would outrank killing one of the world's greatest private investigators at his own private investigator conference?" Helen asked, sarcastically. "Don't be absurd, Geri. And besides, the Mona Lisa has already been stolen and found. That's old hat. This is something new."

"That's it?" asked Martha. "That's what you wanted to test on us? To see how we'd react? That was worth the wrath of a grieving Roberta Steiner? Helen I'm having serious concerns about your sanity right now."

"No, no, no!" Helen waved her away. "That's just the start of it. You see, we, that is to say Tom and I, we had that idea nailed down."

"We wanted to see what your reaction would be if we told you we think that Murray has, in fact, been murdered," said Tom.

A cold chill ran through Martha. It made her shiver, despite the balmy summer heat in the park. Those words, exactly what she'd imagined before. It was enough to make her teeth chatter.

"Oh, this is absurd," said Geri, dismissing the notion right away. "Murray Steiner was murdered? Don't talk rubbish. Next you'll be supposing that I was the one who killed him."

"Goodness, no," said Helen. "You wouldn't have the means. You're my sister, Geri and I love you to the ends of the Earth. But if this is true, it would take something a bit more cerebral than you dazzling him with your looks and charm."

Tom laughed. Even Martha afforded herself a little smile.

"So where do we fit in?" she asked. "And what was the test?"

"The test is conclusive," said Tom. "You two are still standing here listening to us. Which means there's at least *some* plausibility to what we're thinking. I don't pretend to be the world's greatest detective, Martha, but I'm a pretty shrewd judge of character. And when somebody like you, and Geri for that matter, the guests of honour at SteinerCon, don't laugh at the idea. I reckon there's a good chance it might not be complete cobblers."

Tom's logic was sound enough, Martha couldn't argue with that. Tom Hopgood was growing on her. She liked his attitude, his easy-going manner. She wouldn't mind him at all as a brother-in-law.

"This proves nothing," said Geri. "So what? We don't think it's *so* crazy that it's impossible. We've got nothing else to go on. Not that we're even investigating it."

"True," said Helen, tucking her hands behind her back and pacing around the grass." But as Tom's contact at the Met has said, there *is* heightened security around Murray's body. And while you're absolutely right ladies, you can't just walk in and take a peek at a corpse any time you wish. It would beg the question that there's some sort of extra worry that the results of

Mr Steiner's post mortem may *not* be as straightforward as it would first seem."

Martha furrowed her brow.

"Just supposing there *is* foul play at work, here," said Martha. "Just *supposing* that you two are correct. What does that mean?"

"It means that there's a killer on the loose," said Helen. "Now, here's where it gets a little more serious."

A darkness fell over her. She stopped her pacing and looked gravely at Geri.

"If there *is* foul play," she said ominously. "Then that would mean there would be suspects. And top of that list would *have* to be Geri Parker."

Martha's head snapped around to look at her youngest sister. Geri stood perfectly still. She blinked a few times and suddenly she was no longer the fierce, fighting, fiery twenty-one year-old who took everything in her stride. The weight of Helen's words appeared to strip her of her armour.

"Steady on, Hel," she just about managed, her voice weak. "We don't even know the old boy's been snuffed out yet, eh? Don't go pointing fingers at me."

"No, we don't," said Helen. "We don't know for sure that it was murder."

Martha reached over and squeezed Geri on the shoulder. The touch seemed to wake the youngest Parker from a daze. She smiled.

"Then we should probably find out, shouldn't we," she said. "I assume you two lovebirds have some kind of plan."

Helen and Tom looked at each other once more. He raised his phone and waved it at Geri and Martha.

"Rule number one of being a gumshoe, ladies. It always pays to have a man on the inside."

Eighteen

AMBULANCES SEEMED TO be in steady supply around University College Hospital. As silly as it may seem, for some reason Martha had always worried there would be a shortage. Something about there being so many people tightly packed into the one city. The numbers didn't add up in her head.

This afternoon it was busy. The tall, shimmering glass and steel of the hospital rose up above all the more traditional buildings surrounding it. It looked more like an office block than a place for the sick. Just another way this city perplexed Martha.

"Is this the right place?" asked Geri, huddling behind the others. "I thought UCH was, you know, a hospital, not a morgue."

"It's a security thing," said Tom. "Seems that this place is a bit better at looking after you than any of the more traditional resting places for the dead."

"How macabre," said Martha.

They lingered a little while across the road, watching for anything out of the ordinary. The hospital seemed normal—no signs of extra security or police outside its entrance. No journalists either. The steady flow of ambulances in and out continued, and everything seemed quite regular. Which worried Martha, as it always did.

"Okay, so what's the plan?" asked Geri.

"We need to rendezvous with Tom's contact," said Helen. "She'll give us the inside scoop of what's going on."

"Why doesn't she just call or message him?" asked Martha, suspicious.

"That'd be a paper trail then, Mart," said Tom. "You can't track a conversation between two old friends meeting up quite by chance, can you?"

"Makes sense," said Geri. "So where is she? Can she come up and meet us?"

"We'll have to go inside," said Tom. "It might look quiet, but that building over there, right now, is probably one of the most secure in London."

Martha glanced over at the hospital again. Its looming tower and endless spring green windows suddenly seemed quite sinister—like a serial killer who dressed in a smart suit.

"And how, Romeo and Juliet, do you plan on getting us in there?" Geri asked. "The most secure building in London is *probably* going to be able to turf the four of us out with no problems isn't it? Especially Helen."

"Hey!" Helen protested. "Why me more than anyone else?"

"You're hardly the most inconspicuous looking punter Helen—what with those sandals and that head of hair that looks like you were dragged through a hopper backwards… twice."

"And you're one to talk! With your… your… face!"

"Enough you two," said Martha.

Helen and Geri were quiet on demand. Tom smiled and sidled over to Martha.

"We need to get inside and…" he pulled out his phone and checked his messages. "Up to the fourteenth floor. Apparently the whole floor has been closed off. If we get up there then we can meet my contact and get the hell out of Dodge."

"Okay," said Martha, looking up at the glass tower across the street. "Any ideas how we do that?"

Tom grinned devilishly. He tapped the side of his nose and started towards the hospital. Helen followed after him, Geri close behind.

"Is this a good idea?" Martha asked the youngest Parker.

"I think I'm the wrong person to be asking, Mart," she replied. "I'm hardly full of great ideas at the moment. In fact, if

I was, we wouldn't be up to our necks in this mess right about now."

Martha agreed. But she didn't say. Geri had taken enough of an emotional kicking over the last day or so. She didn't need another boot.

"Come on then," she said, taking Geri's hand, as if she was going in to school. "Let's see what these two characters have got planned for us."

They hurried across the busy road after Helen and Tom. The rear of the hospital housed an open ambulance bay. The street was narrow and barely wide enough to let the huge vehicles in and out. The steady flow of traffic was only interrupted by the sudden burst of a siren. The whole area worked like clockwork but Martha imagined it wouldn't take very much to bring it all crashing down.

Tom signalled back to her to stay where they were. They stopped at the corner of the huge hospital, as Tom and Helen headed for the bay.

"What are they doing?" she asked Geri.

"God knows," she answered. "This is what happens when you let Helen's libido do the thinking. We end up here, watching her and some Australian bit of totty walk up to an ambulance… open the back door… and steal a wheelchair."

Helen and Tom came running back towards them, wheelchair flailing behind them. It skidded and bobbed on the pavement, catching on his heels. With all the finesse of an Olympic relay team, he passed the wheelchair to Helen who unfolded it and pushed it out in front of her.

"Get in, Mart," she said, panting.

"What?" Martha blurted.

"Get in, sit down," said Tom. "Come on, quickly, before somebody notices it's gone."

For some bizarre reason Martha didn't argue. She sat down in the wheelchair and was shoved, unceremoniously, down the street at pace.

"Do you ever get the feeling that you made a wrong turn somewhere along the line?" Martha asked. "I'm having that feeling right now."

"Be quiet," Helen hissed. "You're supposed to be the sick one."

Martha shook her head in dismay. How had it come to this? Being taken into a busy hospital in a stolen wheelchair to steal confidential medical information about a possible murder victim. All while one of the world's most famous women hunted her down for dog meat. It had been strange enough being invited to London in the first place. She hadn't dreamt it would get *this* strange.

"Remind me, if we ever get out of this mess, to officially retire from the private investigations business," she said. "I don't think my nerves can take much more of this."

"Hush down there, Mart," said Tom. "Stick to the plan. We're your family and we're taking you back to the ward."

"Oh there's a plan is there?" asked Geri. "I thought this was all being done on the hop, by two of the greatest undiscovered improv minds of their generation."

"Shut up, Geri," Helen barked.

"This isn't going to work," Geri added.

"Not with that attitude, it's not," Helen hissed again. "Come on, let's show a little optimism here."

"Hah," Geri laughed.

"Just try to look ill, Mart," was Tom's advice. "And keep your wrists hidden, we don't want to give away you don't have a tag."

"Oh we'll be getting plenty of tags," said Geri. "The ones that go around your ankle and let the police know where you are at all times."

"Geri Parker I'm going to biff you in the face with a—"

Helen stopped her threat before it got to the good part. Two nurses came walking out of the main hospital door and eyed the companions up. She smiled as best she could and urged them on a little quicker.

"There we go, first obstacle tackled," said Tom reassuringly. "We're in, and all we need to do now is find an elevator up to the fourteenth floor."

Martha looked around the lobby. The hospital was busy, packed with people in various states of distress or care. She had never been in a place like this before. Growing up she had been used to the Victorian charm of Glasgow's old facilities—the ones that oozed character but were falling apart at the seams. This place felt more like an office block for some international bank. Coffee bars, interactive screens, huge tinted windows that let in balmy summer light. It was almost pleasant.

"Over there," said Helen, trying to keep her voice down but failing miserably. "In the corner."

A row of lifts sat opening and closing their doors. Medics, nursing staff and patients all filtered in and out in polite rushes. Martha felt a jolt of excitement at the chase being on once again. But she had to contain herself, she was supposed to be ill.

"Pity about the front desk," said Geri.

She nodded to the long row of the hospital's reception area. In order to reach the lifts they'd have to pass the entire length. The admin staff were busy, furiously trying to keep the massive facility working. People asked them questions and they answered, directing traffic, taking calls. Martha felt awful as she watched them work so hard, knowing she was there under false pretences. She had to keep justifying it all in her head. They *had* to find out if Geri was going to be in trouble.

"Okay," she said. "Let's go. Just keep calm and don't draw any attention to yourselves. That means you Helen."

"Me?"

"No tripping, no falling, or general clumsiness, at least not until we're in the lift. Then you can trip, fall and roll around as much as you like."

"I don't know what you're talking about," she replied indignantly. "I'm perfectly capable of walking two hundred yards in a straight line. And I won't hear anything else about it."

She lifted her head high and strutted out in front of the others. Martha laughed a little.

"You've got yourself a real catch there, Tom," she said.

"Don't I know it," he laughed.

They moved on, starting past the long reception desk. Martha felt her heart thumping in her ears. She kept her head low, and tried to look how she thought someone ill might look. She wasn't convinced it was working. But that didn't matter. The lifts drew closer and closer until they were within touching distance.

"We made it," Geri whispered.

The nearest lift pinged and the doors opened. It emptied and Tom wheeled Martha inside. As they turned, a small, elderly man with a long, white beard and bright red nose came hobbling over.

"Eh, sorry, you can't come in here," said Geri, trying to hold him back.

"You what?" growled the old man, his eyes a brilliant blue.

"You can't come in this lift mate, you'll have to get the next one," said Tom.

"What the 'ell are you lot talking about!"

Geri stepped to block the door. Martha felt a wince of discomfort. This was getting out of hand.

"You can't come in here because…" Geri said. "Because she's infectious."

"Infectious?" the old man asked. "She looks alright to me."

"Yeah but she's filled with pus, mate," said Tom. "And bugs and viruses, everything. The ones that look the healthiest are usually the worst."

"Yeah, he's right," said Geri. "She's infectious like you wouldn't believe man. Horrible stuff."

The old man peered over Geri's shoulder at Martha. She tried to look like somebody who was full of pus, as Tom had so eloquently put it. She gave a quick shiver, just to stress the point.

"She doesn't look very infectious. And what about you lot?" asked the pensioner. "How come you're allowed to be around her if she's that bad?"

"Look mate, just sling your hook would you?" bellowed Helen, stomping forward. "You're not coming in this lift so get the next one. End of."

She mashed the button with her hand and the door closed. The last thing they heard was the old man swearing as they started to climb the floors.

"Nice Helen, really nice," said Geri. "Subtle as always."

"Well, he was asking too many questions. Actions speak louder than words, am I right?"

"Bloody hell," said Geri, leaning against the wall. "That's all we need. Some angry geriatric going and blowing the whistle."

"He won't do anything," said Helen. "Trust me."

Martha sighed in frustration. She was doing that a lot.

"Okay, what do we do from here?" she asked, trying to focus on the task at hand. "What's the next move Tom?"

"I'm just texting my mate now," he said. "Once she knows we're here, she can come and get us. And then we can ask her as much as we want. She's a good lass, you'll like her."

"Okay," said Martha. "We just need to keep our heads low, get what we came for and get out of here. Then we're going straight back to the hotel and apologising to Roberta Steiner. Hopefully she'll only flay the skin from our backs and nothing more. Does that sound like a plan?"

"Yeah," said Geri.

"It does," said Helen.

"Good," agreed Martha.

With the plan settled, the lift came to a slow stop. Martha was starting to feel a little better about herself—despite everything going on around her. They were going to get answers. And answers always helped.

The elevator doors opened. And Martha's optimism disappeared as quickly as the ping of the buzzer faded. There, on the other side was a huge, burly man, the word 'police ' emblazoned across his mile-wide back.

"Bugger," said Martha.

Nineteen

EVERYONE IN THE lift stood motionless. None of them dared to breathe.

The police officer stood perfectly still too, like a mountain just outside the door. Martha thought about hitting the button to close the doors again. But the cop's instincts kicked in before she could react. He spun around, eyes darting around the lift from the middle of his meaty face.

"Who are you?" he asked, his voice like a steam engine thundering through a tunnel.

None of them answered. He gave them all another look, each in turn. Then he asked again, crossing his mighty arms across his barrel chest, fluorescent jacket squeaking at the seams.

"Who are you?"

"Eh…" Geri was the only one with enough about her to answer. "She's sick."

"She? Who?" asked the cop.

"Her… my sister here, she's ill, infectious," said Geri, remembering something from the past ten minutes. "We're just here to drop her back off at her ward. She wanted a smoke, can't get enough of them. And you know what all these new rules are like, well, of course you do, you're a police officer."

Geri laughed a little, more out of nerves than any disarming charm. She stepped out of the lift and Tom took her lead, shoving Martha over the lip with a rattle of the chair.

"Woah! Woah! Hold it there, you can't come out here!" said the cop, batting them back. "This is a restricted area. Off limits to anyone without strict clearance. You're on the wrong floor. Get back in the lift."

"Restricted area? That sounds intriguing, Officer," said Tom. "Why's it off limits?"

"Yeah why's it off limits, Officer?" asked Helen, like a trained parrot.

"Yeah what gives, Officer? Why's it off limits?" Geri chimed in.

The youngest Parker sister picked up on what Tom was attempting. She started bobbing around the cop, peering down the empty hallway.

"What's going on here then? Is it a crime scene? A murder? Has one of the doctors flipped and gone on a rampage? Or what about one of the patients? Have they spontaneously combusted or got their head stuck in a set of railings? What's going on here, eh? Are you going to tell us? Are you?"

"Enough!"

The whole building seemed like it was shaken to its foundations as the officer let out a roar. The companions fell silent and stood in his shadow.

"Enough," he said again, much softer this time. "This area is restricted to civilians. That means you lot. And if it's restricted to you, you can't be here. So I'm going to have to ask you to go back downstairs and try another door. Because I'm not going to listen to any more questions from her."

He thumbed at Geri. Martha stayed silent, silently resigned to being sent packing.

"Ah, that's a shame," said Geri, sounding philosophical. "I suppose we should just hit the old dusty trail then and get out of your… hair."

Geri leapt as high as she could. She snatched the policeman's hat clean off his head and landed behind him, boots thumping hard on the polished hospital floor. She looked back over her shoulder and smiled at the others.

"You better run," she shouted, then took off down the hallway." Catch me if you can, Officer."

She was already halfway down the corridor by the time the cop and the others knew what was going on. Like a cartoon character, the officer pawed at his bald head for his hat, still confused as to what Geri had done. When he realised she had his headgear, he shouted loudly.

"Oi!" he yelled. "Get back here with that!"

The cop gave chase. Martha and the others could only watch on in total shock. Then the penny dropped.

"She told us to run," Martha said. "She's distracting him while we find your contact."

Helen and Tom groaned in agreement. Martha pushed herself up from the wheelchair and snapped her fingers at the Australian gumshoe.

"Your friend, where is she?" she asked. "We don't have much time, I don't imagine Geri can outrun that officer forever, or any of his friends. Even Geri can't do that."

"Will she be alright?" asked Tom. "I mean, does she do this sort of thing a lot?"

"Yes," said Martha and Helen at the same time.

Tom had no reason to disbelieve them. Walking a little away from Helen and Martha, he started looking around the place for directions. A cool wave of fear passed over Martha. She tugged on her sister's sleeve and drew her in a little closer.

"Can we trust this guy?" she whispered.

"Tom? Of course!" said Helen, flatly. "Why do you think we can't trust him? He's been perfectly straight with us so far. Not to mention a real good sport about, you know, him now also being on the run from Roberta Steiner. Why? What's wrong with him?"

"Nothing, nothing at all," said Martha. "I just, I don't know, I've been on edge a lot these past few days. Ever since we came down here—heck ever since the whole Coulthard business—I just feel like I'm chasing my shadow. Everything that's gone on here at the conference and with Murray. Now this, here, in the hospital. I just wonder if I'm losing my better sense of judgement."

Helen smiled back at her sister.

"Tom is one of the good guys Martha, he's been nothing but a gentleman to me," she said. "He's been very helpful, he seems to enjoy our company. And if what we're thinking is true, then we have to be ahead of the game. We have to be prepared for *any* eventuality, if for nothing else, then for Geri's sake."

"I'm worried about her," she said, looking down the empty corridor. "I'm worried that this whole thing is doing untold damage to her mind. Waking up to a corpse would be a test for even the strongest of us."

"Geri *is* the strongest of us. You know that."

That thought eased Martha a little.

"You're right, she is," she said.

"That's why we're here now, Martha. We're protecting her, by bending the rules a little. I'm not exactly over the moon about that fact. But she's our sister. And we have to do what we can. She'd do the same for either one of us. She already has."

"You're right," said Martha. "As usual. You're right, Helen."

"Okay, we're on," said Tom, interrupting them. "Down this hallway, my mate will meet us at the back entrance of ward five, it's on the other side of the building from here. She says we need to be careful, the place is swarming with cops and security people from the hotel. They're not letting anyone in. So keep it quiet ladies. If that's possible for you lot."

He started down the corridor where Geri had led the cop on her wild chase. Martha and Helen gave each other a reassuring look and then followed after him. They had work to do, no matter what the result. This was where they thrived.

Twenty

THE FOURTEENTH FLOOR of UCH was surprisingly sparse. The rooms were empty and all the wards that Martha and the others passed looked deserted. The further the group travelled the more suspicious she grew.

"This isn't right," she whispered to Helen and Tom. "There should be more people here, we haven't come across anyone?"

"But it's locked down, remember?" said Helen, equally quiet. "Apparently Steiner's people have the clout to close down an entire floor of a busy central London hospital."

"Now *that*'s power," said Tom. "Remind me again why you guys wanted to mess with them?"

"Don't Tom. Just don't," said Martha.

They carefully made their way along the empty corridors and hallways following signs for Ward Five. The place was airy and light, the large spring green tinted windows of the hospital tower paying off. It only served to creep Martha out more. Nobody about and a strange ethereal light at the end of the hallway. There was something rather foreboding about that image.

At last they came to a crossroads of hallways and what appeared to be a nurse's station and reception area. The faint sound of voices and a hard crackle filled the cool air. Martha and the others slowed down.

"Where are those voices coming from?" whispered Helen.

"Down to the right, I think," said Tom.

"And where's Ward Five?" asked Martha.

They all looked up to the sign bolted onto the wall beside the nurse's station. It unhelpfully indicated that Ward Five was on the right side of the adjoining hallway.

"Struth," said Tom, wiping sweat from his tanned forehead.

"What are we going to do now?" asked Helen.

"I thought you had a plan," said Martha.

"Hold on, all isn't lost. I'll text my mate and see if she can come meet us here."

Tom was interrupted by heavy, thumping footsteps. Helen looked at the others, her eyes as wide as dinner plates. The steps were growing louder and Martha sprang into action. She grabbed her sister and Tom and pulled them into the nurse's station. Sliding under the desk, she held her finger to her lips to tell them to keep quiet.

"This is a bloody nonsense all of this," came one gruff voice.

"I should be at Stamford Bridge this afternoon. I had the Chelsea game and everything," replied another, a woman.

"Who they got?"

"Everton."

"Tricky one that," said the first. "Don't know if I fancy them. Still, better to be out of the sun, ain't it. And this place isn't too bad."

"You should see it later on tonight, mate," said the second voice. "A and E is like something out of a war film. Honestly, I don't know how people behave these days. They're like animals."

A loud crackling interrupted the two voices.

"Sierra one-four, Mike Whisky go ahead, over," said the woman.

"They're police," whispered Helen.

"Your deduction skills really are world class," Martha whispered back.

"Okay we'll keep an eye out for her. Young Caucasian female, about five feet five, cropped bleach-blonde hair, with an officer's hat, is that right? Over."

"That's Geri they're talking about," Helen whispered again.

"Yes Helen, I know that," said Martha, rolling her eyes.

"At least they haven't caught her," said Tom.

"Yet."

There was another crackling on the radio.

"A missing girl with a police hat—there's something you don't hear every day, eh?" said the female officer.

"It gets stranger and stranger this assignment," acknowledged her partner. "First they pull every unit within a five mile radius to guard a corpse. Now we've got random members of the public nicking headgear. What's next?"

Tom looked at the Parker sisters. He held up his hand, fingers outstretched and mouthed the word five at them. Martha didn't like the sound of what was going on.

"Anyway, who are we to argue," said the male officer. "We just do as we're told, don't ask questions and hope they let us home early."

"A real ambitious attitude, that," said his colleague.

They both laughed and then started off down one of the corridors that stretched from the nurse's station. Martha and the others waited a moment until the footsteps were faint. Then, plucking up enough courage, they emerged from their hiding place beneath the desk.

"Bloody hell," she said. "This is serious."

"I don't like where this is going," said Helen. "It all smells a bit fishy. Pulling police officers from all across the city just to guard a dead body. Something's wrong."

Tom's phone buzzed. He checked the message.

"Okay, down here, let's go," he said.

They hurried along the corridor where the cops had come from. Following the signs, they reached Ward Five. The doors were closed, but through the small windows they could see the brightly coloured jackets of more police. They hesitated for a moment, not sure what to do.

A door opened suddenly behind them. Martha, Helen and Tom all spun around at the same time. It was about all they could do to stop their skeletons from leaping out of their skin.

"Wow," came the response.

A tall, slender woman in a pale white forensic jumpsuit and safety goggles was standing behind them. Her bright red hair was tied neatly back in a bun, and her face narrowed to a point at her chin. Despite the less than flattering, highly clinical outfit, she seemed to ooze an elegant style.

"Hell's bloody teeth," gasped Tom. "You scared us half to death."

"I frightened *you*?" she asked, opening her arms for a hug. "I nearly had a heart attack. Which isn't something you'll hear regularly from a woman who takes pictures of dead bodies."

Tom laughed and took up the offer of a hug. He held the woman by the shoulders, beaming.

"Good to see you Daisy. Really good to see you, mate," he said.

"Daisy?" said Helen under her breath. "What is she? A photographer or a flower?"

"Now, now," smiled Martha. "Is that the green-eyed monster rising up in you Ms Parker?"

"Jealous? Me? Have you lost your mind, Martha? I'm above all feeble human foibles like jealousy. You should know that by now."

Martha kept smiling. She stepped forward and offered her hand to the forensic photographer.

"Pleased to meet you," she said. "I'm Martha Parker and this is my sister, Helen."

"The pleasure is all mine," said Daisy, taking her hand. "Tom has been telling me all about you. Although, isn't there one of you missing?"

"Yeah, there is, what of it?" said Helen spitefully.

"What Helen means, Daisy, is that Geri is about here somewhere," said Martha more diplomatically. "As you can imagine this isn't quite how we would have liked to be introduced. And time is pressing. I can't thank you enough for taking this risk for us. But if you don't mind, we'd very much like to hear everything you know."

Daisy smiled. She pulled her goggles off and let down her hair. It spilled over her shoulder, shimmering in the cool light of the hospital, a stark contrast against the sanitary white of her jumpsuit. Martha could almost feel the anger radiating off Helen.

"I can't tell you much," she said. "Only that I was pulled off a job in Peckham to come here. Now that doesn't usually happen, I can tell you that much. Snappers like me are ten a penny, you could get anyone to take a picture of a body."

"You do yourself a disservice," said Tom. "You're the best in the business Daisy."

"Too kind as always, Tom," she giggled. "Anyway, I get pulled off the grisly business south of the river and hauled all the way up here. The team come with me, the forensics officers, everything. We're told that it's a matter of urgency and maximum security abounds."

Daisy paused for breath. She looked about the empty corridor to make sure nobody else was listening.

"We arrive at the hospital and there are all these cops here," she continued. "We're ushered in through a back door and up one of the service lifts. I think it brought us out over there, I don't know, these places all look the same to me. I'm used to dingy morgues and basement graveyards, I'm afraid."

She pointed down the hallway. Helen snorted.

"Anyway, when we get up to the fourteenth floor, the place is deserted, save for all the cops. They walk us into this ward here, Ward Five, and there's a trolley set up in the middle of the room. Single body, no fuss. Some high flying police woman then appears. She's got the uniform on, the braids over the shoulder, looks like a real tough cookie. We're told it's a man in his seventies, died suddenly overnight, just go about your business and file a report. Only the thing is, the closer I get to the body, the quicker I realise who it is."

"Murray Steiner, yes we know," said Helen impatiently. "In fact we knew that before anyone else did!"

"Helen," Martha warned her sister. "Daisy, please go on."

"Yeah, like I was saying," the photographer gave Helen a strange look, then continued. "The cop isn't giving us any detail. In fact, she's wandering around the place like this has ruined her

Saturday afternoon—sour faced and grumbling. I don't question it, even though I know who's on the slab. I start taking my pictures and upload them to the system as the doc gets to work. It's the usual sort of thing, taking blood, examining the liver, kidneys, all of that. Now, I know Murray Steiner, you'd be very hard pressed to come across anyone who *hasn't* heard of him. But I know what he was like too."

"What do you mean?" asked Martha.

"Come on," Daisy smiled. "He might be one of the best known men on the planet. But he's also been a jack the lad all of his life, hasn't he? That rock and roll lifestyle was going to catch up with him sooner or later. And here we are. Or at least, that's what I thought anyway."

Martha had that gnawing, uncomfortable feeling again. It felt like a boulder rolling around in her stomach.

"What are the police saying Daisy?" asked Tom.

"Seems they're treating the whole thing as suspicious," she said.

It was the hammer blow that Martha had been dreading. That word, that singular, devastating word. Suspicious. How could a single word cause so much damage, heartache and turmoil?

"I don't know the results of the post mortem, that'll take a few hours while the lab boys finish up," said Daisy. "And there will be samples taken from all over Murray's body, his stomach, brain, that sort of thing. But as soon as I know I can let you guys know."

"Thanks Daisy," said Tom, the colour draining from his tan.

"Sorry about dragging you guys in here like this," she said apologetically. "But, well, if there is something up, I thought you should know, Tom. And I didn't want to be spreading this sort of thing on a message. You don't know who's watching or listening in a case like this. The whole thing is pretty tight with security."

"Well," Helen sniffed. "*We* were able to get in without any problem. So it can't be as tight as *you* say it is, can it?"

Daisy didn't reply. And Martha didn't chastise her sister for being rude. She didn't have the energy. All of her thoughts had now turned to Geri.

"I'm sorry I can't be of more help guys," said Daisy. "I had better get back before they miss me."

"I owe you a pint Daisy," said Tom, embracing his friend once again. "Thank you for this."

"Don't mention it," she said. "And I'll let you know as soon as the toxicology report comes through. Good luck in whatever you have to do."

She hugged Tom again and gave him a peck on the cheek, then disappeared through a door that led back into Ward Five. It closed with a click, leaving the three of them alone. Martha rubbed her forehead. She could feel a headache coming on. In truth it was the least of her worries.

"Bad news guys," said Tom, puffing out his cheeks. "Looks like Helen and I were right. And I don't think I've ever wanted to be wrong so much in my life."

"Still, we *were* right," said Helen.

"So, what are we going to do?" asked Tom.

His words seemed to trigger something deep in Martha's mind. She wasn't exactly sure what it was they were going to do. But a little switch had been flicked. Maybe it was instinct. Maybe it was practice. She didn't know. Suddenly she felt motivated, the cobwebs blown away.

"We need to find Geri," she said. "And we need to get back to the hotel."

"Back? Why?" asked Helen.

"If we keep on running then it looks like we've got something to hide," she said. "And we have *nothing* to hide. This has all taken a very serious turn Helen. A man has died and the police are treating it as suspicious. It doesn't matter that he's famous. Justice needs to be served. And I don't want the blame being laid at Geri's feet when she's completely innocent. We've been here before—good people being made scapegoats. I'll be damned if it's my own sister who is punished this time."

"So what's the move?" asked Helen.

"Like I said," answered Martha. "We need to find—"

"Yoo-hoo!"

Geri came running around the end of the corridor, interrupting Martha. She saw the others and waved the policeman's hat high above her head.

"If you guys know of a quick way out of here, now would be a good time," she said, out of breath and bathed in sweat. "I don't know how long I can keep outrunning these coppers."

"What coppers?" asked Helen.

Before Geri could answer her sister, a gang of policemen and women came thundering into the hallway. Martha and the others quickly started running in the opposite direction.

"Oh God," moaned Geri. "Not again."

"Down here!" Tom shouted. "Daisy said there was a service elevator somewhere."

"Where?" asked Helen.

"There it is," said Martha pointing ahead.

They hurried to the lift as the shouts and commands from the small police force filled the hallway. The doors of the lift slid open with a rusty creak.

"Hurry," Helen shouted.

The companions bundled themselves in and hit the bottom button on the control panel. The doors juddered and closed just as the cops reached them, their fluorescent jackets vanishing with a split second to spare. The elevator dropped quickly as Martha caught her breath.

"Well," said Geri. "I must say it's good to see you all again after such a long time."

She popped the policeman's hat on her head and put her hands on her hips.

"Tell me. How's your trip to London going?"

Twenty-One

"OKAY, LET'S JUST take a timeout here," said Geri. "Just pretend for a moment that I'm a total novice at this whole private investigation malarkey. And explain to me again what we're doing?"

The underground was hot and stuffy. Martha wasn't sure there should be so many people all tightly packed in like this. What if there was a power cut? Or the train came off the tracks? They'd be trapped like sardines in a tin can, miles under the ground.

She tried to put that thought out of her head. There were enough, *real* problems to be dealing with at the moment without her imagination getting away from her.

"Don't you ever pay attention?" asked Helen. "I mean if, just once in your life, you listened you might know what it is we're talking about."

"Alright then smart arse," snapped Geri. "*You* tell me the plan again without help from these two."

Helen unfurled herself from the little corner near the door. She looked about at the other passengers all crowded around them. Nobody seemed to care what they were saying. Headphones in and blank looks on their faces.

"Alright then," she said. "It's perfectly simple. We're going back to the hotel and we're going to make a grovelling apology to Roberta Steiner for running out on her."

"We?" Geri asked.

"Fine, *I* am going to make a grovelling apology," said Helen. "Then we're going to tell her that we know what's going on with Murray—she deserves to know the truth. And we'll tell her that we're more than willing to cooperate with the police in any of their investigations."

"*We* are going to cooperate?" Geri asked.

"Yes, *we*," said Martha interrupting her sisters. "We are going to cooperate. All three of us. We're a family and we're in this together. I'm not having you take the fall for something you clearly didn't do. We've been through all of that before."

"Don't I know it," said Geri. "So what about Dash Dingo here? Where does he fit in?"

Tom smiled, his neck crooked as he tried to stand up at the curve of the cabin.

"Tom's got nothing to do with it," said Helen sharply. "He's just a friend who was happy to help us out. Absolutely no reason to get him embroiled in all of this."

"That's very kind of you, Hel," he said. "But I'm not going to let you girls face the music on your own. Besides, as soon as I ran out of that exhibition hall with you lot, my card was marked."

"We'll put it all straight Tom," said Martha. "The easiest thing in the world is to tell the truth. And we've done nothing wrong, none of us. That's what we're going to tell Roberta and all of them. Simple as that."

The group stood in silence as the train rocked back and forth. It ground to a halt at their station and they all trudged off. Martha sensed a nervous defeat hanging over them. She could hardly blame the others—she was feeling rather apprehensive too.

Her mind kept ticking back to the hospital and Daisy's brief information dump. Murray Steiner's death was *suspicious*. That meant there was potentially a killer on the loose. And if it wasn't Geri then who could it be? And how had they done the deed while she slept in the same room?

They climbed the stairs and emerged into the beaming light. The balmy, beaming sunlight was intense and Martha could feel herself burning already. Outside Piccadilly Circus was teeming with tourists, workers and the whole of the world it seemed.

"Oh cool, look Martha," said Helen, tugging on her sleeve and pointing far away down the street. "It's The Ritz."

The huge structure of the famous hotel stood proudly in the daylight. Its immaculate veneer seemed to tower over everything and everyone in the rest of the busy street. Martha smiled weakly at the thought of going in there right now. They were all tired, ragged, drained and filthy. She didn't suppose the staff would take too kindly to four scarecrows settling down for afternoon tea.

"Come on," she said, grimly.

They made the short walk around the corner and back towards their own hotel. Everything looked quiet from the outside. There was no sign of any police outside the main entrance. Taxis came and went in regular intervals, slipping in and out of the thoroughfare, carting the rich, the great and the good to and from the resort.

"I don't like this," said Geri.

"What's there to like?" asked Helen.

"There shouldn't be this many people here," she said. "I mean, surely Roberta knows that the cops are treating Murray's death as suspicious. Surely the conference shouldn't be still going on."

She nodded at a group of delegates gathered outside the main entrance of the hotel. They huddled together and posed for a picture with a few of the embarrassed looking doormen.

"This is big business, Geri. Every year," said Tom. "Sponsors, ticket sales, you're probably looking at a turnover in the millions of dollars for the Steiners. You couldn't just stop it, even if you wanted to. Besides, it is probably worth even more, given the death of the host."

"Really?" asked all three Parker sisters in unison.

"Oh yeah," Tom continued. "This is huge business. I was reading up on it on the flight over. This summit forms the backbone of the whole annual revenue of Murray and Roberta Steiner's company. Oh God, what's it called again? Kronos Productions, I think. That's their holding firm, the one that all their comings and goings go through so they're not taxed out the wazoo."

"And they're the sole proprietors?" asked Geri. "I knew they were rich. And I knew this was a big thing. But millions in turnover?"

"Definitely," said Tom. "They're a couple of shrewd business people, don't forget that. SteinerCon is like their big end of year party. But it's also a huge cash cow. The money they make here can be the difference between them having a good year and a great year. And it all comes down to bums on seats and big corporate sponsors. Who do you think paid for your rooms?"

"The Steiners," said Martha, although she was doubting herself now.

"No chance," smiled Tom. "Your rooms, your meals, your everything will have been covered by the hotel. And if not them, then whoever is doing the video production for the summit. Or the caterers. Or one of those corporations who have set themselves up in the lobby, you know, the security firms, the CCTV people, the tech giants trying to flog their wares to budding PIs like myself. It's all covered and keeps the overheads down. The networks in the US probably have a good crack at the whip too. This is a huge money spinner for the Steiners. And as you've seen, everybody laps it up."

"But he's dead," said Helen bluntly. "Surely something as tragic as the main host's death would be enough to call it quits."

"You'd think so," said Tom with a wry smile. "I mean, any decent human being would take exception to the fact that the star of the show passed away in the night. Not here though, not with SteinerCon. This thing has been running for decades. And there's a lot riding on it turning over at least *something* for everyone involved. The corporations might be putting up the cash for the convention, but they'll be expecting a good bit in return. Murray's death means more attention, and more attention is more publicity for the sponsors. There's no point in paying a fortune if you're getting nothing back. Which means the show *must* go on, no matter what. It's all in here, hold on."

He pulled out his phone. Swiping through screens, he brought up a lengthy tome from a financial website. Martha couldn't follow him, he was moving too fast. She only caught brief sights of more glossy pictures of Murray and Roberta Steiner smiling out from some more glamorous locations.

"Can I see that?" asked Helen.

"Sure," said Tom, handing over his phone. "Here's the thing though. SteinerCon isn't what it used to be. There are certain commentators, critics if you will, who think that the whole thing is haemorrhaging money and that the Steiners are just putting a brave face on things. They point to statistical analysis that says footfall is down, there are less punters buying tickets every year, yet every time it rolls around it's not getting any smaller. In fact it's the opposite. More sponsors, more events, more speakers, more everything. The graphs don't add up."

"What are you trying to say?" asked Geri. "That this is some giant ruse on the part of the Steiners to con people out of money."

"I don't think so," he said. "I think it's the jewel in their many, many crowns. But I don't think everything is as hunky dory as they would have you believe. Like I said, Murray Steiner died less than twenty-four hours ago. But it's as if nothing has happened at all. You guys were still thrust on stage to address the conference as planned. And there are still talks going on, still events this evening. Hell I was meant to be going to them all. And I'm a nobody."

"Not to us you're not," said Helen, handing back his phone. "You're very helpful and a thoroughly nice chap too."

"Steady on, Helen, that almost sounded like a compliment," droned Geri.

Martha drank in everything Tom had said. She hadn't really thought about the corporate sponsors of SteinerCon and what the financial implications of stopping the conference could mean. She had always just assumed that Roberta Steiner was a consummate professional. Even while her husband was a cad. A dead one at that.

"Okay, let's gather our thoughts, shall we?" she said. "I think we just go in there, announce ourselves to the reception desk and wait for—"

"The inevitable bollocking," said Geri.

"Wait for Roberta to do what she sees fit with us. Simple really. What could go wrong?"

"You *always* have to say that Martha," said Helen, rolling her eyes. "And that usually means *something* goes terribly wrong."

"She's right, Mart, something *always* goes wrong when you say that," added Geri.

Martha grabbed the stolen policeman's hat off Geri's head and stuffed it into a bin. Then she led her merry band towards the hotel reception, and the unknown.

Twenty-Two

THE SULLEN, NIPPY face of Eleanor David was waiting for them. And she wasn't happy. Although Martha and the others suspected that she was never, in fact, happy.

She was flanked by her security team—now swollen to a dozen tall, mean looking men and women who wouldn't be out of place guarding a president. Martha was sure it was an analogy Eleanor would have approved of. While she presented herself as a subservient, loyal member of Roberta Steiner's staff, Martha suspected that, deep down, she longed for the power, for a chance to step into the limelight. Bossing people around, ordering them what to do, it could be intoxicating.

Nothing that Martha had seen of the ferocious Eleanor David had indicated she wasn't partial to a bit of bossing around. Now, as Martha and the others approached her, it felt suspiciously like they were mice, walking straight into the waiting, drooling jaws of a crafty cat.

"Oh boy," said Helen, a little breathless. "Oh boy, oh boy, oh boy."

She slowed down, falling behind the others. Martha turned to her.

"Helen?" she asked. "What's wrong with you?"

"I don't… I don't think I can do this," she said. "I mean, there's lots of them, isn't there? Maybe this was a big mistake, yeah a huge mistake, you were right Martha. We should have just got on that train and headed home. Yeah, in fact, let's do that. Let's do that right now."

She turned to head back out of the main doors. Martha was about to grab her when Geri got in first.

"Hey," shouted the youngest of the Parkers.

Helen stopped. She stared down at Geri, her eyes glassy.

"Hey, Helen, stop," she said. "Listen to me. You've *got* to hold it together here. There's no use messing around. We can't have you taking one of your turns and having a wobble. Not anymore, the stakes are too high. You've got to stick with me on this. If we're not all united and you go running about London again then none of this plan works. We're here to tell Roberta Steiner that we know Murray might have been killed. And that I, we, none of us, had anything to do with it."

"Geri is right, Helen," said Tom, stepping forward. "You've got to put on a united front."

Helen swallowed her tears. She sniffed and nodded her head. Slowly, Geri let go of her arm. Martha panicked for a moment, thinking she might take off. But she didn't. She took a deep breath and nodded again.

"Okay," she said. "Sorry. I just… well, you know what I'm like."

"Don't we just," said Martha. "You okay now?"

"Yes, fine," said Helen.

They started off towards Eleanor and her brood. A look of satisfaction had now replaced the bitterness on the woman's face. The closer the companions drew to her, the taller, more imposing her entourage of security staff seemed. They loomed like mountains as they reached her.

"Well, well, well," she said. "Look what the cat dragged back in."

Martha wasn't surprised she'd use a cat metaphor. She looked like the type who probably sharpened her claws.

"We're here to see Roberta," she said. "We want to set a few things straight with her."

"Ms Steiner is in a state of mourning, she won't be accepting any visitors," she said coolly. "And I hardly think you lot are in any position to be making demands of her, after the stunts you've pulled."

She cocked an eyebrow at Tom.

"And you are?" she sneered.

"Tom Hopgood," Helen butted in, clumsily. "And he's got nothing to do with any of this."

"Very good," said Eleanor. "I had no idea you could train a loudmouth like her so well, you should be proud of yourself, Mr Hopgood. A pity her sisters couldn't take a leaf out of your book."

"What did you say?" Helen stomped forward, suddenly unperturbed by the security heavies.

"Easy Helen," said Geri, holding her back. "You don't want to get into a fight with an *older* woman, would you?"

That one stung. Martha could see Eleanor David's right eye twitch ever so slightly. It wasn't a lot, just enough to crack her thick makeup. She moved quickly on, her driving gaze falling to Martha.

"What is it you wish to speak to Mrs Steiner about?" she asked. "Not that it matters of course. You and your sisters have caused quite enough trouble already. You're lucky I don't have the police here waiting to arrest you."

"Actually, it's the police we wanted to speak to her about," said Martha calmly. "Some information has come to light in our absence."

"Absence?" Eleanor scoffed. "You went rogue, AWOL, we were about to send out a search party. And I don't need to remind you how it went against your agreement, one that should have been absolute, with Mrs Steiner—on this, the day of her husband's death. You lot should be ashamed of yourself."

Martha couldn't really argue with that. They *had* run out on the deal. But they were back now. That had to count for something.

"Like I said before, Ms David. We're here to apologise. But we also have to speak urgently with Mrs Steiner about Murray's death."

Eleanor looked at them all in turn, her contempt growing. Her phone began to ring. She stared at the screen and then up at Martha.

"Is that her?" asked Martha.

Eleanor held up a stiff finger and answered the phone

"Hello," she said, her face stoic. "Yes. Yes I have them here in the reception of the hotel. They look like a bunch of vagrants."

"Is that Roberta?" Geri asked. "If it is, tell her we need to speak with her."

"No it's all in hand," Eleanor ignored her. "My security team managed to catch them on camera before they were anywhere near the hotel and alerted me. I was down here with plenty of time. They haven't disturbed any of the other delegates."

"We have to speak with her," Geri shouted. "We have to tell her we know there's something deeply suspicious with Murray's death."

Eleanor stopped talking. It was just for a split second. Blink and the others would have missed it. Martha saw it though. It was shock, surprise even. Did Eleanor not know? Could it be that the most organised woman in the world was actually in the dark?

"Would you mind if I called you back," she said. "Something's just come up that I really need to deal with."

She hung up the phone.

"I have absolutely no idea what you're talking about," she said, clearing her throat. "Mr Steiner's death has been a shock to us all. But there is absolutely *no* hint of impropriety."

"Oh yeah?" said Helen. "Well we've just come from the swanky university hospital that's looking at his body. And our source says that there's something very fishy with what's happened to him. What do you think of that? Eh?"

Helen puffed out her chest. She looked at the others for approval, raising her eyebrows up and down with glee.

"This is preposterous," laughed Eleanor nervously. "That's private information. Completely private, you shouldn't know anything like that."

"So you admit that we're right," jabbed Martha.

"What?"

"We're correct then. You did know about this. You've just said it yourself."

"Yes, no, I mean," Eleanor was flustered.

The strong, confident dictator who had met them only moments ago was falling apart. Martha almost wanted to give her a hug. But she stopped just short.

"This is very serious," she said. "These are serious allegations. No matter how we came about the information, we know now, Ms David. And we're here to tell Roberta that we're innocent and have nothing to do with any of this. That's why we came back. I don't want Geri or the rest of us getting phone calls from the police or worse, being bundled into the back of a waiting van when we're done absolutely nothing wrong. I need to assure Roberta Steiner that we'll cooperate fully with the proper authorities. But we won't be held accountable for something we haven't done."

"Not to mention the killer that's still on the loose," said Geri.

Eleanor furiously rubbed her head. As if to compound her frustration, two of her phones started to ring at the same time. She quickly cancelled the calls.

"What?" she asked. "What killer? What are you talking about?"

"The killer," said Helen, still buoyed by her earlier victory. "You know, somebody who commits murder. Or culpable homicide sometimes, if you want to get all American about it. There's somebody out there who's done the proverbial dirty on old Murray Steiner. They need to be caught."

"Yes, yes, yes, all in good time, I know," said Eleanor.

The director of SteinerCon's steely veneer had been shattered. She looked like someone on an out of control train that was barrelling towards a brick wall. More than aware of the situation, but stricken with the knowledge there was nothing she could do.

Martha reached forward and touched her elbow. Eleanor jumped. She looked down at Martha's hand and then back up to her, as though the gesture was completely alien.

"We want to help Ms David," Martha said. "But you have to let us. We don't want to cause any more trouble, believe me that's the last thing we want to do. So let us help in any way we can. You have a conference of thousands of people here. They could be in danger. The authorities need to be brought in so this can be taken care of quickly and precisely. The longer we dally and fight among ourselves the more dangerous this whole situation becomes. Do you understand?"

Eleanor moved to speak. She stopped herself and laughed a little.

"You know, I've been organising SteinerCon for what feels like centuries," she said, her voice a little softer than before. "And I normally pride myself on how seamless the whole thing is. This year however, has been nothing short of a nightmare. From one disaster to another—it's just gotten worse and worse. Now this."

She threw her hands up in the air, looking for help. Martha was full of sympathy for her. She wasn't sure about the others.

"Okay," said Eleanor. "Okay. I think we need to get you to Mrs Steiner. I think that would be a good idea."

"Yes, it would," said Martha.

"At last," Helen rolled her eyes.

"She has instructed me she is not to be disturbed in her suite. So I'll have to phone ahead. If you want to follow me, we'll get you guys out of the way and ready before I can put together a meeting. Does that sound okay?"

Martha looked at her sisters and Tom for approval. They all nodded.

"Yes, that's fine with us," she said. "We're not going anywhere. And this needs to be sorted out."

"Good," Eleanor took a deep breath. "Follow me, I'll clear a green room and have a security guard placed on the door to make sure you're not disturbed."

She started off towards the main concourse of the hotel. Her guards parted and waited for the others. As she set off, Martha was struck by a sudden thought.

"Tom," she said, turning to the Australian gumshoe.

"Yes Mart?" he seemed perplexed.

"Stay here, stay out here with the rest of the delegates."

"What? No, I'm coming with you guys."

"You're not caught up in any of this Tom, and you've already done *more* than your share," said Helen.

"She's right mate," said Geri. "You've been a big help. But we can't have you traipsing into this wasp's nest with us. It's our cross to bear and all that."

"It's more than that though," said Martha quietly. "We need you to be on alert for the results of Murray Steiner's toxicology report. As soon as your friend hears anything we *must* know."

"Ah," said Tom, winking. "Gotcha. Will do Martha. You can rely on me."

"I know we can," she smiled.

"Take care," he said. "Don't do anything I wouldn't."

He bid them farewell and hurried back towards the doors of the hotel. Martha took Helen and Geri's hands and guided them off to follow Eleanor David. The security heavies closed in around them and kept them closely under guard.

Twenty-Three

ANOTHER FACELESS ROOM and another long, drawn out wait. Martha, usually the voice of reason and sensibility, couldn't muster up enough of her usual calm to be still. She paced back and forth near the door, while the others sprawled on the couches, tucking in to the free snacks and drinks.

"You can't help yourself, can you Helen?" asked Geri. "If there's a free sandwich, free packet of crisps, free lecture on the breeding habits of the star-nosed mole—you'll be front and centre."

"You what?" asked Helen, speaking with her mouth full.

"Just look at you," Geri pointed at the empty packets and crushed cans littered about Helen's feet. "You've ravaged the spread here in record time. You can't help yourself."

"I haven't eaten anything since breakfast," said her sister, draining a bottle of water. "And besides, it's not like we're not *supposed* to eat and drink this stuff. It's a spread, that's what it's there for. Right?"

Geri shook her head. She folded her arms and kicked her legs over the arm of her chair. Turning to Martha, she let out a sigh.

"So what's wrong with you then?" she asked. "Seems like I'm the village problem solver this afternoon."

"Nothing's wrong," said Martha, deep in thought. "Nothing more than the obvious."

"Obviously," droned Geri. "I have fifty pence in my pocket that tells me you're worried, stressed and anxious all at once, Mart. And I don't have to be a detective of world famous proportions to know that. The threadbare line you've worn in the carpet is enough."

Martha hopped a little and looked down at her feet. The carpet was fine.

"Made you look," laughed Geri.

"Very good," said Martha. "Fine, yes, something's wrong. Something's *always* wrong with us. I just can't let it all go. Not until we're out of this, cleanly, with nothing hanging over us."

"She's trying to say it's your fault Geri," said Helen, reaching over for a free banana. "She's just too polite to say it in as matter-of-fact a way as I would."

"That's not true," said Martha. "Well, it *is* true, of course I'm worried about Geri. But it's not your fault Geri. Not at all."

Helen shrugged and peeled her banana. Geri remained worryingly quiet. She kicked the side of her chair with her heels. Letting her head lie back on the opposite arm, staring up at the ceiling.

"Who would have thought trying to further your career would cause so much bloody trouble," she said, wistfully. "And one night humouring an old man would see me in the frame for murder."

"It's not that bad Geri, don't say things like that," said Martha. "That's why we're here. We're setting the record straight and you'll cooperate with the police."

"As long as they don't realise it was her who stole one of their hats," said Helen.

Geri threw a cushion at her sister.

"A minor indiscretion," she said. "But worth it in the end."

She swung her legs back over the arm of the chair. Resting her elbows on her knees, she drummed her fingers against her cheeks.

"Do you think Roberta will play ball?" she asked the others.

"What do you mean?" asked Helen. "She's got just as much on the line here as we do. Surely, she'll want to know who killed her husband."

"We don't know he was killed, Helen," said Martha. "His death's just being treated as suspicious at the moment."

"Do you think Roberta will see it from our perspective?" Geri asked. "Even after we bailed and went out on our own? I wouldn't blame her if she didn't."

"Nor would I," said Martha. "But what does she have to gain by throwing us to the dogs? We're nobodies, we've caused a minor stir in the grand scale of things. If, and only *if*, there's skulduggery afoot with Murray Steiner's death, then she needs to know about it."

"Do you think she knows already?" Geri looked up hopefully at Martha.

"I don't know," said Martha. "I can only *hope* that we're going to be bringing her more bad news. I'm not sure we could sink any lower in her estimations, but that would just about do it."

"Of course she knows," said Helen.

Martha and Geri peered over at their sister. Helen was polishing off the last of her banana, chewing methodically and folding the skin over on itself.

"How can you be so sure?" asked Geri.

Helen placed the skin on the arm of the sofa, leaned over and pulled a yogurt and spoon from the small fridge that was now nearly empty. Peeling back the lid, she tucked in before pointing the spoon at her sisters.

"Who would have the most to gain from Murray Steiner's death?" she asked them.

"Hold on, Helen," said Martha. "Just hold on, before you start making any more wild accusations. We don't want to cause any more fuss."

"It's a perfectly logical, pertinent question," she said, mouth full of yogurt. "If Murray Steiner died, who would stand to gain the most?"

"Roberta," said Geri. "His wife."

"Exactly."

"I don't like where this is going, Helen," said Martha. "And I'm nipping it in the bud right now."

"Why?"

"Why?" Martha said. "Because she said she loved him. And I, for one, believe her."

Helen shrugged and went back to her yogurt. Martha could feel her heart pounding in her chest. She decided to sit down. Geri rubbed her back.

"You okay?" she asked.

"Yes, I'll be fine," she lied. "Just been a long few days is all. Would much rather be back in the house with the door locked, the curtains drawn and the world left to run its course a long way away."

Geri kept rubbing Martha's back. It was comforting and warm. Just what she needed. Helen finished her yogurt and put the empty carton on the floor. She let out a long, exaggerated sigh and stretched out on the sofa.

"How much longer are they going to keep us waiting?" she asked.

"Why, have you got somewhere you need to be?" asked Geri sardonically.

"About a million other places spring to mind. I don't like being at someone's beck and call like this. Especially when there's a murderer on the loose."

Geri stopped rubbing Martha's back. She cracked her knuckles and rolled her neck, like she was about to start boxing.

"You know there's something that's been bothering me all day," she said. "Something I just can't shake and it's really bugging me."

"What is it?" asked Helen, her interest piqued.

"I don't know," she said. "Just something about Murray. You all saw him at dinner, you've seen him on TV and all the rest of it. Big, boisterous, the life and soul of the party. Take your pick from any number of platitudes all the social media tributes have been saying. To die in his sleep. It just feels so… anticlimactic."

"Yes!" Helen leapt forward, snapping her fingers. "Doesn't it?"

"Geri," said Martha, drawing out her sister's name in warning. "Don't encourage her."

"But don't you think so too Martha?" she asked. "Somebody like Murray Steiner wasn't meant to pass away quietly in his sleep. He should have died at some sordid sex party. Or parachuting over the Grand Canyon out of a crashing plane."

"Or fighting an escaped rhino that was rampaging through the streets of New York, causing all kinds of mayhem and madness," said Helen, bouncing up and down with glee.

"He was big, loud, and overzealous. It all feels wrong. And I'm inclined to side more and more with Helen that he was bumped off."

"Suspicions," said Martha. "That's all we've got at the moment. It could be anything. Literally anything at all. You know what the police are like and that's before you factor in the fact he is—he was—one of the most famous people on the planet. We're here with a plan. And we're sticking with it."

Geri and Helen settled back in their seats. Martha was hoping she'd poured cold water on their fanciful thinking. She loved her sisters dearly. But they had a tendency to spiral out of control with their shared imagination when the appetite took them. Still, at least Geri was staying upbeat all things considered. That had to be a positive.

The door opened. A flood of noise came rushing in from outside. Loud voices, raised, the sound of a crowd. A security guard stood taking up the doorway. She was about as tall and wide as Martha, Helen and Geri put together.

"You the Parker sisters?" she asked with a grunt.

"No, we're the halftime show," said Helen.

The guard's eyes widened. Martha stepped in before it turned ugly.

"Yes, that's right," she said. "We're waiting to see Roberta Steiner."

"Come with me," she said.

Martha did as she was told. Geri and Helen followed close behind her. She was about to chastise her middle sister when the guard held up a hand the size of a boulder.

"What's wrong?" she asked.

There was a crackle of static from the guard's radio. She pulled it off her shoulder, staring down the long, faceless hallway somewhere in the bowels of the hotel.

"What's the problem, central?" asked the guard.

Another burst of static. The voices of the crowd seemed to be growing. Martha had a terrible sense of *Deja vu* from the morning. It brought her out in a cold sweat.

"Trouble?" asked Helen. "Has the buffet run out of seafood or something?"

"Just hush up," said the guard, a vein pulsing in her temple.

They stood in nervous silence for a moment. The guard's radio crackled back into life.

"Okay. Roger," she snarled. "Right you lot, follow me and stick close."

"What's going on?" asked Geri. "I think if we're in some sort of danger we have a right to know."

"Seems your presence has caused a stir outside," said the guard, marching quickly down the corridor. "There's a bit of a crowd waiting to get a glimpse of you three superstars."

"No way," said Helen. "You're pulling our chains."

"It's as much a surprise to us as it is to you, believe me. Not something we were planning on. So you need to stay close to me, keep your heads down and whatever you do, don't look at the people between here and the lifts."

"This is unbelievable," laughed Helen. "I feel like I'm in The Beatles."

"Wow, what a current reference," scoffed Geri.

"Quiet you two," said Martha.

This was the last thing she wanted. This whole exercise was meant to be quick, clean and simple. Being the centre of attention was fine for anyone who wanted to be a celebrity. Martha just wanted to go home.

They reached the door at the end of the corridor. The crowd noise was loud here, like a football match or concert just on the other side of the doorway. The security guard reached for her radio.

"Okay, Central. We're ready," she said, one hand on the handle.

A final crackle from the radio and they were off. The guard shouldered the door hard and the afternoon light flooded into the hallway. Martha wasn't quite sure what to expect. But the noise flooded over her like a crashing wave.

As her eyes adjusted to the brightness, she saw hundreds, thousands of people split into two solid walls either side of the room. Security personnel were holding them back. Some were shouting, screaming even. Others were booing, cursing and volleying insults at the Parkers.

"Keep going," the guard shouted at them. "Almost there."

"How did they know we were here?" Geri yelled.

"Just keep moving!" the guard barked.

Two more security people joined the sisters, flanking them as they burrowed their way across the main hotel concourse towards the lifts. Martha clung on to her arms for comfort. She was cold, ice cold, her skin frosty to the touch even through her cardigan. This was as close to Hell as she could ever imagine. When would it be over?

Then she heard a familiar voice over the din. She looked up and saw Tom Hopgood jumping up and down from behind the crowd to their left.

"Martha," he shouted. "Helen. Geri. The results."

Martha stopped dead. Helen and Geri bumped into her back. They unfolded themselves and were about to scold their older sister when they spotted Tom too.

"Tom," Helen yelled.

"The results," he shouted again, trying to be heard over the din. "I've got the results."

Martha felt her mouth open. And it didn't want to close again. She'd never felt more conflicted or uncomfortable in her life. As the baying crowd's rapturous voice came crashing over her, she wanted to turn and run away forever. But she couldn't, not while Tom was dangling such a tempting carrot. In the end, the decision was made up for her.

"What are you doing?" screamed the female security guard. "Don't stop. Keep moving."

Two big hands grabbed Martha by the arm and hauled her down the small channel between the crowd. The others were pulled away too, protesting and shouting at their manhandlers.

"Tom," she shouted. "What are the results?"

She could see Tom shouting back at her but his voice was lost among the noise. His tanned face grew further away as the tides drew them all apart. He waved his phone high above his head, pointing at the screen. But it was no use—none of them could see.

The security guards dragged them to the lifts and bundled them inside. Martha didn't take her eyes from Tom who was little more than a speck amongst the crowd now. He was still pointing at his phone, the tendons in his neck flexed as he shouted at them.

As the doors of the lift slid closed, he finally vanished. Martha couldn't be sure what their friend had been saying. But she thought she'd picked something up from him before they'd been dragged, kicking and screaming, into the lift.

"What did he say?" asked Geri, breathless.

"I couldn't hear him properly," said Helen. "He said something about the results of the report. Did you hear him Martha? What did he say?"

Martha looked at her sisters, the security guards all tightly packed into the lift around them. She couldn't be sure. Not at all. But she had heard something.

"Poison," she said slowly. "I think Murray was poisoned."

Twenty-Four

"AAARRRGGHH."

"It's in my eyes."

"Aaaaaargh."

The three security guards tripped and fell out of the lift. They scrambled around on the floor, clawing at their faces as tears streamed down their cheeks. A foul smell seeped out of the elevator and into the small reception area. With it stumbled the Parker sisters, coughing and spluttering and in no fit shape.

"Bloody hell, Geri," Martha wheezed. "Where the hell did you get that spray from?"

"I feel like my eyes are on fire," said Helen, between fits of coughing and retching. "It's all the way down the back of my throat."

"You think that's bad?" said Geri, peering through bleary eyes. "I didn't even get any on you."

Martha fumbled her way across the small room and managed to steady herself. The pepper spray Geri had let off in the lift had been altogether too much for her. She kept rubbing at her eyes, trying to clear them. But the potent mixture was still powerful enough to render her almost completely useless.

She saw the security guards bent double in pain. She only wished she could help, but there were more pressing problems. Namely what had happened to Murray Steiner.

"Blimey Geri, that stuff is powerful alright," said Helen, helping her sister across the room to join Martha. "Where did you get that from? The SAS?"

"Not a million miles away actually," Geri sniffed, her nose running.

She held the small, empty can up to her sisters. Martha blinked some more and could just about make out lots of skull and crossbones stickers on the container.

"A guy I was seeing for a while a couple of years ago used to be in the Territorial Army," she explained. "He was really into his self-defence classes and he gave me this stuff. I always carry it on me, just in case. You can never be too careful."

"Remind me to have a word with you about the company you keep," said Martha. "But we've got work to do."

Her eyes were starting to work properly again. Or as close to properly as they could get. She rubbed her wet face on her sleeve and looked about the reception room. The fire exit was across the way and she started for the door.

"Hey, Mart, what about them?" asked Helen, still blinking madly.

She thumbed down at the security guards. They were a writhing picture of misery.

"They'll be fine," said Geri. "No permanent damage, just knocks you on your back until the police get here or you can run away."

"Run away it is then," said Martha.

They bolted for the fire exit. A cool draught was blowing up the airy stairwell, taking with it the pungent odour of the pepper spray. The sisters hurried down the stairs, taking two and three at a time. Helen was at the back as usual, her sandals clapping against the concrete.

"So we think Murray was poisoned then?" she shouted after the others.

"That's what Tom was saying, right Mart?" asked Geri.

"I don't know," said Martha. "But we need to be sure."

"Won't this put us even further in the bad books with Roberta Steiner?" asked Helen. "I mean, this is what, the second time, or is it the third, that we've run out on her. She's bound to lose the plot with us now."

"It doesn't matter," said Martha. "If we have a method then we *know* it's murder. And where there's a method then there's a motive. So get your thinking caps on and quick."

"Aren't you worried about Roberta?" asked Geri. "If somebody has bumped off her husband, she might be next."

"She's got an army protecting her," said Helen. "Those three you just blasted in the face with your weapons-grade pepper spray are just the tip of the well-organised security machine. Besides, Eleanor David is no slouch. I imagine Roberta's bulldog has a nasty bite to her if she puts her mind to it."

"Bite."

Martha stopped suddenly. Geri and Helen caught up with her, breathless.

"Bite, bulldog," she said.

"What are you talking about, Martha?" asked Helen, leaning on the handrail of the staircase.

"Eleanor David, you said she probably had a nasty bite on her. That's what you said."

"Yeah, so what? It's just a turn of phrase."

"Bite, hook, bait," said Martha.

Helen and Geri looked at one another. Then they turned back to their older sister.

"You okay there, Mart?" asked Geri. "Are you feeling okay?"

Martha smiled at her sisters. Then she laughed a little.

"Nothing," she said. "No, nothing. I just thought of something. It's fine. Don't worry about it."

Before Helen and Geri could question her further, a door opened from beneath them. They all peered over the guardrail and saw shadows flooding into the stairwell. The familiar luminous yellow of the security guards flashed past and they all jumped back away from the edge.

"Damn," said Geri. "I thought we might have had a little more time."

The footsteps sounded like rumbling thunder booming up the draughty stairwell. Being chased by angry mobs had become a rather nasty habit in the last few days and Martha was getting a little sick of it.

"Quick, in there," said Geri.

She darted over to the nearest door. Pulling it open with a creak, the sisters slipped through and huddled on the other side. The small army of security guards hurried past. Martha, Helen and Geri watched them through the crack in the door.

"Good spot Geri," said Martha. "Helen, where's your phone?"

"My phone?" Helen asked.

"Yes, your phone."

"What do you want my phone for?"

"Is she serious?" asked Geri. "Your phone. To call Tom."

"Yes, to call Tom," said Martha. "We need to know everything that he knows."

"Why would you want my phone for that?"

Martha threw up her hands. She loved Helen dearly. In fact, she doubted there was another person on the Earth who loved her as much as she did. That didn't stop her from wanting to strangle Helen where she stood sometimes.

As the de facto leader of their troupe, she refrained from launching any attack on her younger sister. Geri, however, was not nearly as restrained.

"What the hell is wrong with you Helen!" she hissed, lunging forward. "Why can't you just give us a straight answer now and again."

"Bloody hell." Helen tried to fend off Geri. "Martha, she's gone mad! Call those security people back, they can have her."

"Enough."

Martha wedged herself between the pair. She separated them, and they stood glaring at each other menacingly.

"Honestly, this is the very *last* thing we need right now," she said. "Bickering, fighting. I'm surprised you haven't brought the whole place down on us."

"She started it," said Helen.

"You started it with your nincompoopery!"

"That's not even a word, Geri. That doesn't make any sense."

"Stop."

Martha's voice echoed down the corridor. She only realised then that they were in the bowels of the hotel. Blank looking doors lined either side of the corridor, soft, warm lighting giving it a friendly, welcoming glow.

"Helen," she said with a sigh. "We need your phone to call Tom. We need to fetch him quickly and learn everything he knows. From there we can plot our next move."

"Right, yes," said Helen, scratching her head. "See, the thing about that is, and you're going to laugh when I tell you. I don't have his number."

Silence. Martha didn't know if she wanted to laugh or to sob uncontrollably. Geri, once again, was much more open with her emotions.

"Wonderful," she said. "Absolutely bloody wonderful."

Helen shoved her hands in her pockets and shrugged.

"Guess I just hadn't got around to asking him yet," she said, sounding almost bashful. "It's not the thing you do these days anyway, is it? You don't just ask people for their phone numbers. That might have been alright what five, ten years ago maybe, when people were a little less frosty about relationships. But my students—"

"*Ex*-students," Geri interrupted.

"Ex-students were forever telling me about all these new-fangled apps and programs people use for dating. You swipe up and down, left and right, that's how you get to meet folk these days. So I *assumed* that's what would have to happen with Tom and myself. Not being the type to break from social convention of course. Heaven forfend."

"Heaven forfend, indeed," said Martha, leaning her aching body against the wall.

"Helen," said Geri, doing the same. "You are, by a very long stretch, the single most infuriating person I've ever had the misfortune of calling my sister."

"You what?"

Geri pulled her phone from her pocket. She began clicking and tapping the screen, smiling.

"Social convention," she laughed. "That's a good one. Name me one time when you've been anywhere *near* a social convention."

"This is a convention isn't it?" smiled Helen.

"Yeah and look at how this has turned out."

"Well I'm here, *we*'re here aren't we?"

Martha could feel her whole body crying out for rest. Her eyelids were heavy and she just wanted to lie down on the comfortable hotel carpet and sleep for a century.

"What are you doing Geri?" she asked her.

With a final flourish, Geri stopped. She turned the phone around and handed it to Helen.

"Here you go," she said. "Your Prince Charming awaits on the other end of the line."

"What?" Helen blurted. "What do you mean he's on the other end of the line."

"It's ringing Helen," said Geri. "You see some of us aren't too proud, shy or indeed technophobic to be able to find the number of a good looking Australian private eye. I think that might have been a new record, was anyone timing me?"

"Hello?" Tom's voice came from Geri's phone. "Hello? Who is this?"

"Hello! Tom! It's me Helen. Helen Parker."

Geri flashed Helen a thumbs up and then rolled her eyes at Martha.

"Young love, eh?" she said.

"You didn't do anything… illegal there did you?" Martha asked.

"No," she replied flatly. "Not that time, anyhow. You really should get clued up on this whole social media and interconnectivity thing Martha. I can just about stomach Helen's reluctance but I don't know if my grey matter can cope with *both* of you."

Martha ruffled her youngest sister's hair. She was becoming the woman that Martha knew Geri was capable of. Resourceful, calm and cool, even under terrible strain. The little tiff with Helen a moment ago was the exception to the rule. She was very proud of her youngest sister. And she knew Helen was too.

"Okay, okay that's great, wonderful. Yes, yes we'll see you soon. Oh hold on, where will you be?" asked Helen. "The kitchens, okay, brilliant, yes. We'll be there shortly. Okay, see you soon. Bye, bye, bye… bye."

She hung up the phone. Passing it nervously between her hands, she looked at the others with an anxious smile on her face.

"Well?" asked Martha, pushing herself off the wall.

"Go on then," said Geri. "Out with it."

"Well," Helen started. "He sounded *really* happy to hear my voice. Which means that there just *might* be something there."

"Helen!" Martha and Geri said together.

"What?"

"We don't care about your bloody personal life," said Geri.

"Murray Steiner. What about Murray Steiner?" Martha begged.

"Oh, right, yeah, sorry," she clapped her hand to her forehead. "Yeah he was poisoned. Quite a nasty amount of potassium in his system by all accounts. It was enough to finish him off apparently."

"Potassium?" asked Martha.

"Blimey," said Geri. "That *is* nasty."

"You didn't feed him any bananas did you?" asked Helen, handing back the phone.

"Of course I didn't."

"I was joking, Ger."

"Potassium," said Martha again. "That's what killed him?"

"Too much potassium. It's like our teachers always said, too many bananas can kill you."

Martha was surprised. It wasn't the first time this weekend she'd felt that strange sensation of being completely bewildered.

Every time she thought she'd had a grasp on things, something else popped out of nowhere and completely sideswiped her.

"I said we'd meet Tom at the kitchens," said Helen. "He's heading there right now."

"Why?" asked Martha.

"It's hardly the time to get something to eat," said Geri.

"If you two could stop talking your stupid pills for a bit. Murray Steiner died from potassium poisoning. Which means he probably died from something he ate. And if Geri promises that she didn't force feed the old man a hundred bananas during their midnight rendezvous, then clearly somebody was messing around with his meals. And who creates meals? Chefs. And where do chefs work? Altogether now class… kitchens."

"Sarcasm doesn't suit you Helen," sneered Geri. "Although a surgical collar might if you try to be a smart arse again."

"Let's go," said Martha. "It feels like we're finally making some progress. If we can get down there without Roberta finding—"

She opened the fire exit door but was immediately halted. Standing in the doorway, looking fabulous as always, was Roberta Steiner.

"Going somewhere ladies?"

Twenty-Five

MARTHA HAD BEEN expecting a frosty reception from Roberta Steiner. It would have been foolish to think anything otherwise. Still, as she and the others were frogmarched through the corridors of the hotel, she thought things weren't quite as bad as first anticipated.

For one thing, they were all walking of their own free will. The amount of messing around and bother that Martha, Helen and Geri had caused, she wouldn't have blamed Roberta for manifesting her anger in a physical manner. Beaten to a pulp sprung to mind.

Yet here they were. All very civil, if a little cold. Roberta at the head of the procession, Eleanor David by her side. A few other dark-suited aides had joined the entourage, all looking for guidance from their fearless leader. Mrs Steiner wasn't in a chatting mood. She strode on purposefully, her pace unbroken.

"You think she's mad at us?" whispered Helen.

"Yes I'd say so," said Geri. "We're the three idiots that have ruined an already bad day for her. Would you be mad?"

"Probably," she shrugged. "Although I'm not really the emotional type, as you two can attest to."

"Oh brother," groaned Geri.

Roberta pushed open a wide set of doors. Like a hatch being opened in a submarine, the sound of the conference erupted like water pouring in the hole. The entourage followed her at a safe distance, and Martha and the others found themselves on a wide, balconied walkway high above the main concourse of the convention area. Roberta took long, elegant strides over to the glass rail and spread her arms out, leaning on the edge. She surveyed the busy summit still unfolding below her, like a mighty Roman Emperor ready to address the mob.

"Leave us," she called over her shoulder, not turning her head.

There was a moment's hesitation. Nobody was quite sure what their fearless and fearsome leader was talking about. After that microsecond of inactivity, Roberta shouted her orders again.

"Leave us."

Her entourage didn't need another dressing down. The aides quickly ushered the security personnel back through the door that led to the balcony. In record time, everyone was gone, leaving the Parker sisters and Eleanor David alone with Roberta Steiner.

"This isn't good," whispered Helen, shuffling about, her sweaty feet sucking against her sandals. "I've got a bad feeling about—"

"What's that?" asked Roberta.

She spun around, facing the four women congregated about her. Her sharp eyes glared down at Helen, cutting through the air between them.

"Nothing Roberta," said Helen. "Or is it Mrs Steiner. I can't remember how we left it the last time. Sorry."

"Sorry?" she said. "You're telling me you're sorry."

"Well, yes, that's what I said," Helen continued. "I'm sorry for not remembering what formal standing we're on at the moment. It's been a bit of a long day you see."

Martha had to close her eyes at that point. If only the ground could swallow her whole, this would have been a good moment for it.

"Yes, well, that's all in the past now, isn't it?" Roberta said.

Martha opened one eye first. Then the other. Roberta had turned to look out over the balcony again. Far below, the main concourse was still heaving with people. They bobbed in and out of side rooms and visited exhibition tables and stalls. They carried coloured bags of swag and other memorabilia all branded with SteinerCon or the Steiners' wordmarks.

"They seem happy, don't they?" she asked the group. "Down there, going about their business like nothing has happened. They call themselves private investigators, detectives. Yet you flash a free T-shirt or fridge magnet in front of them and they're just like kids. Glued to the shiny treats that will rot their brain and dilute their focus."

Eleanor stood looking at her boss with an almost god-like admiration. It was the longest Martha had seen her not using a phone or a tablet.

"Thousands of them will pass through the doors today," Roberta continued. "Tens of thousands by the time the weekend is out. They come from all over the world, from all different backgrounds and professions. Some long in the tooth, with long careers behind them. While others are just fans, with nothing else better to do than sit through lectures and talks and listen to me speak at them for a while. It's incredible really, when you think about it. Murray and I started this convention as a bit of a lark, another money-spinner and a way to promote the show. We had three hundred at the first SteinerCon. Now look at it. Bigger and better than ever and filled to the rafters with people who are or who want to be detectives."

She tapped her hands on the metal rail, rings making the polished steel rattle.

"So tell me this, Parker sisters," she said, turning back around to face them. "Out of the thousands of people here, all claiming to be detectives, why is it you three are the only ones who thought to investigate my husband's death?"

Martha was dumbfounded. Once again she struggled to stop her jaw from dropping and hitting the floor with a bump.

"Pardon me?" she managed to squeeze out.

"You three," laughed Roberta. "You three women from the back-ass end of nowhere. You three are the only ones out of everybody in this place that thought there might be something odd about Murray's passing."

"Glasgow isn't the back-ass end of nowhere, lady," said Helen, defensively.

"Whatever," said Roberta. "My point still stands. I'm curious. If nothing else, I'm curious. I want to know what it is that's caused the three of you to be such a thorn in my side today. Why is it that you just can't let any of this go?"

"We haven't done anything wrong," said Geri, stepping forward. "In case you've forgotten Roberta, I'm the one who found your husband dead. I'm the one that had to wake up and see his bloated corpse sitting at the other end of the bed, eyes bulging like a pair of eggs from his stupid, meaty face."

"Geri," Martha and Helen held their sister back.

"I'm the one who had to see that Roberta. I had to see that for God's sake."

Her voice cracked and she began to cry. She pulled herself free from Martha and Helen and paced up and down the balcony.

"I promised myself I wouldn't get angry," she said. "Out of respect for you Roberta. Out of sheer bloody respect. I mean look at you, just *look* at you. You're one of the most glamorous, famous women in the world. You're a role model for millions of people, not just your fans or the people down there. You've got fame, fortune and everything that goes with it. You're a walking, talking, breathing example of the American Dream—that no matter where you come from, you can make it. And yeah, I don't mind admitting it, you're hot as hell."

That drew a wry smile from Roberta. It quickly vanished.

"So whatever long-winded speech you want to give us, just get it over with, okay," Geri continued. "We came back here to tell you, to *warn* you that the police forensics team believe Murray was poisoned. And that means somebody is out there willing to commit murder. You could be in danger Roberta, real danger. If whoever did this to Murray got to him, then they can get to you too."

Geri stood, breathing hard. Martha dearly wanted to hug her and tell her how proud she was. But Roberta acted first.

"You're quite the little firecracker Geri," she said slowly. "I'm starting to see what Murray found so attractive in you."

"Didn't you hear what I said?" asked Geri. "I'm telling you, *we* are telling you, that you could be in danger. The police need to get involved in this."

"The police," Roberta laughed mockingly. "You've got to be kidding me. What you lot call a police force, I wouldn't trust to run security at a county fair. I've spoken with your police, and believe me when I tell you, they stand a better chance of catching a cold than they do my husband's killer."

"So you know then?" said Martha. "You know that Murray's death was suspicious? That he was poisoned?"

"Ms Steiner is a grieving widow," said Eleanor, stepping forward. "And the information surrounding her husband's death is completely confidential and—"

"Put a sock in it, Eleanor," Roberta barked. "I've just about had it up to here with you and your goddamn red tape. You're worse than the cops. They know, I know, we *all* know. Why do you think I sent everyone else away?"

Eleanor retreated a little. She looked like a scolded dog who just wanted somewhere to hide. Martha stifled a satisfied smirk.

"I know all too well what's going on here ladies, believe me," Roberta went on. "And if I truly believed that my life was in danger, I'd be on the plane back to LA before you could chase my shadow. Now the fact remains, you still haven't answered my question. Out of all the sleuths, gumshoes and bloodhounds at SteinerCon, why was it only you three decided that there might be something worth investigating?"

Geri was silent this time. As was Helen. Martha tried to steady her breathing. She was nervous, excited and terrified all at once.

"Self-preservation," she said.

Roberta twisted to face her.

"Self-preservation? You Martha?" she asked. "Now I admit I haven't known you a long time, though it's still too long in my book, but you don't strike me as being the selfish type."

"Self-preservation, Roberta," she said, again. "The preservation of my family, of my sister Geri. I told you before that she has done nothing wrong. And she hasn't. It was Helen and her friend Tom Hopgood who thought there might have been something wrong, something not quite right. And through a little sleuthing, we've established that is the case. Now, as Geri said, we came back here to warn you, and to tell you also that we have no qualms about helping the police in their investigation. We'll cooperate. But I'm warning you, as I'll warn them, I won't stand idly by while a murder charge is laid at the feet of Geri or anyone in my family."

"And you think you can do a better job than the police?" Roberta sniffed. "You think you can do better than professional law men and women whose job it is to catch murderers and killers. You three think you can do that better."

"With all due respect, Mrs Steiner," said Helen, stepping forward. "We're the guests of honour at *your* convention for private investigators. Why don't *you* tell *us* if we're qualified or not?"

Roberta's glare turned to Helen. Martha had noticed that there was a special look of total contempt reserved for Helen and Helen only. Nobody else seemed to get under the great Roberta Steiner's skin more than the middle Parker sister.

"Alright," she said, folding her arms across her chest. "Alright. I'm convinced."

"Convinced of what?" asked Geri.

"Convinced that you three aren't anywhere near as dumb as you look or act," she said. "Convinced that despite all of my best efforts trying to get you out of my sight, you actually might be onto something. So I'm going to make you an offer."

"Another one?" asked Helen.

"Yes, another one, Helen," the poison dripped from her tone. "I'm going to offer you three a chance at redemption. A shot at glory. One last hurrah before I turn you over to the police and let that sorry-ass force fumble and pick their way through a mystery that'll take them a century to work out. All the while my poor Murray lies in pieces on a slab somewhere letting the flies collect around him."

She narrowed in on Martha. Like an adult speaking to another while the children played.

"I'm letting you go," she said. "I'm letting you go to see what you can turn up. The police have already told me Murray's death was no accident. I can only assume that you have leads, contacts, everything at your disposal. So go and do it. Prove to me that you have the chops, that you're not just some bumpkin outfit from the territories. Find me Murray Steiner's killer."

"And what do we get when we do?" asked Helen.

"*If* you do," said Roberta. "If you do. You'll have my respect."

"Is that it?"

"Helen," warned Martha.

"You'll have the respect of Roberta Steiner, the woman, the myth and the icon, as Geri so aptly described it. But most of all, you'll have your freedom. You won't ever hear from me again. I'll be out of your life, everything forgotten, everything forgiven. We draw a line in the sand and nothing else can change it, not the betrayals, not the numbskullery, not the millions of dollars you've probably already cost me in sponsorships for next year. Nothing. End of the line. Does that sound fair?"

Eleanor cleared her throat politely. Roberta gave her a hawkish look.

"It's time Mrs Steiner," she said, tapping her smartwatch.

"It seems I don't have any more time to waste with you," said Roberta.

She adjusted the cuffs of her suit jacket and licked her teeth. Straightening her shoulders, she looked at every one of the Parkers in turn, with varying degrees of contempt.

"Don't disappoint me again, ladies," she said. "The cops are slow but they're not *that* slow. In fact…"

As if on cue, a series of loud clangs rose up from the concourse. Martha and the others peered over the edge of the balcony railing. Police officers stood at the entranceways, guarding the exits that were being locked by hotel staff. The hustling, bustling crowd oozed a nervous energy. At the far end of the concourse, a hotel manager was speaking through a megaphone, trying to bring some order to the mass of delegates.

"Right on time," said Roberta. "Her Majesty's finest, locking down a crime scene hours after it's been contaminated and the killer probably long gone from here."

"What are they doing?" asked Helen, staring wide-eyed at the crowd.

"Witnesses," said Martha. "Everyone here at the summit could be a potential witness."

"Or suspect," added Geri.

"Whatever you three have planned, I suggest you don't dawdle," said Roberta, making for the door with Eleanor in tow. "Remember, if the deal is to be honoured, it's you three who bring me Murray's murderer. Not the police, not any of those idiots down there. *You.*"

The crowd was being filtered into long columns, queues snaking out across the concourse with a team of police officers at the head all furiously scribbling down statements already. An uneasy if docile panic had set in amongst the delegates. Martha could feel their cautious energy drifting up towards them.

"What about…"

She turned to finish her question but Roberta was gone. They were alone on the wide balcony, with only the glittering chandeliers for company.

"Potassium," she said to the others. "Potassium overdose. That's what killed Murray Steiner."

"That's what Tom said, yeah, we know," answered Helen.

"Let's go talk to the Chef, then," said Martha. "Come on."

The Parker sisters broke into a run as they headed for the kitchen and a date with a possible murderer.

Twenty-Six

"DO YOU HAVE any idea where we're going?" gasped Helen. "It feels like we've been running forever."

"It's been five minutes, Helen, and yes, of course Martha knows where we're going," said Geri. "Right Martha?"

Martha didn't have the heart to say 'no'. They'd hurried down into the main concourse and were edging their way through the crowd. The security staff were struggling, but slowly the delegates were being wrangled into some sort of order. Formal queues now stretched from one end of the main convention area to the other. The stalls and stands of merchants and promotion people were abandoned, a haven for unsupervised swag should anyone want to nab a free T-Shirt, hat or keyring.

There were more police down here than she had expected. Containment was clearly, finally, high on their agenda. The men and women of the Met looked stern, eyeballing everything and everyone.

"Stick to the walls," said Martha, guiding her sisters through the maelstrom.

"You *do* know where the kitchens are, don't you?" asked Helen.

Again Martha didn't answer. They hugged the wall that ran directly below the balcony they'd come from. Travelling in the opposite direction of the forming queues, they passed unnoticed behind and below the ever watchful gaze of the gathered police force. They reached the end of the concourse. Nowhere left to go. Martha looked about, trying to find some sort of direction, somewhere to point them towards the hotel's kitchens.

"These damn hotels," she said, frustrated. "They do so well to hide all the mechanics of a place like this. Unless it's shimmering and chic, there's no place for it in the public eye."

"Oh come, come Martha, you wouldn't want all the international delegates, business people and rock stars to come in here and see where the dirty laundry is kept, would you?" asked Geri. "As we've seen from the Steiners, people who stay here don't live like us. They don't live like *anyone*. It's a total fantasy world."

"As long as they are the centre of attention," added Helen.

"Okay," said Martha. "Give Tom a ring. We're not going to find this place. Maybe he can direct us."

Geri pulled out her phone. She scrolled through the numbers and selected the last one called.

"Eh… excuse me?" said Helen.

"What?" asked Geri, putting the phone to her ear.

"I think I should be the one who calls Tom. Not you."

"And how do you figure that one out?"

"He's *my* contact."

"He's not *your* anything, Hel, come on now."

"He wouldn't be helping us if it wasn't for me."

"And we wouldn't have his number if it wasn't for me."

"Yes, but *I* am the one who made first contact. I should be the one who speaks to him."

"It's *my* phone."

"Would you two just get on with it," said Martha exasperated. "Honestly, you two weren't like this as kids. I don't know what's gotten into you."

"It's ringing out," said Geri, hanging up.

"I hope nothing has happened to him," said Helen.

"He'll be fine," said Martha. "He can take care of himself. He's a big boy."

"Oi!" The voice boomed out from the crowd like a locomotive charging through a tunnel. When Martha saw who the voice belonged to, she was surprised there wasn't steam coming from his ears just like the train.

Pushing his way through the well-organised lines was the policeman from hospital, less his hat. His face was purple with rage, big arms trowelling through the convention-goers like a paddle-steamer on a river.

"Stop right there," he bellowed.

"Leg it," Geri shouted. And they were off again. Martha didn't dare look back. She knew the officer would be hot on their tail.

"Down here, quick," said Helen. "Through there."

They barrelled into a service door on the far wall. The soft, luxuriant lighting of the concourse was replaced by a sterile, hard glow from above. A narrow little passageway that reeked of disinfectant opened up ahead of them. A woman with a mop looked as surprised as the sisters when she saw them running towards her.

"Look out," called Martha.

They whizzed past, kicking over her bucket in the process. She let out a torrent of expletives as they pressed on. Left, right, left, another left, a right and then a final left. The passageways went on and on, the next as mistakable as the last. Until finally they came to a small opening with tables, chairs and a tatty old couch.

"It must be a break room," said Martha.

"Where are they?" came the cop's booming voice from the corridor behind.

"We can't keep running like this," said Martha. "We're going to tire long before he does. Not to mention there are hundreds of his mates upstairs."

"You're right, we need to hide," said Geri. "Come on guys, think."

She snapped her fingers, looking all about the silent break room. She spied a large, frosted glass window on the near wall, a pair of drab curtains untidily hanging over it.

"Quick, here," she said, racing to the window.

She unlatched it at its hinges. The wafer thin glass spun on its axis, almost knocking her backwards. A warm wind blew in from outside, the throbbing sound of machinery drifting into the breakout room.

Martha leaned through the gap. A sheer drop fell away four or five stories to a small, grotty courtyard, the tall, sleek walls of the hotel rising up on all four sides.

"Come on," said Geri, climbing through the opening.

"We can't go out there," said Helen. "We'll fall and break our necks."

"Have you got a better idea?" she asked. "Come on, hurry up."

A narrow ledge, barely wide enough for a foot, ran along the wall outside the window. Geri eased herself out, sidling along to make room for her sisters.

"You can't be seriously thinking about this Martha," said Helen. "That's got to be a thirty foot drop."

"Now that I'm out here, probably closer to forty," said Geri. "Would you two hurry up."

Martha was uneasy about it too. But that was nothing new, not for this weekend. They had work to do and couldn't afford to waste any more time. She let out a loud sigh and threw her leg through the open window.

"This just gets better and better," she said.

The hot wind blew up and about her. She tried not to look down but there was little else to do out here. If she didn't look down, up was the only other option. The huge structure of the hotel vanished into the clear blue sky with a dizzying effect. Down it was.

"Oh god, oh god, oh god," said Helen. "My vertigo is acting up. I'm going back inside."

"You're not even out yet," snapped Geri. "Get onto this ledge and close that bloody window behind you."

"Oh god, oh god, oh god."

Helen stepped onto the ledge and faced outwards. A little of the masonry crumbled and fell away from beneath her sandal.

Martha grabbed her arm and gently pulled her towards her, clearing the window. On the other side, Geri grabbed the frame and closed the window with a click. They all stood in silence, not sure what to do next.

"Look," Geri whispered, barely audible over the pulsing sound of extractor fans in the courtyard below.

Martha peered over to the frosted glass as much as she dared. The brilliant yellow of the police officer moved back and forth across the frosted glass. Even as a smudge he looked big and imposing.

The cop moved inside, clearly searching the breakout room. He turned away, as though about to leave, and the Parker sisters heaved a collective sigh of relief, still holding on by their fingernails. But he stopped, facing the window again. Stepping up to the frosted glass, his huge mass seemed to fill the large frame. He pressed his face against the glass, looking out.

Martha instinctively reached for Helen's hand. She grabbed it, feeling her sister squeeze back. They all stood perfectly still, staring outwards ahead at the row of windows on the far wall on the other side of the courtyard. A curtain twitched over there.

A woman appeared. When she spotted the Parkers she jumped back. Martha wasn't sure what to do. What *could* you do in a situation like that? The woman reappeared, her husband being dragged by the elbow. She pointed furiously at them, mouthing unheard expletives through the double glazing of their hotel room window. Martha thought about waving, something to acknowledge that they had seen her, and they were okay. But that would involve letting go, and she wasn't about to do that. She silently willed the couple to go away, hoping the cop wouldn't see them and realise what was going on. They argued with each other, a heated back and forth broken only by quick, sharp pointing sessions. Eventually she disappeared, leaving the man to stare at the Parkers for a long moment. Then he pulled the curtains closed again and wasn't seen again.

Thankfully nothing else happened. The window didn't open. There was no booming voice from the hatless cop. Nothing. Martha dared to look over to the window. The giant yellow smudge was still there. And for a brief second she thought she'd been spotted. Then she realised that the cop had turned around, the smudge was made up of his huge, broad back.

She was about to start breathing again when she felt something crack beneath her foot. A huge chunk of the ledge dropped away, taking her with it. For the briefest of moments she was floating in mid-air. As gravity took hold, she reached out and grabbed on to the ledge, stopping herself from falling to what would have been certain death.

"Martha," Helen shouted.

"Quiet," Martha whispered. "He's still there."

Martha felt the strain all the way down through her shoulders. Her fingertips burned as she tried to support her own weight. She didn't have the strength to pull herself back up. Helen and Geri watched on helplessly as the cop stood guard on the other side of the window.

She thought about shouting for help. Nothing would be worse than falling at this point. Surely not even being arrested, and the whole plan scuppered. Martha looked down between her dangling feet at the drop below. She was about to scream for help when she spotted a door opening down in the courtyard.

A bald man in white tunic and checkerboard trousers emerged. He was swearing as he pulled something heavy out through the door behind him. Rocking it back and forth. A huge cart on castors emerged from the building—filled to the brim with sheets and linen. As the wheels cleared the lip of the door, the man gave up and patted the sweat from his glistening head. He skulked back into the hotel and slammed the door behind him.

Martha looked back up at her sisters. Gritting her teeth, she took her weight on one hand and pointed down below her with the other.

"I think I've found the kitchens," she whispered.

"No," said Helen.

"Don't do it Martha," said Geri.

It was too late. Martha had made up her mind. She took one last, deep breath and closed her eyes. Letting go of the broken ledge, she dropped fast. The journey was over in seconds. She landed among the linen with a hollow thud. More importantly, she was unhurt, everything still moving, working, apart from her sore shoulders.

She let out a yelp, half in disbelief and half in celebration. She looked up at the others and beckoned them down.

"Come on," she said, a little giddy. "The linen's lovely."

Helen and Geri looked at each other, a knowing sense of inevitability spread across their faces. Even all the way down here Martha could see it. She clambered out of the linen cart and made sure it was ready for them.

They reached across and took each other's hand. Much like Martha before, they closed their eyes and stepped off the ledge. With a whistling scream, they soared majestically before landing in a heap among the sheets, tablecloths and pillowcases.

"Bloody hell," Helen gasped, floundering. "Bloody hell, I'm never doing anything like that again."

"Wooo," Geri laughed. "What a rush."

Their celebration was short lived. Martha hurried them out of the cart as the window high above them clicked open. The Parker sisters slipped in through the door that led back into the hotel before the angry cop could notice they were there. All that met him was a grotty looking courtyard and a linen cart significantly flatter than it had been before.

Twenty-Seven

MARTHA WAS GETTING to see so many new things, new experiences, even new smells on this trip. Maybe when it was all over she could reflect on these eye-opening few days. As it was, as it *always* was, there was no time for gentle reflection.

The kitchens of the Imperial were something altogether different. Not since she had been on the spirited adventure of student life around Japan had she been met with such a sudden sensory invasion. Everywhere she looked, there was something being chopped, boiled, fried, sautéed, drizzled, poached, sliced, diced and minced. It was a literal mixing pot, jam-packed from ceiling to floor and wall to wall with people preparing meals.

"We've found the kitchens then," said Geri.

All about them chefs, cooks and waiters were winding and weaving between workbenches. Plates were spun, quite literally, as the expert staff kept the well-oiled machine moving. A drop anywhere in the line would spell disaster, Martha could tell. She'd never seen such concentration on so many faces before. The fact that they had been ignored as they stood aghast at the hotel kitchens was testimony to that.

"Can you see Tom anywhere?" asked Helen, peering across the chaos.

"What's wrong, your Tom-dar not working?"

"Shut up, Geri."

"I can't see him," said Martha. "Although this is worse than a needle in a haystack. At least the hay stays still."

"We should hurry," said Geri. "That goon without a hat is still looking for us."

"We need to find the Head Chef," said Helen. "We know that Murray had a potassium overdose. We need to know what he ate and who prepared it." She held her arms wide to the kitchens. "Do you want to start asking or shall I?"

Martha drummed her fingers on her chin. She didn't know where to begin. The place was awash with people, all busy, all focussed. In the end she resorted to the simplest method. Whoever was closest.

"Excuse me," she said.

"Burger for room two twenty," said a flushed faced woman in spattered chef's whites.

She hoisted a plate up onto a waiting food warmer and mashed a bell. It pinged and a waiter came hurrying over to the work station.

"Two-twenty," she said to him, then turned to Martha. "Yes?"

The chef eyed Martha up and down suspiciously. She hurried over to a nearby sink and washed her hands. Martha followed, a little intimidated by this woman's no-nonsense attitude.

"I was wondering if you could help me?" she said. "Can you direct me to the Head Chef."

"Why?" she asked. "Who are you?"

"I'm… a curious guest," Martha lied.

"Guest?"

The chef dried her hands. She caught sight of Helen and Geri milling by the door and her look turned even more suspicious.

"You three don't look like guests," she said. "And you didn't come in the main door."

Martha tensed. She had to think quickly.

"What seems to be the problem here?" Geri appeared at her shoulder. The chef wasn't fast enough to conceal her sneer.

"I'm asking your friend here who you guys are and what you're doing in my kitchen," she said.

"Health inspectorate," said Geri, pulling out her phone.

"Health inspectorate? But your mate here just said you were guests."

"She did," said Geri, not breaking sweat. "We don't like to advertise the fact we're dropping in for a random inspection, sort of takes away the element of surprise, doesn't it, Ms Parker?"

Martha gritted her teeth. This was never going to work. More rules broken, maybe even laws. Was this misrepresentation? Falsely pretending to be a member of a government backed public office.

"Yes, you're right Miss… McGillicuddy." It was the first name that popped into her head.

"Yes, see, there you go," said Geri, unfazed. "Now we're here to speak to the Head Chef. And we're on a very tight schedule, so if you could help us out that would be great."

"Have you got ID?" asked the chef.

"ID?" Geri squeaked. "Do you have any idea the number of police officers are outside at the moment madam? The hotel is positively crawling with them. Myself and my colleagues were practically strip searched to get access to the hotel for this random inspection. If you're going to keep us standing around here, then I suggest you start getting your story straight madam. This is a random inspection of one of the finest hotels in London. I would hate to think that we weren't introduced to the proper people in a timely and orderly fashion because we were being asked for red tape trivialities. But… if that's how you want to play it then I'm happy to make a note in my report."

"Okay," said the chef, throwing her towel down hard. "Fine. Whatever. I've got too much work to do to be standing around here all day. This is all above my paygrade."

She started up a long row between busy workbenches. Martha, Geri and Helen followed her.

"McGillicuddy, seriously?" whispered Geri.

"I know, I'm sorry," Martha replied. "I panicked and that was the first name that sprung to mind. And you had used our actual name. So technically it's your fault."

"We'll call it a draw."

"What fun name can I have?" asked Helen at the back. "Can I be Aristotle? Oh wait, Wagner, yes Wagner, I like the sound of that. I'll pronounce it with the 'vee 'at the start too. Yes, lovely."

"Parker, Wagner and McGillicuddy, we sound like some seventies prog rock trio," said Geri.

"It'll have to do, we're too far through the looking glass to change it," said Martha.

The chef took them across the main kitchen. Along the back walls ran a series of small offices, their glass doors and walls misted up with condensation from the heat. The chef who had escorted them stood to one side.

"Here you go," she said. "Marcel Blanc, Michelin star chef and our boss. Good luck."

She didn't wait for further introductions, retreating back into the madness, cursing under her breath. Martha gave a quick pep talk to the others.

"Remember, keep cool," she said. "For all we know this guy could have murdered Murray Steiner. We have to be clever, not crass. Think fast and stay sharp. Got it?"

"You bet," said Geri.

"Clever is my middle name," said Helen.

Martha knocked once on the misty glass door. There was no answer so she tried again.

"What!" came a gravelly voice from the other side.

She opened the door. Inside was a cramped, confined space filled with loose folders, papers and filing cabinets. A small desk and computer dominated the little office. And behind it sat Marcel Blanc, scarlet-face beaming out from behind a thick beard whose grey hairs were winning the fight against the dark. His chef's tunic was unbuttoned at the top, the rest of the fasteners straining against the push of his massive gut.

The head chef of the Imperial looked far too big to be housed in an office this small. Everything around him seemed to be trying to claw at his shoulders. Even the scattered papers on his desk were making a concerted effort to launch an attack on his stubby little fingers.

"Mr Blanc?" asked Martha.

"Who are you?" he asked. "Who let you back here."

Martha slipped into the office. Geri and Helen were close behind her and shut the door, drowning out the mayhem of the kitchen.

"What is this?" he shouted.

"Mr Blanc, you don't know us."

"You're damn right I don't know you! How the hell did you get into my kitchen? I'm calling security.

He looked about for his desk phone, scattering papers and files all over the place.

"Mr Blanc, please, hear us out," said Martha. "You don't know us, my name is Martha Parker. We've been sent by Roberta Steiner."

At the mention of Roberta's name, Blanc stopped.

"Roberta Steiner?"

"Yes," said Martha. "Mr Blanc, her husband Murray died last night. And we have it on good authority that he suffered from a potassium overdose."

"Potassium?" asked Blanc, rising from his chair. "I had no idea. I mean, I saw that he was dead, how could you miss that? It's everywhere. But potassium? Are you sure?"

"Yes," said Helen. "The toxicology report says he had an unusually high amount of potassium in his system when he died. And that it was likely this that brought on a fatal cardiac arrest."

"He's been a guest at this hotel for the past few days Mr Blanc," said Geri. "I don't imagine he was ordering his food in. We have good reason to believe that he might have been deliberately poisoned. Which means his food was tampered with, food that would have come from your kitchens."

Blanc's face went slack. He ran a hand through his thinning hair as he rounded his desk. Taking heavy steps, the huge man thudded his way towards the door.

"This is unbelievable," he said. "I'm absolutely aghast."

"We need you to think Mr Blanc. Think very hard," said Martha, putting her interrogation voice on. "Who has been preparing Mr Steiner's meals? Is it a team, some of your junior staff maybe? Whoever it is, we need to speak to them straight away."

"You can, of course you can," said Blanc. "It's me."

Martha paused her questioning.

"You?" blurted Helen. "You cooked all of Murray Steiner's meals?"

"Yes I did," he said, flatly.

Martha wasn't sure if it was her imagination, but she suddenly became very aware of Blanc's size. He was a massive man, tall and wide. His heaving gut hung over his trousers, but his arms were as thick as pylons. He took up most of the office, even standing still.

"You prepared *all* of Murray Steiner's meals?" asked Geri.

"Yes, of course. Didn't you hear me?" The flash of anger from Blanc made the room even more tense. "He and Mrs Steiner were favoured guests of the hotel. I personally cook for all the friends of this business. They are generous with their time, not to mention their business. It's the least I can do for them."

He stared out of the misty glass door. Deep in thought, he pinched at the hairs of his beard.

"I'm bereft," he said. "The thought that Mr Steiner could have died from my cooking. I shall never live this down, never. And what will the press think? I'll be ruined."

Much to the Parker sisters 'surprise, Blanc began to sob uncontrollably. The huge chef who had, only seconds before, seemed so imposing and intimidating, now blubbed away close to the door.

"Bloody hell," said Geri.

"I wasn't expecting that," said Helen.

Martha looked at her sisters. They were just as shocked as she was. She sighed and walked over to Blanc and put an arm around his mighty shoulders. The thought that this was Murray's murderer seemed more ridiculous by the minute. Blanc looked pathetic now, embarrassed. Could he really have killed Murray? Martha wasn't so sure.

"There, there," she said feebly.

"I'm ruined," he said. "Absolutely ruined. It won't be long before the journalists get a hold of this. I'll be all over the newspapers and magazines. Not to mention social media. My empire, it'll be thrown to the dogs. My beloved restaurants, my delis, everything. All my sponsorships, they'll be pulled. I'll be destitute."

While Martha had sympathy for Blanc, she couldn't help but feel a pang of frustration. He may lose everything. But Murray Steiner was dead and his killer was still on the loose.

"We have to ask you this, Mr Blanc," she said. "And I have a feeling I know the answer. But before the police arrive, do you have any idea who might have laced any of Murray's meals with poison?"

Blanc stopped his crying momentarily. He lifted his face from his hands and looked at Martha with bloodshot eyes.

"The police?" he said. "You mean you're not the police?"

"No," said Martha.

"We're private investigators," said Geri.

"From Glasgow," added Helen.

"You're not police detectives?" asked Blanc.

"No, we're the guests of honour here at SteinerCon," said Martha. "Roberta Steiner has given us this commission, to catch the suspected killer of her husband and—"

Blanc grabbed her and threw her across the tiny office. It was as hard a force as she had ever felt—like a child's doll thrown off a bridge. She clattered into Helen and Geri and the three of them collapsed into a pile of files.

"Look out! He's getting away," shouted Helen, muffled with a mouthful of Martha's cardigan.

Blanc didn't waste time. He moved with surprising speed, bolting out of the office.

"Hurry! After him," shouted Martha, scrambling to her feet.

The sisters gave chase. Blanc thundered through the busy kitchen clearing a path in his wake. Martha, Helen and Geri started to gain on him as he burst through a door. The blinding light of the outside world dazed Martha. But she kept going.

"There!" shouted Geri, pointing at Blanc.

He blundered his way across a road. The street was quiet, the huge hotel looming up behind them. Delivery lorries and vans were parked up all around. Martha led the charge as Blanc started to pull away, heading for the end of the road.

Then he was stopped. A small scooter came whizzing around the corner. Neither the driver or Blanc had time to think. Or more importantly react. The scooter smashed into the chef, sending him rolling away across the road before stopping in a heap in the gutter.

"Crikey!" said Helen. "I didn't see that one coming."

"Come on," said Martha.

They raced across the street to where Blanc was untangling himself. The scooter whizzed past behind them, the driver shouting as he went.

"Arsehole, watch where you're going next time!"

"Up yours!" Geri shouted after him as he sped away.

"Are you alright?" asked Martha, propping Blanc up.

"Damn it," he panted, face still scarlet and covered in dirt. "I used to be a champion sprinter in school."

"Yeah, well, school was a long time ago for all of us, wasn't it," said Helen.

Blanc looked up at her, eyeballs a brilliant white against the broken capillaries of his cheeks and forehead.

"For some, longer than others."

Twenty-Eight

TIME WAS PRESSING, Martha knew that. The police wouldn't take long to process everyone in the conference. They had already stretched their luck as far as they could. Sitting in a small cafe across from the hotel, helping Marcel Blanc nurse his cuts and bruises didn't feel like progress. But she had to trust her gut.

"Nothing broken then?" asked Martha.

The Michelin-starred chef winced as he held an improvised ice pack over his knee. He shook his head and reached for the last remnants of the coffee the Parkers had bought him.

"Good," said Martha. "I think that was a lucky escape, Mr Blanc."

"Lucky? Hah, tell that to my aching joints and pounding headache."

Martha's sympathy for the chef had returned. She was fully aware of how painful joints and headaches were. She'd been nursing enough of them both since the break of dawn.

The sun was still beating down outside, although its brightness was beginning to fade. Long shadows were beginning to creep across the street and into the cafe. It was only now that she realised the time—five o'clock. Roberta's big speech was coming up, her address to the conference. She wondered how different it would be now, given everything that had happened. There was supposed to be a ball tonight, a dress and heels specially packed. She doubted she'd get to waltz around the dancefloor now.

To her surprise, she found that the thought had made her quite forlorn. For the first time during the trip she lamented that it had not been a success. If things had been different, maybe she would have come around to the fame and fortune idea of working as a private investigator. Both Helen and Geri were well onboard with that idea. So much so that Geri had ended up in Murray Steiner's bedroom the night he was killed.

Her mind came racing back to the present at that thought. Like a bucket of ice water being thrown at her, she was shocked back into the cafe and Marcel Blanc licking his wounds in front of her.

"Why did you run?" she asked.

Blanc winced again. She was sure he was hamming up at least fifty per cent of the pain he was in.

"Because I don't want to go to jail," he said. "Is that reason enough?"

"Only if you've done something wrong," said Geri sceptically.

"I didn't kill Murray Steiner if that's what you're alluding to," he said adamantly. "I may be many things but I am not a murderer. And I told you before, I was good friends with Murray Steiner. We used to drink together, go clubbing, that sort of thing."

"Clubbing? At your age?" Helen snorted.

"It was a long time ago now," said Blanc. "When we were both much younger. I knew all the best places to go in London and Murray liked to party. We shared the same zest for life, the same taste in fine dining, fine wine—"

"Fine women?" asked Martha.

Blanc looked a little embarrassed. He fidgeted with the ice wrapped up in a sandwich bag that was doubling for a pack. The edge of the bag was dripping, leaving a puddle on the floor beside his shoe.

"We were young and foolish," he said. "And I never saw any indiscretion from Mr Steiner. He was always faithful to his wife, absolutely. When I was there."

Geri tutted loudly. Helen did the same. As the lead interrogator, Martha refrained. Although she agreed with her sisters.

"You still haven't answered our question properly," she said. "If you're innocent of his murder, then why did you run when you realised we weren't with the police."

Blanc went to drain his mug but realised it was empty. He pushed the mug away, eyes turning glassy.

"I am ashamed," he said. "Ashamed to admit this terrible secret to three complete strangers."

"Secret? What secret?" asked Helen, sitting forward.

"I am a Michelin star chef, I own a dozen restaurants across central London, even more across in France. I live in Chelsea, drive a Ferrari and have three beautiful children that adore me. I have *everything* to lose, you have to understand that."

"Yes, yes, what about the shame?" Helen coaxed him.

Blanc started to cry again. Martha offered him a stained paper napkin. He blew his nose loudly, attracting the attention of the other cafe patrons.

"I am an illegal immigrant," he said, every word hard and heavy as he spoke. "I should not be here, I don't hold any citizenship. Can you imagine? The shame of it all."

"What? That's it?" asked Helen. "That's your great shame, that you don't have a British passport."

"No, no, I have *no* passport at all."

"And?"

"I came over here in the wheel arch of a lorry twenty-five years ago. Everything I've got has been through sheer hard work. I scrubbed toilets and cleaned dishes in the best restaurants and learned to cook by watching the masters at work. I'm a self-made man, a minor celebrity. And yet I carry this terrible secret around with me everywhere I go."

Helen threw her hands up, exhausted. She leaned back in her chair and tutted loudly.

"I thought at the very least we would have got some juicy, illicit affair with somebody."

"Like Roberta Steiner," said Geri.

"Exactly. Not that he's an illegal immigrant who's become one of the wealthiest chefs in London. That's something you should be proud of Marcel. You shouldn't be ashamed of your past."

"She's right," said Martha. "Like you said, you're a self-made man. You're a role model for everyone out there that with a little hard work and determination, you can do anything with your life. A bit like Roberta Steiner."

"Oh, that reminds me," said Geri, fetching her phone and untangling her earphones. "I'll listen to Roberta's address to the conference. It's being streamed on social media."

Martha offered Blanc a hand. He looked at it like it was some foreign object he was afraid to touch. Then his sad face settled and he took up the offer.

"Never be ashamed of who you are," said Martha. "I tell that to Helen, Geri, my family, everyone in fact. Your history is what makes you who you are today. You can't change it but you should be proud of it. Don't wear it around your neck like a ball and chain. Let it define you, sure, but let it go too."

"My reputation would be shattered if I were arrested," said Blanc. "The indignity of the charges, the public scandal. It would be too much for me to bear. That's why I ran. I panicked, thinking maybe I could somehow get away, before you asked any more questions. Before the police came sniffing around asking questions of the foreigner who might have killed poor Murray Steiner."

"That question still remains," said Helen. "He ingested too much potassium and you cooked all of his meals. That makes you a suspect, Marcel. Unless you can categorically point to somebody else who might have been involved, we're going to *have* to turn you over to the cops."

"No, please," his jowls jiggled with fear. "I'm begging you, please don't do that. I'm innocent. Why would I kill him? It doesn't make any sense. I have no reason to do something like that. Murray Steiner was a friend of mine."

"And to millions of others around the world, but he's still dead," Helen said, flatly.

"Please Marcel," said Martha, trying a different approach. "Help us to help you. If you didn't lace Murray's food with poison, who might have? Could it be one of your team maybe? Another chef or a waiter?"

"No."

Blanc's voice made the cutlery rattle. He shook his head, vehement and sure. "Absolutely not," he said.

"How can you be so sure?" Helen cocked an eyebrow. "A minute ago you were certain that nobody could have killed Murray. Now you're saying he could have been killed, but *not* by one of your staff."

"I can assure you all that nobody on my team would have done this," said Blanc, his sadness turning to anger. "My staff are hand-picked by myself and my assistants. We interview every chef, cook, kitchen porter, waiter and waitress. We run one of the busiest and best kitchens in all of London, maybe even the world. You've seen it for yourself, everything works in harmony, we are like an orchestra. All of the parts work together, or none of them work at all. That's how I was taught and how I will *always* run my kitchens."

"And you're certain nobody would do something like this?" asked Martha.

"Absolutely not," said Blanc again. "I would put my *life* on it that nobody from my staff had anything to do with this."

"But how could you possibly know that?" Helen asked.

"Because everyone in that kitchen has gone through the same ordeal as I have."

Marcel's words hung in the stuffy warmth of the cafe. A balmy glow had bathed everything in a homely orange as the sun began its journey towards the horizon. Blanc sighed again, shifting uncomfortably in his hard chair.

"They are or have been like me in their lives," he said, voice low. "They have come into my kitchen with nothing and worked their way up. They've been given the opportunity that was handed to me when I arrived here, had no money, didn't speak English and was sleeping rough at St Pancras Station. My staff know what it is like to have nothing. And they are appreciative, just like I was, to be shown some faith, time and respect. None of them, and I mean not a single one, would be capable of poisoning Murray Steiner. They have everything to lose, just as I do. They wouldn't dare risk it all over some petty grudge or trivial matter. My people are better than that. That's why they're my people."

Martha was convinced. Even Helen seemed to call off her dogs.

"Okay," she said. "Your passion speaks volumes Marcel. We appreciate your honesty too. It clearly means a lot."

"It does. Thank you," said the chef. "I have no idea who would do something like this. It's a tragedy, truly a tragedy."

Martha was frustrated. She had hoped their lead would be sound. She had hoped that somebody in the kitchen staff would harbour a grudge or even have a motive to murder Murray Steiner. With every passing second their window of opportunity was getting smaller and smaller. She could feel the anxiety building in the back of her mind.

"When you served Murray his food, what was the process?" she asked, clutching at straws.

"Process?" asked Blanc.

"Yes, procedure. I don't suppose you actually delivered it to him."

"He didn't," said Helen. "We were at dinner last night with the Steiners, we didn't see him once."

"When I had finished with Mr and Mrs Steiner's meals, I would call on a waiter or member of my team. That would be the last I would see of it, unless there was something wrong with it of course."

"Something wrong?" laughed Martha. "You're a Michelin starred chef Marcel, what could possibly be wrong with what you had prepared for him."

Blanc's face went a little slack. He looked at Martha and then over to Helen.

"You don't know?" he asked.

Martha felt her stomach knot. She leaned forward.

"Know what?" she asked, her voice barely able to push over her lips.

Blanc stared at her. Then he laughed a little.

"Murray Steiner was allergic to almost *everything*," he said. "He always had to be careful. Nuts, white fish, eggs, wheat, soybeans, even peas for God's sake. Can you imagine? Peas. It was one of the reasons why I would always prepare his meals. One chef, less chance of contamination. But you guys really didn't know, did you?"

"No we didn't," said Martha.

"It's true. A proper challenge, and one that I always relished, of course, for such a dear friend. Still, that's why precautions were always taken."

"Like what."

"Well, for starters, all of his meals were vetted by Roberta."

Martha didn't say anything. Neither did Helen. They both pushed back their chairs and stood up. Blanc looked back and forth between them, unsure what was happening.

"What did you just say there?" asked Helen.

"Roberta. She vetted Murray's meals. She knew every allergy he had. She knew what he could and couldn't eat. She vetted everything that was prepared for him before it reached him. It is one of their rider demands, they were famous for it, all around the world. When you cook for Murray Steiner, better make sure Roberta likes it first. Yes, yes."

Martha and Helen didn't say anything to the chef, or each other. Heading for the door, they each grabbed one of Geri's shoulders and hauled her with them.

"Hey, what gives?" she protested. "I was watching Roberta's speech, she was quite good actually, thanked everyone for helping with the police investigation. She didn't really talk about what happened, kept it nice and simple, elegant really. I suppose that's what we've come to expect from her during all of this, haven't we?"

"Geri," said Martha, as they hurried out of the cafe, the hotel across the street. "We don't want to alarm you."

"Actually we *do* want to alarm you," said Helen.

"What? What's happened now? Are you two okay? You look like you've seen a ghost, or something equally terrifying if less cliched."

The Parker sisters walked across the road and headed for the looming hotel tower. There was a murderer to catch.

Twenty-Nine

"THIS CAN'T BE happening," said Geri. "There's no way that this can be the world that we're living in. Tell me that I'm having a nightmare. Tell me that I've had a nasty bump on my noggin and I've been heavily sedated and this is just the product of my imagination running wild."

"It's none of those, Geri. None of them," said Martha. "We're actually doing this."

"Bloody hell," she said, taking a big gulp of air. "What about you? Are you onboard with all of this?"

She slapped Helen on the arm.

"Ow," she said. "What was that for?"

"I was checking you were still awake," said Geri.

"Of course I'm awake. You didn't have to hit me Ger, that's going to bruise. You know I have very sensitive skin. The slightest little nudge and I bruise like a peach."

"You didn't answer me."

"Yes, I can believe what's happening. I can believe it quite easily actually."

"What?" asked Martha. "You're not surprised, even a little bit? We're going to confront Roberta Steiner and accuse her murdering her husband."

"No, can't say I am," she shrugged.

They reached the back entrance of the hotel. Delivery drivers and staff were still loading and unloading heavy crates and boxes of provisions. Huge bins and containers filled with more laundry were carted out from waiting trucks. Martha said a silent prayer of thanks again to their cushioned landing.

There were no police about, that Martha could see. The Parker sisters sought refuge behind a long row of bins. Peering over the edge, Martha waited for a gap when there were no staff coming and going.

"When we get the chance," she said to the others. "We make a run for that big entrance over there."

She pointed forward across the small courtyard where the deliveries were made. The place was cool, steeped in shadow by the overhanging behemoth that was the hotel. Martha shivered, although she suspected that it was about more than just the setting sun.

"No, hold on, wait a minute, time out," said Geri. "I'm not letting this go. Helen Parker, you're telling us that you're not surprised in the slightest about what we suspect?"

"No," said Helen, peering over the bins. "Why would I be?"

Geri looked at Martha for some backup.

"Because it's Roberta Freakin' Steiner, that's why," she said. "She's… she's… she's…"

"One of the most famous people on the planet, an inspiration to millions, a self-made woman, blah, blah, blah, blah, I've heard it all a thousand times before Geri. It's tiresome to say the least."

"Martha, help me out here, would you?"

Martha sighed. She wasn't quite sure she shared Helen's confidence. In the mere moments since it seemingly had all fallen into place, she was doubting herself more than ever. But some innate sensibility deep inside her, told her that they were on to something.

"Geri has a point Helen," she said. "I mean, if what we think is true, that Roberta is in some way linked to this. That would be pretty shocking right? You're trying to tell us that you wouldn't be surprised."

"Yes I am," said Helen, bluntly.

"Yes, you're surprised?" asked Geri, smelling she was onto something.

"No."

"What are you talking about then?"

"I'm saying yes, I'm *not* surprised. Why would I be surprised when it seems like the most logical explanation."

"Logical explanation?" Geri blurted. "How do you come to that one?"

Helen turned around and sat down against a bin. Licking her lips, she started picking something out of her teeth.

"Damn poppy seeds," she said. "I don't know why I always go for those rolls. They get stuck in my incisors all of the time. I never learn."

"Helen!" Geri shouted. "We're at a bit of a crossroads here. Can you try to focus?"

"Fine," she said with a huff, flicking away a stray poppy seed.

"Roberta Steiner," said Martha. "You're not surprised she's maybe involved."

"No. For two very simple reasons."

"Which are?"

"She hated her husband," said Helen casually. "And she's broke."

Martha blinked. It felt like the first time in a long while.

"Broke? How can you say that Helen? She's one of the richest women in the world?" she asked.

"Assets Martha, merely assets," said Helen dismissively. "Remember what Tom was telling us earlier, about the sponsorships and ticket sales for this cavalcade convention. They're rock bottom, she's haemorrhaging money. Think about it for a second. If you woke up to the news that your husband had died overnight and said husband was one of the most recognised faces on TV on the planet, would you still want to talk to us on a stage in front of ten thousand fans? I know I wouldn't."

"You're not married," said Geri.

"No, I'm not," Helen said. "But I know that doesn't make a difference. Forty years together, that's a long time, longer than I've been alive. Getting that sort of news is enough to put anybody in a state of catatonia. Not Roberta Steiner though. She had her face done, power suit on, out in front of the lights with the smiles and the thanks. And why? Because if she pulled the plug on all of this, there would be bills to pay that she just can't afford. Which leads me on to my first point."

"That she hated Murray," said Martha.

"That's the obvious one," said Helen. "I mean, I certainly can't blame her. We were in his company for a matter of hours and he tried to get Geri to sleep with him. While his wife was sat at the same table. What does that say about the man? And, more importantly, his marriage. Motive isn't really a question for Roberta, she's got everything to gain from Murray popping his clogs to use a rather vulgar turn of phrase."

She wrinkled her nose. Martha had to take a moment to stop her mind from racing away from her.

"If Murray dies, she's free of him," she said to the others. "And there will be a hefty life insurance pay out too, I would imagine. In one fell swoop she clears a large chunk of debt and can get on with her life without having to put up with him."

"Not to mention the adulation she'll receive from the fans," said Geri, warming to the idea. "The brave widow, still soldiering on despite all of the tragedy that's befallen her. It's a public relations masterstroke."

"See," said Helen. "A little logical thinking goes a long way to seeing the bigger picture. You can send me your apologies on a postcard."

"She can't think she would have gotten away with it surely," said Geri. "I mean, surely Roberta Steiner wouldn't have been stupid enough to think that a post-mortem wouldn't show the increase in potassium in Murray's bloodstream or what have you. You can't just kill somebody and think you can get away with it."

That drew silence from the others. Martha had to agree with Geri. There didn't seem a lot of sense in that, no matter how awful Murray Steiner was. There would be consequences of his murder, no matter who was responsible.

"I don't know," she said. "But we've got a lot to go on just now. I think we carry on with the plan."

"Which is what?" asked Geri. "Citizen's arrest?"

"No. We put these accusations to her," said Martha. "See what she has to say for herself. Maybe we'll get lucky and she'll confess. I don't know. We're all out of ideas and I don't think we have too much time left."

"What are you three doing?"

Martha, Helen and Geri all jumped. So did Marcel Blanc when he saw their reaction.

"Marcel," said Martha, patting her chest. "You scared the life out of us."

"What are you doing hanging around by the bins?" he asked them.

He offered Helen a hand up. She thanked him and patted him on the back. The chef almost stumbled forward, wincing at his sore knee.

"We have to get up to Roberta's penthouse suite," said Martha. "But we can't just very well walk in there."

"We've been waiting to sneak in while those delivery men aren't looking," said Geri, nodding over at the large lorry near one of the hotel's back entrances.

Marcel looked over at the deliveries being unloaded. Then he smiled as he turned back to the Parker sisters.

"I have an idea," he said. "Come with me."

Thirty

MARTHA PUSHED THE trolley, her new shoes squeaking almost as badly as the wheels. She tugged at the collar of her uniform shirt, the tie in the hotel's colours feeling like a noose. Her sisters appeared to be struggling just as badly with their disguises. Helen, her frizzy hair tied back into an unruly ponytail, had a face that would turn milk sour.

"You really should wash behind your ears from time to time Helen," she said. "As mum always said when you were little, you could grow spuds back there."

"Thanks for that Martha, that's the confidence shot in the arm that I've been longing for all these years."

She too twitched and fidgeted with her collar. Geri, riding shotgun with the trolley, started to roll up her sleeves.

"Get those cuffs done up missus," said Helen. "You heard what Marcel said. The hotel prides itself on the punctuality and precision of its staff. Have you seen any of them wandering around with their sleeves rolled up past their elbow?"

"No," said Geri. "But we're not members of staff. And these aren't our uniforms. So I'm trying to make an exception to the rules—which are stupid by the way."

"I agree with that," said Helen. "What difference does being trussed up in a shirt, tie and waistcoat make to how good your service is. Surely it's all in the manner and efficiency."

"And getting the order right," said Geri. "Speaking of which."

She lifted a lid off one of the trays laid out on the trolley. Pinching a chip, she offered it up to Martha and Helen.

"Oh yes, please, I'm starving."

"You just ate Helen," said Martha.

"I know but I'm hungry again. And this is free."

She nabbed another handful of chips before Geri put the lid back down. Martha despaired.

"Honestly, I can't take you two anywhere," she said.

She didn't tell them but she agreed with her sisters. The orders Marcel had given them when he'd provided their disguises were nothing short of Napoleonic. A lengthy speech about pride in the uniform and the ideals that it carried, had tested even Martha's patience. She couldn't fault his passion for his place of work, but they were only using it as a disguise to get up to Roberta Steiner's penthouse.

She had politely listened while Marcel had gone on and on. And when he was finished, quickly exited the changing rooms without giving him another chance to launch into a new lecture. Still, she had to compliment the chef's ingenuity. The ruse that they were delivering food to the penthouse was practically watertight. The police wouldn't suspect anything from three members of staff doing their jobs. Even in the exceptional circumstances.

"I'm surprised Marcel wanted to help us," said Helen, as if reading Martha's mind.

"Why's that?" she asked.

"If he was such a good friend of Murray's, why would he want to get Roberta into trouble."

"Keeps his nose clean," said Geri. "If we catch the real killer then he's in the clear, no matter who that is. And besides, if he was such a good friend of Murray's then he'll surely want his murderer brought to justice, no matter who it is."

"No matter who it is," said Martha again.

Geri and Helen looked at her. She was staring off into the distance, pushing the trolley ahead of her.

"You okay there, Mart?" asked Geri. "You've gone all doe-eyed on us again."

"Sorry, yeah," she said. "Just what you said. No matter who the murderer is. It's very true. I can scarcely believe that this is what we're doing, this is where everything has led to. It's been quite a day."

"Yeah, not been great has it?" said Geri.

"I don't know," shrugged Helen. "We could be about to apprehend the killer of a proper celebrity. And the murderer herself is as *big* a famous face as he was. This could be the making of us."

"I thought we were already made," said Martha. "I don't think I could handle seeing my ugly mug on any more posters or billboards."

"There's always Hollywood, Mart. Always Hollywood," winked Geri.

"I wonder if Tom will still be interested in me if I become a Californian millionaire?" pined Helen.

"Who says he's interested in you now?" Geri scoffed.

Helen bowed her head a little.

"I wonder where he is, anyway? she said. "He's not tried to call you has he?"

"Nope, but my phone signal has been shocking since we arrived at this place."

A genuine worry seemed to creep across Helen's face. Martha felt her own heart ache a little. As much as they had all joked about Tom and Helen's relationship, if it could be called that. There were clearly feelings there from her for him. Helen's confidence with men was low at the best of times. Martha only hoped he wouldn't hurt her.

"He'll be fine," she said, squeezing her arm. "He's a big boy and can look after himself. We'll find him again when we're finished with all of this. I promise."

"Yeah, he'll be fine, Hel," said Geri. "We'll catch up with him. He won't have gone back to Australia tonight. Don't fret."

"Thanks guys," said Helen. "I thought for a minute there I'd have to jump on a plane and chase him across the world. And you know what I'm like on a long-haul flight. I get the most dreadful gas."

The three sisters laughed. It was nice to be able to share some humour with them, Martha appreciated it. This had been a sorely testing weekend. She'd come to London worried and everything had gone downhill from there. Here they were, wandering the bowels of a luxury hotel, dressed as staff, about to accuse a powerful woman of killing her husband. Strangely, when she thought about it that way, it sort of made sense. Maybe this was the way that her life was going. Maybe this was their destiny.

The corridor Marcel had directed them down came to an abrupt end. Using the labyrinth of staff tunnels and hallways that ran alongside the main hotel thoroughfare, they had navigated their way to below the main lifts of the reception area. They'd come across nobody on their journey. And there had been no sign of any police or security guards.

"There's the service lift," said Helen, pointing towards the big, heavy, industrial doors that marked the end of the corridor.

Martha pressed the button and the doors juddered open. They guided the trolley in and Geri pulled the shutters closed behind them. It smelled of oil and old, stale cooking in here. Damp ran down the walls and collected in small puddles in the corners.

"This isn't as nice as the other lifts is it?" she commented.

"Practical and with a purpose," said Helen. "The ugly side of the hotel industry."

"And what do *you* know about the ugly side of any industry, Hel?" asked Geri. "You've spent your life in academia, with all of its leafy avenues and dusty old books."

"You should spend more time with dusty old books, maybe you'd learn a thing or two."

"Okay, enough you two," said Martha. "Time to sharpen up and focus. I know we're tired and hurt and everything else. But this is it. This is our big test. I need us all to be on the same page. We don't know what's going to be waiting for us on the other side of that penthouse door. So let's stick together, stick to our guns and remember, we're the Parker sisters, got that?"

"Oh blimey," said Geri, smiling. "I came out in goose pimples when you said our name there Martha."

"Yeah, me too," said Helen. "I'm positively quivering here."

"Good," Martha laughed. "I'm glad at least you two are feeling the good vibes. Personally, I'm bricking it."

The service lift shuddered and creaked to a halt. Geri got the shutter and the door slid open. Outside was a kitchen.

"Oh," said Helen. "I think we're back in that lovely restaurant."

Martha pushed the trolley. Its wheels wobbled as it shunted over the lip of the lift. She was no expert in this waitressing lark. In fact, she was anything *but* a waitress. Her first job while she was at school had been waiting on tables at a local tea room in the south of Glasgow. She'd lasted all of an hour into her first shift —those sixty painful minutes seeing her blunder every order and almost scald an old lady with her coffee.

Many decades had passed since then. And she was still terrible at it. She was about to start shouting at the trolley, when she spotted movement in the corner of the kitchen. She froze, Geri and Helen doing likewise.

On the other side of a long workbench, two police women were bent over something. When they heard Martha's trolley rattle, they quickly stood up, mouths full, a guilty look on both of their faces.

"Bugger," whispered Geri.

"I agree," said Helen.

"Quiet," said Martha.

"Who are you three?" asked one of the cops.

They both stopped chewing and wiped sauce away from their lips. Adjusting their utility belts and jackets, they hurried over to the Parkers.

"What's this?" asked the taller of the two.

"Dinner," said Geri, sniping. "What does it look like?"

That drew the ire of both police women. They rolled their eyes towards the youngest sister, their chests puffing out a little more.

"Is that so?" asked one.

"Who for?" asked the other.

"Mrs Steiner," said Martha. "We've been sent up from the kitchens downstairs. Been told to deliver this to the penthouse suite."

"So here we are," said Helen, feigning a smile. "We've got a delicious hamburger here and some chips, although Mrs Steiner might want to call them fries, being of an American disposition."

She lifted the lid off the main course. The plate looked a little bare close to the edge where Helen and Geri had picked at it.

"And for afters there's a traditional English trifle, as a send-off to our dear American cousin."

"Three Jocks," said the tall cop.

"Pardon me?" asked Helen.

"You three, you're all Scotch."

"Scottish, yes," said Geri. "Is that a problem officer?"

The cop was about to answer her but thought better of it.

"And if you'll let me finish ladies," said Helen. "There's a lovely bottle of Beaujolais chilling under the trolley there. We understand that it's Mrs Steiner's favourite champagne. I would offer you both a sample to make sure it's up to standard, but I fear you're both on duty and, by the looks on your faces when we got off the lift, you've probably had your fill already of what was left by the cooks up here."

Both officers blushed. They gave each other a quick look of reassurance before standing aside.

"On your way," the taller one said.

"Thank you," said Helen, giving a little bow.

She replaced the lid and Martha pushed the trolley onwards, praying the wheels wouldn't stick again. They eased out of the door, and all breathed a sigh of relief.

Outside was the main foyer of the restaurant. The long central aisle of the venue stretched out in front of them. The place was still deserted. No waiters, no concierge, nothing. Nothing, except a single figure sat at the wide top table at the opposite end of the restaurant.

The tinted windows gave the whole place an earthy, beige glow. It was eerily quiet, tables and chairs all set up for service on either side of the aisle standing empty and silent like tombstones. The stillness was only broken by the gentle scraping and tapping of a knife and fork on a plate.

Martha, Helen and Geri abandoned their food trolley. They slowly marched up the central aisle, heading towards the person sat at the top table. As they drew closer, they realised who it was.

"The Parker sisters," said Eleanor David. "I wish I could say that I am glad to see you all. But I'm not taken to telling lies while I'm having my dinner."

Thirty-One

"CUTE," SAID GERI.

"At least you lot've smartened yourselves up," she said, taking a long sip from a glass of red wine.

Martha didn't like this. There was a strangeness to Eleanor's tone. She knew something she wasn't saying. It wasn't quite arrogance, but certainly confidence. And that made Martha uncomfortable.

"To what do I owe this pleasure?" Eleanor asked, coolly.

"We're here to see Roberta," said Martha, trying to match the confidence.

"Is that so. And why would that be?"

"We've reason to believe, strong reason in fact, that we may be a step closer to catching Murray's killer."

Eleanor let out a laugh, although it sounded more like a screeching cackle. Martha realised that this was the first time they'd seen Eleanor David smile. It wasn't a particularly pleasant sight. She threw her head back, guffawing loudly. Then she started to clap slowly.

"Bravo," she said. "Bravo indeed. You know, you don't expect to get many laughs in this job. And believe me there *aren't* many to be found. But it's nice to see you three still have a sense of humour after everything you've put us through."

The sky beyond the tinted windows was darkening as the sun dropped lower in the city sky. It seemed to cast a long, dark shadow over the proceedings. Martha wondered if the police officers were still tucking into the leftovers in the kitchen. She hoped they were.

"I'm glad we entertain you, Eleanor," said Martha. "But we really do need to speak to Roberta. It's urgent."

"Mrs Steiner is not available, to you or to anybody else. I have strict instructions on that matter. You won't be seeing her again."

"Where is she?" asked Helen.

Eleanor didn't look in her direction. She kept her gaze fixed firmly on the remnants of her dinner.

"She's on her way to the airport," she said. "She's leaving London tonight to be at the family home in California. Mr Murray's remains will be flown over, too, when his body is released from police custody. That's all you need to know."

"Well I think you should get her on the phone," said Helen. "Because what we've got to say to her is going to put a crimp in that plan."

Eleanor slammed down her cutlery. This time she looked at Helen.

"Is that so?" she said.

"Yeah, it is," said Helen, stepping forward a little. "So if you wouldn't mind, could you get on one of your five hundred devices and ring her up. We want to talk to her."

Eleanor raised a napkin to her mouth and dabbed it gently. She raised an eyebrow and steepled her fingers, levelling her gaze at all three Parkers.

"You don't get it, do you?" she said with a smirk. "You three really don't get it."

"Get what?" asked Geri. "Come to think of it, what a stupid question. You're clearly going to tell us, seeing as you're in your whole full Bond villain mode."

"I don't know what that means," said Eleanor.

"You don't know what a Bond villain is?" Geri yelped. "Are you kidding me?"

"I must admit, I don't get it either," whispered Helen.

"Savages," said Geri.

"Roberta doesn't have any time for people like you, not really. She gives you a place because she chooses to. She can make you, and she can break you, just like that." She snapped her fingers.

"Hey, watch it," said Helen. "People like us? What's that supposed to mean."

"Where is she Eleanor?" said Martha.

"I told you," she said.

"We know."

Eleanor composed herself. She stood up from behind the table and drained her glass.

"And just what do you know exactly?" she said menacingly. "What is it you three bumpkins think you know, eh? I'm desperate to hear this. Because I've spent the better part of two months listening and reading about how you three are supposedly the next big thing when it comes to private investigation in this country. I keep seeing things online, reading magazine features, pictures of all three of you looking slovenly and dishevelled, like something the cat dragged in. And I'm yet to see any evidence of the brilliant investigative minds that you all apparently possess. Stop me if I'm wrong."

"You should have stopped a long time ago love," snorted Geri.

"Ah yes, the baby of the group," said Eleanor with a sneer. "The one who thinks it's acceptable to spend the night with another woman's husband. The one who's always quick with a quip and a sarcastic putdown, even though she's got no qualifications, no background and absolutely *no* life experience."

"You can't talk to her like that," said Helen. "That's bang out of order, and I don't care who or what you are, lady."

"Oh no, have I brought on the wrath of the great sleeping giant," Eleanor pretended to quiver. "I wouldn't want to be absolutely *bored* to death with another one of her lectures. Or worse still, the seemingly endless tomes you call your blog posts on your university department's website. Not that you'll be doing those any time soon, you've been terminated as far as I'm aware, isn't that right?"

Helen didn't reply. She was too affronted. Her cheeks flushed, and her mouth goldfished. Martha remained silent. She was thinking, or at least trying to think. It wasn't easy when she was feeling so angry.

"And that brings us to the leader of this motley crew," said Eleanor, turning on her. "Martha Parker, the blandest woman in the world. The one who claims to shun the spotlight, but is perfectly happy to be plastered all over this conference, *my* conference, and takes everything that's offered on a plate to her. The woman who pretends to be a virtuous bastion of truth and as straight an arrow as you can find. Only to run out on promises—and contractual agreements I may add. Yes, I think that about covers it. I can't *wait* to hear what you three have got to say. And I'm sure Roberta will adjust her busy schedule to listen to it."

She rounded the table, collecting her phones and tablets. Shoving her way past Martha, Helen and Geri, she marched down the central aisle of the restaurant.

"She killed him, didn't she?" said Martha. "And you know she did it."

Eleanor came to a gentle stop. She shook her head, her back still to the Parkers.

"I have absolutely no idea what you're talking about Martha," she said with a laugh. "And it's absolutely ludicrous that you would make such an accusation, both to me and about Roberta."

"We know about Murray's allergies," Martha volleyed back. "And that Roberta was the *only* person who would vet his meals before he ate them. That's information that's not out there in the public domain Eleanor. But the chef here at the Imperial told us. And he's willing to testify in a court of law should it come to that."

"Blanc? That old drunk? There's no jury in the *world* that would listen to a word he has to say," said Eleanor, finally turning to face the others. "And if you think that's supposed to scare me, then you're sorely mistaken."

"Scare you?" asked Martha. "We're not trying to scare you. We're asking for your help. Roberta Steiner is a prime suspect her husband's murder. You can't stand in the way of justice, no matter who is to blame."

"Justice? What would you lot know about justice?" she laughed. "It's just another word to you. You wouldn't know what it meant if it came up and slapped you in the face."

"You can't protect her, Eleanor," said Geri. "We know that she had access to Murray's meals. We know that she was the *only* one who did. He was poisoned, he died from too much potassium. It all adds up."

"You don't know what you're talking about!" Eleanor screamed.

Her voice echoed off the grand walls of the rooftop restaurant. The place fell silent when it had faded into nothing. And the calm veneer of the SteinerCon director was broken.

"Do you have any idea what he put her through?" she said, her breath short. "Can you even begin to imagine what it was like being married to that pig? Day in and day out being made to feel like you're six inches tall. And being forced to go out there, into the limelight and protect him, help him, put him on that pedestal that all of his fans, all of *you* people put him on. Oh yes, the great Murray Steiner, the rogue with a glint in his eye and a smile on his lips. He's your best friend, your big brother, your kindly uncle and loving dad all rolled into one. Isn't he? And the world loved him back. But all the while he was a monster, a tyrant, one of the worst people I've ever had the misfortune of meeting. Let alone working with.

"How Roberta put up with him for all of these years I'll never know. Even on phone calls he would be dismissive of her, talk over her, make her sound like some cheap bimbo who didn't know what she was talking about. He believed, and I know this as he told me often enough, that he was responsible for her fame and fortune, for everything she had achieved. He always used to say to me that, if it wasn't for him, none of us would have a job—and that included Roberta."

"Why did you put up with it?" asked Helen. "Why the hell didn't you tell this creep where to go?"

"Because he was Murray Steiner," said Eleanor, with a caustic laugh. "He thought he was untouchable, and so he was. He was a relic from a time gone by. He was a dinosaur, brought up to see women as objects and people as disposable."

"But scumbags like that are being brought to order now," said Geri. "Nobody has to put up with that kind of treatment. Nobody ever should have, right enough. But the time for hiding from bullies like Murray Steiner is over."

"And so, now, is Murray Steiner."

There was a finality to Eleanor's words. Martha felt like she'd been kicked in the chest. She looked down at her hands and saw they were trembling. She tried to compute everything that had been said, everything that Eleanor had just thrown at them all. And she tried to think of what to do next.

A door from the kitchens opened, surprising them all. The two police women came out, serious looks on their faces. They were tense and taut, cautiously fanning out when they saw the others.

"What's all the shouting about in here?" asked the taller of the two.

"I thought you guys were staff?" asked the other.

"I'm sorry officers," said Martha. "We're not staff. We've come here to apprehend Mrs—"

"Me," said Eleanor.

"What?" stuttered Martha.

"They've come to apprehend me officers," she turned to face the cops. "These three women, they're private detectives, investigators. They're Martha, Helen and Geri Parker. They're guests of honour at this convention and I'm its director, Eleanor David."

"Eleanor, what are you doing?" asked Geri, stepping forward.

"Stay where you are," the taller officer warned.

They both drew their batons, their hands held up in front of them for protection. Martha thought her head was going to burst. She didn't know if she could compute what was going on.

"I believe you have an open investigation into the murder of Murray Steiner in this hotel," said Eleanor. "I'd like to confess to that murder. I poisoned Murray Steiner, laced his final meal with potassium. Check the toxicology report, that's what will have killed him. I did it and I'd like to be arrested."

"Eleanor," Helen and Geri exclaimed. "What are you doing?"

"I said stand back," demanded the cops.

Eleanor placed her phones and tablets on the ground. Then she offered her wrists to the police women.

"Control, we have a situation in the top floor restaurant," said the taller of the cops, speaking into the radio mounted on her vest. "A woman called Eleanor David has just confessed to the murder of Murray Steiner."

There was a garbled message of static and the cop's face went white.

"Roger," she said.

Pulling her cuffs from her belt, she stepped forward and slapped them on Eleanor's wrists with a click.

"Eleanor David, I'm arresting you on suspicion of murder. You don't have to say anything but it may harm your defence if—"

"You can't do this!" Martha shouted at them.

She had no idea where the voice had come from. She felt like she was operating on autopilot.

"Stand back," said the other officer, grabbing her.

"But she's innocent, she didn't do it. It's not her."

"I said stand back, madam."

The cop raised her baton and threatened Martha. She settled down as Helen and Geri pulled her back. The taller of the officers led Eleanor away towards the lifts, talking into her radio. As she went, Eleanor looked back over her shoulder at the

Parker sisters. A wry, knowing smile made her face twitch. And then she was gone.

Thirty-Two

THE PRESS HAD managed to break through the barriers. The brave hotel staff had locked all the doors and hoped that guests not attending SteinerCon would understand. They didn't. These were some of the most important people in the world after all. They had business meetings to go to, shopping to be done, football matches to attend. The list was endless.

In the end, the management had caved. They made their pleas to the police and opened the doors regardless. And as one open door provides an escape for the gilded elite, it also swung the other way. Newspaper reporters had been waiting outside all day. TV camera crews had gathered in a makeshift shanty town of open-backed vans with giant dishes and hi-tech equipment on the pavement just outside the boundaries of the hotel. When the police had closed the place down their numbers had swollen.

First they were a trickle, just a few of the well-known braver souls among the press pack. Seeing their colleagues get great success in cornering passers-by and convention attendees already interviewed by the Met, the others chanced their arm. It didn't take long for the main concourse and lobby of the Imperial to become a fully-blown media circus. The staff were overwhelmed, the guests were happy to chat and the journalists were shooting fish in a barrel.

Martha had never seen anything quite so manic. Even the kitchens of the hotel seemed positively calm compared to this. In there it was organised chaos. The main concourse was pure bedlam, unfiltered bedlam that would drive even the most placid of people mad.

Thankfully Martha had passed beyond the realm of all halfway sensible thought. Eleanor David's performance in front of the police was perhaps the strangest few minutes she'd ever been a part of. Now, as she, Helen and Geri were led out of the lift by the police, she felt like she was walking on air. Everything felt that little bit more detached than before. She didn't really believe in out of body experiences. Although the last ten minutes had given her more than enough evidence that they might, in fact, be real.

"Come on, keep moving," said the officer.

She nudged them onwards away from the lift. The noise was louder down here, every voice felt like it was competing with the next to see who could talk and shout the loudest. Only there would never be a winner. It was non-stop, endless, a cavalcade of sound.

Camera flashes went off here and there, punctuating the sensory overload. They made Martha wince as she passed by. Occasionally there would be a news anchor talking into a camera. Artificial light made their faces ghostly as they spoke in different languages, beaming the news all over the world. News that, she suspected, would be incorrect.

"Where are you taking us?" asked Helen.

Her voice was comforting to Martha, even over the din. The cop remained stoic. Martha had noticed they had a habit of that down here in London.

"Debrief," she said. "We'll need to get statements from all three of you. You're witnesses to the confession and we need to make sure nothing goes unchecked."

"We know," said Geri wearily. "We're private investigators, remember? We have a fairly good idea as to how all of this works."

The cop didn't answer her that time. They carved a path through the journalists and guests, now all mixed together like ingredients of a cocktail.

"Do they know?" asked Martha.

"Know what?" asked the cop.

"That you've made an arrest."

"I wouldn't have thought so," she said. "But you can never be too sure. The Met is as leaky as a watering can. All my colleagues will know now, it's just a matter of time. Plus there's the media team. I'm sure they're getting off their arses as we speak to cobble something together for these vultures. If you want my advice, you'll do yourselves a favour and not talk to them."

"We learned that the hard way," said Martha. "Believe me, we learned."

The cop led them through the maelstrom, all the way past the front reception and out to the front courtyard. The whole area that had earlier been packed with taxis and hotel cars was now awash with police vehicles. A huge articulated lorry decked out in the Metropolitan Police colours and livery sat across the small parking section close to the main road. On the back was a mounted command centre, officers standing guard near the doors.

The officer led the Parker sisters towards the glorified portacabin and ushered them up the narrow metal steps that led inside. A flurry of camera flashes and volleys of questions came from the contingent of journalists still lingering outside. Martha didn't answer them. And thankfully, neither did Helen or Geri.

Inside a gust of cool, recirculated air brought Martha around a little. The command centre seemed bigger on the inside than the exterior would have suggested. There was a conference table, desks, computers and a communications station. Half a dozen police men and women passed paperwork between then, coordinating their whole operation from the safety of their temporary war room.

At the top end of the cabin was a distinguished looking man. His white hair was combed neatly across his forehead, dark blue eyes scanning a stack of files in front of him. The cop led the Parkers up to his desk and stood to one side.

"Excuse me sir," she said. "But I had a request from command to bring these three to yourself immediately."

The older officer looked up. He took off his glasses, pinched his nose where they'd been sitting on it and thanked the policewoman.

"Wonderful," he said with a half-stifled yawn. "You can be on your way now constable, I'm sure you'll be relieved to get something to eat."

"Sir," she said, clicking her heels together and bowing a little.

As the officer left, she gave Martha a knowing smile.

"Take a seat, ladies, please," said the senior cop. "My name is Superintendent Henry Ghosh, I'm the officer in command of this operation. Sounds like you three have been through it today."

There was an easy friendliness to Superintendent Ghosh. His voice was gentle and he seemed quietly in control of everything he surveyed. A reassuring presence among a whirlwind of unruliness.

"You could say that, yes," said Martha, allowing herself a little laugh. "Not exactly what we'd signed up for when we came down to London for the weekend."

"I'll bet," he said, leaning back in his chair. "Just a shame that you've come all this way down from Glasgow to spend it surrounded by death and misery. Such is life I suppose, although I would say that, I'm a police officer."

Junior cops kept coming and going from the Super's desk, laying down files, taking some away, some hovering around waiting for a signature. Ghosh was a multitasker, capable of holding his gaze and conversation with the Parkers while everything else was run automatically. His hands were never stationary, there was always something to do.

"I understand you were witnesses to our little confession a short while ago," he said. "A Ms Eleanor David, admitting to murdering Murray Steiner, that's correct, yes?"

"Yes it is," said Martha.

"Are we under arrest?" asked Helen, quite out of the blue.

"Under arrest? No, absolutely not," said Superintendent Ghosh, his white eyebrows arching. "Why do you say that?"

"Well, it feels a little like we should have a lawyer here, or something."

It hadn't occurred to Martha. She had been swept up in the relief of some peace and quiet, and a police officer who treated her like a human being, and, of course, a chair.

"My sister is right," she said, wearily. "I'm sorry Superintendent, but if you're going to take statements and question us, you should probably do it formally. Make sure all the boxes are ticked."

The senior officer leaned forward. He was still calm, still collected, still in control.

"Ladies, I won't mess you around, it's not in my nature," he said. "And I wouldn't take you three for fools, either. Believe it or not, your reputations in this field have preceded you. You're all very capable investigators and I believe there was a reason you were chosen to be speakers at this summit."

Martha was impressed with his depth of knowledge. Maybe he was bluffing, maybe he knew how to keep his cards close to his chest. She knew somebody in his position, within one of the busiest police forces in the country, if not Europe, had to be a capable operator. Maybe this was all part of his ruse.

"What's happened here over the last twenty-four hours has been nothing short of extraordinary. And your involvement, good, bad or indifferent has both helped and hindered our operation. You're not under arrest, far from it. But that's not to say you couldn't be. You were caught and identified in a category one secure area in University College Hospital this afternoon. You gave my officers the run-around, not to mention…"

He quickly replaced his glasses and looked down at his notes.

"Stealing one of my officers 'hats. Which he still hasn't got back yet by the way," he said.

"He's not likely to either," said Geri. "Unless he wants to start raking through the bins."

"Yes, well, I wouldn't want to be the one who has to tell him that," said Ghosh. "And thankfully, I'm not going to be. One of the perks of the job. What I'm trying to say is that your involvement in this incident, while it has ultimately proven useful, leaves me with *many* things still outstanding. You're not under arrest, no, but I'd like to think we could come to some sort of arrangement where we can freely exchange ideas in good faith."

He extended his hands out in front of him. Martha looked at the others for guidance. Neither Helen or Geri seemed remotely bothered. They were both tired, their shoulders rolling, their eyes heavy. Martha had seen that look on their faces all of their lives, from when they were toddlers all the way through to the young women she loved.

"Superintendent Ghosh, this has been a very long day for all of us," she said. "We're tired, emotional and desperate to get home. If sitting here and talking to you is going to get us one step closer to that end point, then ask away. We've got nothing to hide. We just want all of this to be over."

Three cardboard cups of tea appeared on Ghosh's desk, delivered by a young police man. He gave Martha a smile as he retreated.

"Please, carry on," said the Super.

"I don't really know what it is you want us to say," said Martha. "My sisters and I were invited here as guests of the Steiners'. We met them for dinner last night. Geri here was asked to go back to his room for some professional advice."

She paused, expecting some sort of reaction, a raised eyebrow, a clearing of the throat, from Ghosh. But there was nothing, he didn't flinch, his fist remained clenched, chin resting on his knuckles as he balanced his elbow on the arm of his chair.

"When she woke up early this morning, Murray was dead. We spoke with Mrs Steiner. She was devastated of course, but thought it best to carry on with the conference. We, that is to say I, delivered a version of our speech to the summit. All seemed fine, we paid tribute to Murray, then my sister Helen here made the mistake of announcing to the audience that Geri had been the last person to see Mr Steiner alive."

"Ah yes, the speech," said Ghosh with a little laugh. "I've seen it."

"What do you mean you've seen it?" Helen snorted, halfway through her tea already. "How could you possibly have seen it? You weren't there."

"Ms Parker, I may be sixty and if you were to ask my grandson if I'm capable of working his PlayStation he would likely have a laughing fit. But I do know what YouTube is, and as a ranking officer, I'm afraid I know all about social media and how quickly things can spread."

Helen looked hopelessly to Geri. She nodded knowingly.

"He's right, Hel," she said. "You've been viral all afternoon."

"And you didn't tell me?"

"We had so much else on the go, I didn't really want to worry you anymore. Besides, we were trying to clear my name at that point. You don't do well with more than one crisis at a time. You're a bit like the public that way."

"Touché," said Helen.

"Anyway," said Martha, steering the conversation back on course. "We were all set to return home, with our tail between our legs, Mrs Steiner wasn't very happy as I'm sure you can understand."

"Completely."

"But before we could make it, Helen, again, conjured a theory that she thought there might be something suspicious about Mr Steiner's death. We had a source… on the inside… who confirmed to us that Murray's death was suspicious and, eventually, confirmed that he had died from potassium poisoning. Returning to the hotel, my sisters and I came to the conclusion that only one person could have administered a fatal amount of potassium for him to ingest."

"Ms Eleanor David," said Ghosh with a wry smile.

"No, actually," said Geri. "Roberta Steiner."

The Super didn't seem surprised. Or, if he did. he didn't show any of it to the Parker sisters. Which in turn didn't surprise Martha.

"Roberta Steiner was, as far as we know, one of only a few people in the world to know that her husband suffered from terrible food allergies," she said. "Therefore she had complete control over everything he ate. Reasonable deduction makes us think that she would be capable of adding enough potassium to what he was eating to bring on the arrhythmia."

"And you don't believe that Eleanor David could have done the same?" asked the Super. "Despite hearing her confess to the murder. Despite a detailed statement that I've just read before you came in attesting to all the details you've described?

He waved his notes at them. Martha shook her head.

"I don't believe she had a motive," she said. "Murray Steiner was no angel, as I'm sure all the statements you'll have read will show. But I don't believe that Eleanor David had grounds to actually kill her boss. It just doesn't sit right."

"But his wife does?" asked Ghosh.

"She had more reason to kill him than anyone else on the planet," said Helen. "She had to put up with him for decades. Not only him, his antics. I was in his company for a matter of hours and *I* wanted to bump the old codger off."

"Helen," warned Martha.

"Well it's true. What must it have been like to actually live with him?

Superintendent Ghosh nodded. He sucked in a long, deep breath through his nose.

"And what about you?" he said, looking at Geri.

"Me?" she asked. "What *about* me?"

"What do you think of it all? You were, as your sister so correctly announced to the world, the last person to see him alive. Do *you* think he was killed? And do you think Ms David did it?"

"The science and facts are all there, Superintendent," said Geri. "I'm not going to argue with them. Murray Steiner had a fatal dose of potassium. It killed him. Having spent enough time in his company, I'm pretty sure he didn't do it to himself. He was far too selfish for that. My intentions were pure on the night he died. Though I doubt most people believe me. But if you're asking me if I believe Eleanor David killed him, I'd tell you that was a load of baloney. I think, as do my sisters, that she's trying to protect Roberta Steiner. Eleanor's a zealot, Superintendent, a zealot to the Steiner cause. A loyal servant to both the Steiners, a woman consumed by her job, her life *is* her job. And if that means she spends the rest of her life in jail, then she'll do it. Why? To protect Roberta. But that's only how I see it."

Superintendent Ghosh considered everything that the Parkers had put to him. Martha was proud of her sisters. Not just for everything they'd been through today. But for their steeliness, their resolve, their adaptability and their professionalism. She knew, as she had always known, that they were the very best people they could be. And she was lucky to call them friends as well as sisters.

"Okay," said the senior officer. "You've convinced me."

"That Roberta is the murderer?" asked Martha.

"No, absolutely not," smiled the Super. "You've convinced me that you three are genuine. You're not nutters or fantasists. You're not fame hungry loners who just want a slice of the spotlight. You're real people, with real lives, who really care. Maybe you care a little too much judging by our rap sheet. But that's for a different debate."

"But Roberta Steiner killed her husband," said Helen. "She needs to be brought to justice. You can't have a murderer running around—even if she *is* famous. In fact, that's all the *more* reason to bring her in."

"I have a written confession that proves motive, reason and intent for the murder of Murray Steiner," said the Super, his tone darkening a little. "That's where we start. My best officers are interviewing Ms David again as we speak. This will all form part of our case and we will ensure that the justice you're so keen to dish out, will be served. I have a reputation in this force Ms Parker, and it's that of an honest and above all else thorough police officer. We have to take confessions of this nature at face value, and we take them very seriously. Until such time as other evidence presents itself, we *will* be charging Eleanor David with Murray Steiner's murder."

The cloud over the Super appeared to lift. His relaxed and calm manner returned. He bowed his head a little and smiled.

"I understand your frustrations, believe me," he said. "I know what it's like to get close to a nick, one that you're convinced is correct. I've been there, more times than I can remember. Sometimes, however, you have to put your gut instinct to one side and play the hand that's been dealt to you."

He offered them his open hands again. Three officers stepped up from the wings of the command centre. They stood firmly to attention behind Martha and the others.

"It's too late to cart you off to Glasgow this evening ladies," said the Super, rising to his feet. "But we've made arrangements for another evening's accommodation in the hotel. You'll be under strict guard to stop any media getting to you and disturbing your evening. We'll see you in the back entrance too, away from the cameras."

He reached out with his hand, first to Martha who took it.

"I'd like to thank you all on behalf of the Metropolitan Police," he said. "Your assistance in this case has been invaluable, especially given its sensitivity and high profile. My people will be more than happy to offer you some guidance on handling any questions that will crop up in the future from the press. But for tonight, please, get some rest. Thank you again."

Ghosh's tone was friendly but firm. Martha knew there would be no arguing with him, no protesting and no chance to speak up. Not that she minded. The last of her energy had been spent just standing up.

"Thank you Superintendent," she said, turning to go.

Helen and Geri followed her lead. The three officers guided them towards a door at the opposite end of the command centre, different from the one they came in.

"This stinks," said Geri.

"This stinks, big time," agreed Helen.

"I know," said Martha with a long sigh. "I know."

Thirty-Three

THE ROOM THE Met had paid for wasn't quite as lavish as Martha's previous suite. She didn't really care though. It was comfortable and air conditioned, and she could finally take her shoes off without feeling like she was messing the place up.

She was lying on one of the huge beds, watching the television across the room. Helen sat cross-legged on the floor, pawing through one of the complimentary magazines for the third time that evening. She'd tried to inform the others about a very interesting article in National Geographic about Cape Horn, but nobody was paying attention. In a huff, she'd resigned herself to silently reading the rest.

Geri, meanwhile, was lounging on one of the large chairs near the panoramic window. Lazily playing with her hair, her feet bobbed back and forth as they hung over the arm. She was engrossed in the TV and, if Martha squinted hard enough, she could have been no older than six watching Thomas the Tank Engine.

She wasn't six, not anymore. And neither was Helen. They were fully grown women with their own lives to lead. The weekend had taught Martha many things. But her role with her sisters was growing ever clearer. It made her chest hurt and a lump form in her throat.

"Is there anything else on?" asked Geri, breaking her chain of thought. "I think there's only so much Murder, She Wrote that I can stomach. And it feels like I've hit my limit."

"You know you *could* read something," said Helen, not looking up. "Stimulate your mind a little instead of watching that idiot box."

"Firstly, I read plenty," said Geri, getting up to fetch the remote. She sifted through the empty plates and cutlery from their room service, all paid for by the Met. Finding the remote among it, she switched the channel to the news.

"And secondly, nobody has called it the idiot box for thirty years Helen. Certainly not since you've been born, so you can bin the snooty attitude."

"Oh give over, Geri, you've always been the same. You used to get bored reading The Beano."

"Hey, there's absolutely nothing wrong with The Beano," Geri fired back. "In fact you and some of your misery guts lecturers could learn a thing or two from The Beano."

"Oh really?"

"Yes, really. Minnie the Minx, total feminist icon. In fact, if I ever grow my hair out again I'm going to put it in pigtails and start wearing a beret, just in tribute to the sister."

"Unbelievable," droned Helen.

"Besides, you don't know what kind of hairstyle Tom likes, do you Helen?" said Geri cheekily. "For all you know, he might be right into the whole stripy jumper and slingshot in the back pocket look."

"I highly doubt that," said Helen. "I doubt he even knows or cares who Minnie the Minx is. Besides, I'm not talking to or about him anymore. Our relationship was strictly professional and that's all there is to it."

She lifted her nose into the air and thumbed another page of her magazine.

"Is this because we haven't heard from him?" asked Martha.

"Yes," said Helen. "And no. If he doesn't have the courtesy to get in touch. Or indeed be where he says he's going to be. Then I don't have any time for him. Simple economics. He was a great help to our investigations and that was all."

"You don't know what happened," said Martha. "He might have a genuine excuse."

"Then why hasn't he phoned since? Eh? He has Geri's number, we called him on it earlier. He's blanked us. So I'm through with him."

She looked at the others for a reaction. Martha said nothing. Geri was the same.

"What? No sarcastic comments from you both?" asked Helen. "Nothing about the fact I repel men like bug spray? That I'm as successful with the opposite sex as a pair of sunglasses on a person with one ear? Nothing as acerbic as that? You're both losing your touch."

Martha smiled. She could feel her whole body relaxing, despite the discomfort. She'd laid still for too long. She felt rested and peaceful, the antithesis of everything that had happened this weekend. She fought hard to stay awake.

"There's our friend, look" said Geri, pointing at the screen. "Looks like Roberta has released her speech to the wider media."

Martha instantly woke up. She sat up and stared at the screen. Roberta Steiner was standing at the podium of the SteinerCon central hall downstairs. Camera flashes were going off as she waved and blew kisses to the crowd. Ever the professional, she still looked good.

The news reporter spoke over the speech. He talked about Murray's death and how the police had made an arrest on suspicion of murder. The screen cut to various celebrities paying tribute to him, before live scenes from outside the Steiners' mansion in Los Angeles. A shrine had been hastily erected, sobbing fans leaving floral tributes and lighting candles near the gates of the estate.

"I can't believe she's getting away with it," said Geri. "I genuinely can't believe it. We had her. We had her in the palm of our hand. Then that witch Eleanor David snatched it away from us. Why would she do something like that?"

"You know why," said Helen, still on the floor. "She's a disciple. One look at the woman and you can tell she has a screw loose. Must be all the radiation coming from her phones."

"Please, Helen," said Martha. "Don't start with your mobile phone radiation lectures again. Once through that particular series is *more* than enough."

"But why though?" asked Geri. "Why would you put yourself through something like that? If she's found guilty, she's facing a life sentence. That's going more than above and beyond for your employer. It's professional suicide."

Martha had been toying with every possibility. She had turned the situation over and over, trying to see what they'd missed—if they'd missed anything. She slid her way to the edge of the bed and stared down at the carpet between her feet.

"There is a chance, of course, that she actually did it," she said, slowly.

"What?" Geri blurted. "You can't be serious Martha. Come on now, I think some of that wine we had with dinner might have gone to your head."

"I'm just saying it's a possibility," she said. "It's not entirely out of the question now, is it? You heard what Superintendent Ghosh said. Eleanor had motive, and she would have had the means. There was nobody closer to the Steiners than her at this convention. They knew each other well, had worked together for years, decades even."

"If that's the case then why are we ruling out Marcel Blanc?" proffered Helen. "He had even *more* means to slip some pills or powder into Murray's meals or drinks or what have you."

"No motive. He had far too much to lose, and nothing to gain" said Geri. "You saw how he broke down at the prospect of losing his livelihood."

"And Eleanor David doesn't have anything to lose?" asked Martha.

"Of course she does. That's why I'm saying it's bonkers that she would take the fall for something like this."

"Which takes me back to my original point," Martha said. "It seems utterly insane that she would admit to a murder when she didn't do it. And for what? Respect? Loyalty from her boss. But that's what you think she's done, Geri. You think she's covering up for Roberta."

Geri sat down on the arm of the chair. Martha could see she was thinking. She always wore the same expression, somewhere between total concentration and blankness.

"I guess, if you put it like that," she said. "Would she really murder Murray Steiner though? She had as many reasons as plenty of others. What would it be about Eleanor David that would make her snap where dozens, if not hundreds, were able to keep it in check?"

"We don't know what Roberta has promised her," said Helen, closing her magazine. "Maybe the queen of the private detectives has promised to keep her for the rest of her miserable life, when she gets out of prison. Could just be as simple as money. We don't know Eleanor's private situation. Maybe she has a sick mum who needs medication. Perhaps she has *no* life and this was a bit of excitement. Perhaps she's in love with Roberta. We just don't know."

"We *do* know that she's going to be charged with Murray Steiner's murder," said Martha. "And if the evidence is strong enough, which it most likely will be, she'll be convicted, whether it's true or not. The world will have its headlines, Murray Steiner will forever be a martyr and Roberta Steiner will be rid of him and free to live her best life."

Martha stood up, feeling her knees and ankles crack. She stretched and yawned.

"We did what we had to, don't forget that," she said. "Now if you two don't mind, I'm going to have a very long, very hot bath with some of the complimentary soap and maybe fall asleep in there. If one, or ideally both, of you could make sure I don't drown, that would be just superb."

The sisters laughed. Martha ruffled Helen's hair as she tiptoed past her. She was just about to step into the bathroom when Geri called after her.

"Hey I think you're right about Roberta being free of Murray now, Martha," she said. "Maybe she could get something that shows her a bit more love. Like a bulldog."

Martha smiled. But it dropped from her face. She stopped, halfway to putting on the light. Slowly, she turned back to Geri across the bedroom.

"What did you say?" she asked, a penny dropping somewhere in the depths of her mind.

"What?" Geri smiled back. "What are you talking about?"

"What did you just say there, about Roberta Steiner."

"Nothing, I was just having a joke is all."

"What did you say? Say it again."

"Are you having one of your turns Martha?" Helen asked from the floor.

"Geri, say it again," she said. "Say exactly what you just said there."

"Bloody hell Martha," said Geri. "I said Roberta is free of Murray now. She could get something that showed her a bit more love than him. Something like a bulldog."

"Not your best gag," said Helen.

"No, it's not," agreed Geri. "I won't open the routine with it, I think."

"Bulldog," said Martha, stepping back into the room. "Bulldog. You said that before, earlier, when we were in that stairwell. Remember?"

"No," said Geri. "Did I? I say lots of things, as you two know all too well."

"You did, you called Eleanor David Roberta's bulldog," she said. "You called her that and I thought it was strange."

"What was strange?" asked Helen, sitting up straight as though sensing something was afoot.

Martha had to be sure. She had to get the blocks in place in her mind first to make sure they all made sense. She was tired, emotional, ready to sleep for a hundred years. But this was important. She had to be sure.

"A bulldog, that's exactly what Eleanor is. She's an enforcer, someone who does the dirty work for Roberta and Murray. She prides herself on it. Somebody in her position would. She organises SteinerCon for goodness' sake. That's no easy task, even if you've done it before. People like Murray and Roberta Steiner don't do *anything* for themselves. They live in gilded cages. We've seen it ourselves this weekend. So people like Eleanor David usually know *everything* that's going on. But she didn't know about the poisoning."

"How do you work that one out?" asked Geri. "She seemed pretty convincing to those cops upstairs."

"That was later, after we'd told them, after she'd had a chance to prep, had a chance to get up to speed with the truth," said Martha, speaking in short little bursts. "When we first came back to the hotel she was waiting for us, remember. She caught us with her posse in the reception. And we told her that the cops were treating Murray's death as suspicious. The look on her face, she was shocked. It was just a second, a tiny little second, but it was something, I saw it. It was doubt. Doubt because she didn't know. She couldn't have known. She just *couldn't* have known. Because—"

"Because she didn't poison Murray Steiner," said Geri, hopping up from the chair arm. "It *was* Roberta. Like we thought."

"It has to be," said Martha. "It can't be anybody else. Nobody would have enough access to him to poison his meals. Nobody. Not even Eleanor David."

"Hold on, wait a minute here," said Helen, standing up too. "This is all very well and good, the three of us agreeing. But we're not a jury. And we're not the Met Police who have somebody sitting in their cells tonight who has readily offered a confession to killing Murray Steiner. We can't convince them that we're right, just on a fleeting *look* on the woman's face hours before her confession, behave yourselves."

"No, you're right," said Martha.

She hurried around the bed and grabbed her cardigan. Throwing it on, she searched about the floor for her trainers.

"What are you doing?" asked Geri. "Looks like you're, eh, getting dressed."

"I am," she said. "I'm getting dressed because we've got a killer to catch."

"What?" asked Helen. "Not again, Martha."

"Yes, again Helen," she said. "We're going to catch Roberta Steiner and get a confession from *her*. It's the only way we can be sure. And the only way we can be certain that justice has been served."

"But she was heading to the airport hours ago," said Helen. "For all we know she'll be on her way to Los Angeles now to be met with her own darling press."

"We have to try damn it," said Martha.

Helen and Geri stared at her, wide-eyed. Martha bit her tongue. She didn't mean to snap at them. Something had made her so angry suddenly. She shook her head.

"I'm sorry," she said. "I didn't mean to shout. I'm tired and at the end of my tether. This has been nothing short of a bloody nightmare this weekend. And today has been the day from Hell. I challenge anyone who's had a rougher twenty-four hours than the three of us. But I know that what's happened isn't right. Murray Steiner was a pig, we can all agree on that. He didn't deserve to be killed though. He was still a human being. And if we can, in some small way try to bring his killer, his *true* killer to justice then we owe it to him, we owe it to ourselves, to do as much as we can. That's how we were raised. Good or bad, right or wrong, it's the only way I've ever known. I hate bullies. And I hate seeing innocent people being punished for something they didn't do."

She rounded the bed again and stood close to her sisters.

"Now I don't know what we're going to do," she said. "This whole weekend feels like a long string of false dawns and disappointments. But we have to try. That's the main part. And I'd love both of you to help me. If your schedules allow it."

Helen and Geri both laughed. Martha extended her arms out wide. She pulled her sisters in close and gave them both a big hug and a kiss on the top of their heads. The Parker sisters stood, in unison, for an all too brief moment. Then it was over.

"Come on," said Martha. "We don't have much time."

"I hate to break it to you both," said Helen. "Ruining the moment and all of that. But there's a police guard standing outside our door. How are we going to get past them let alone hop it to Heathrow Airport?"

"Just you leave that to me," said Geri. "Never count a good Parker out."

Thirty-Four

TEN MINUTES HAD passed. Ten long, agonising minutes. Martha felt like she'd lived a lifetime in every one of them. Make that every *second.* With every passing moment, their chances of catching Roberta Steiner were getting slimmer and slimmer.

She had to settle down and trust Geri, now more than ever. If her youngest sister said she had a plan then it was going to work. It *had* to work.

There was a knock at the door. Martha shot up from her chair. She wasn't sure why. Her nerves were shredded.

"I'll get it," said Geri, hurrying over to the door.

She pulled it open. A tall, rakishly thin waiter was standing on the other side. He had a kind smile and pushed a trolley, white tablecloth flapping as he passed between the two police officers standing guard outside the hotel door.

"Room service," he said.

"Good, come on in, we're absolutely famished," said Geri, making sure the cops heard her.

"Just put it over by the table, you can collect the empties while you're here."

She clicked the door shut and gave a quick glance through the peephole.

"You shouldn't have ordered all of this food Geri," said Helen, hovering around the latest addition to their feast. "I'm trying to watch my figure."

"Forget about the food," said Geri, rubbing her hands as she came over to them. "I just needed enough to warrant a trolley."

The waiter's smile dropped. Surrounded by the three Parker sisters, he started to fidget.

"Erm… don't you want the food?" he asked. "I can take it away if you like."

"Yes, please," said Geri. "But we need you to do us a teeny, weeny favour while you're at it."

Martha felt her chest tighten. She didn't like where this was going.

"Favour?" asked the waiter nervously. "What kind of favour?"

"We need to hide out in that trolley of yours."

Geri pointed down at the trolley. The waiter choked a half-cough, half-yelp.

"What?" he asked. "Why on earth would you want to do that?"

"It's a very long story, mister," she said, pulling a scrunched up fifty pound note from her pocket.

"Filip," said the waiter.

"Lovely to meet you Filip. This lovely pink note is yours, if you collect the empties, shove them on the trolley and push us out with you without the plod outside catching us. Sound fair?"

"Oi!" Helen shouted. "Where did you get fifty quid from?"

"Never you mind," she said. "It's not for you, it's for our new friend here."

"Geri," said Martha. "This isn't going to work."

"She's right, Ger. This is beyond stupid," agreed Helen. "I mean, how the hell are we all supposed to fit under there anyway. We're not contortionists, and this isn't some sort of Marx Brothers film."

"That almost sounded like a popular culture reference there Helen. Not even a century out of date, I'm proud of you," said Geri. "Anyway, sure we will. Where there's a will there's always a way. And we've got more will than most. Besides, I haven't heard you two come up with any alternatives."

"Hold on, could I say something?" said the waiter. "Now, we're told to respect the wishes of our guests and confidentiality is our top priority."

"I'll bet it is," said Helen, with a little snort to herself.

"But if I do this for you guys, am I going to get into trouble?" he asked.

"Of course you're not," said Geri, slapping him on the back. "Those cops are out there for *our* protection. It's just a precaution is all."

"So why don't you just leave when you want to?" he asked.

"Because… because… look do you want this fifty quid or not?"

"Geri," Martha said, feeling the need to interject before it got ridiculous, although already sensing that line had been crossed.

"This can't work, we can't ask this young man to risk his job for fifty pounds," she said.

"Sure we can," said Geri. "We've got a killer to catch."

"Killer?" the waiter's face turned pale. "What killer?"

"Long story, don't worry about it. They're not after you," said Geri, flapping him away. "Come on Martha, we're against the clock here. The longer we dally, the better chance Roberta has of getting on her private plane and jetting back to sunny California. If she goes over there then we've lost her for good. Time is pressing here. We need to act. Action stations. Come on."

She lifted the tablecloth off the trolley. Nodding over to Helen, she barked out her instructions.

"Come on Hel, you first," she said.

"What, hold on," said the waiter. "I'm not sure about this."

"That's okay mate, you don't have to be," said Geri. "You just concentrate on pushing us through that door, down the corridor and into the lift and we'll be out of your hair. Simple."

Helen rounded the trolley and eyed up the empty space below. She sniffed.

"Going to be a bit tight I reckon," she said.

"You can't be on board with this," said Martha. "You, Helen Parker, of all people are thinking this is a good idea?"

"It's an idea," she answered, hitching up her long skirt and crouching down. "That's all it is. I never said it was a good one."

She shuffled around and pulled her knees up to her chin. Peering out from beneath the cloth, she smiled.

"It's surprisingly cosy in here, actually," said Helen.

"I don't know about this," said the waiter. "I mean, what if I get caught? I could lose my job. And I've got a mountain of student debt I need to pay off. This is a good gig, I don't fancy going back to busking."

"Oh you're a musician?" asked Geri.

"No, mime artist," he said. "I'm a mime."

He stepped away and started pretending he was inside a glass box. Then he pulled an imaginary rope before finishing with a less than perfect robot dance.

"I'm still working on that one," he said. "Four years at RADA."

"Well it was money well spent," she said. "Just think of all the pints you can buy for fifty quid."

"London prices Geri," said Martha with a sigh. "He'll be lucky to get a chaser."

"She's right," shrugged the waiter.

Martha stepped over to the trolley. She looked down at Helen sitting quite content in the lower section. Then she sighed again.

"And we really have no alternative?" she asked.

"Unless you fancy fighting those two cops out there, no," said Geri, flatly.

Martha nodded. That was that, then. She clambered into the trolley. Clearly she wasn't as flexible as her sister and she groaned as she hoisted her knees up as far as they would go.

"This isn't going to work," she grumbled. "Hold on to me Helen, I don't want to explode out of this thing like a coiled spring."

Helen giggled as she wrapped an arm around her shoulder. Geri slipped underneath, her slight frame fitting perfectly in the tiny space left under the trolley.

"Right, you know what you're doing?" she asked Filip. "Straight out the door, down the corridor and into the lift. Easy peasy to a strapping young man like yourself."

"Blimey," said Filip. "You three are nuts."

"You're telling me," said Martha as the tablecloth dropped.

Filip stepped around to the back of the trolley. Martha watched his shadow as the three of them sat in silence. With a grunt, he started to push them towards the door. They wobbled, Geri and Helen balancing themselves on the struts. Martha had nothing to hold on to except her own legs. And she didn't trust those as far as she could throw them.

They came to a halt. Martha panicked.

"What's wrong?" she asked.

"I need to get the door," said Filip from above.

"Calm down, Mart," said Helen. "You're making me nervous. And you know what I'm like when I get nervous."

"I thought you stopped wetting the bed last year," smiled Geri.

"Not as much of it motormouth," Helen batted back.

"Shh," said Filip. "I'm opening the door now."

The Parkers held their breaths. The door opened with a slight creak and Filip slid the trolley over the lip of the frame. The light changed, much brighter—shining through the white tablecloth. Martha felt every bump, every creak, every rattle of the trolley as they moved.

"Who were you talking to back there?" came a strange voice.

The Parkers froze. It was one of the cops. Two long shadows on either side of the trolley loomed through the covering.

"Oh eh… myself," said Filip

They could hear the nervousness in his voice. The longer this went on the greater chance they stood of getting caught.

"Hold up," said the other officer. "Are they not eating any of this?"

The shimmer of a lid sounded like a sword being unsheathed. Martha bit down on her bottom lip, her hands locked tightly around her shins.

"Erm… no," said Filip.

"What a waste," said the first officer. "Still, no reason why the taxpayer's hard earned cash should go to waste, eh Brian?"

"Good point, Eric," said the other.

The rattle of more trays and plates echoed down into the trolley. The sisters all stayed perfectly still, terrified to even sniff should it alert the police.

"Tasty," said Eric, the cop. "Very tasty."

"Here, not as tasty as the older one," said Brian.

Martha's eyes went wide as saucers. Geri had to clamp a hand to her mouth to stop her from laughing.

"Oh yes, now there is a beautiful looking lady. I wouldn't mind letting her investigate my privates, if you know what I mean," said Eric. "Like a fine wine, just getting better with age that one."

Helen started to snigger. Martha elbowed her to keep her quiet. She wasn't sure if she was more terrified or embarrassed. This was truly mortifying.

"Right, on your way pal," said Brian, still chewing.

The trolley trundled along the corridor again, the Parkers still trying to stay as quiet as they could. The familiar ping of the lift sounded out somewhere above them. Shoving the heavy trolley over the ridges of the elevator, the doors closed and finally they could move.

"A fine wine!" laughed Helen.

"Investigate his privates!" bawled Geri.

"Shut up you two," said Martha, unfolding herself from beneath the trolley. "I have absolutely no idea what they're talking about. And if they find me attractive then they're clearly deranged."

"Oh, I wouldn't say that," said Filip, with a cheeky smile.

"You're a good boy, Filip," she said, clapping him on the cheek. "But behave yourself. Now get us as far down to the bottom of this hotel as you can. We need to catch a ride to the airport."

Thirty-Five

"SO I SAYS to the wife, if you want me out the living room for the night, that's fine by me. I'll just leave the whole bleedin' house for a month. What do you think of that?"

The cabbie erupted into a fit of coughing laughter. Martha clung on for dear life in the back as the taxi weaved its way through the central London streets. They'd whizzed past Harrods, Knightsbridge just a blur, before hurtling on by the Victoria and Albert Museum. The delights of Earl's Court, West Kensington and Hammersmith were little more than 'blink and you miss it 'moments fleeting past the window. The driver, clearly enjoying the emptiness of the streets, was determined, it seemed, to get them to Heathrow Airport as quickly as possible.

"Here, I had a young man in the back of the cab earlier today, geeky type, you know the sort, all acne and glasses," the cab driver continued. "I says to him, here, Brains—you remember Brains don't you, from Thunderbirds."

Helen and Geri looked blank. Terrified but blank. Martha had a feeling he was talking to her.

"Yes," she managed between breaths. "Yes I do."

She was silently begging him to stop talking and concentrate on the road. But the cabbie wasn't for doing that.

"So anyway, I says to Brains, here, what's wrong with my phone, it can't take any pictures and I keep getting this message saying the cloud's full. Oi watch it you idiot! Did you get your licence in a lucky bag or something?"

He rolled down the window and volleyed another barrage of abuse at some unsuspecting cyclist decked head to toe in hi-vis.

"Sorry about my language ladies," said the cabbie, roaring the engine back into life. "Where was I? Oh yeah, my phone. I says to this geeky type, what's wrong with my phone. And you know what he says to me? He says, why don't you go to the tech bar and have somebody look at it for you. I says tech bar? Look mate, the only bar I'm interested in is one where I can get a pint of Jack and Coke, a dry sherry for the wife and somewhere to watch Palace. That'll do me nicely, mate. We've got a nice little pub down the end of our road as it happens, do a lovely Sunday roast. The meat's a little on the dry side and sometimes you only get a dozen chips but it doesn't matter, as long as you're out and about, am I right?"

"Yes, you're right," said Martha, appeasing the driver.

Her head hurt. Between the cabbie's inane ramblings and the way he was throwing his taxi all over the road, Martha was feeling quite sick. She knew she didn't have time to be ill. Martha only hoped that they weren't too late to catch their killer.

The cabbie continued on his diatribe. Martha tried to distract herself with the London boroughs that were passing them by at breakneck speed.

"Will he ever just shut up?" Helen asked, her tone hushed. "He's a walking, talking caricature."

"I feel for his wife," said Geri, bouncing about the back seat. "Not to mention the bloke who got both barrels earlier."

Then Martha saw it. In a city already famed for its light pollution, Heathrow Airport appeared to be vying for the title. Like a great big dirty blot on an already neon-saturated landscape, the famous airport came looming on the horizon. Lights twinkled from aircraft all lining up to make their final approach high above. And below them planes taking off, destined for the very furthest reaches of the Earth.

Like the huge, gaping mouth of a whale, the campus seemed to swallow their taxi and all the other traffic whole. Suddenly the airport and its outbuildings were all around them, a hard white light illuminating the concrete roads and tunnels that led to the fortress-like structure.

"What terminal are you ladies wanting dropped off at?" asked the driver.

"Terminal?" asked Martha. "Oh, I'm not sure."

"Well where is it you're going to? Who's your airline?"

"We don't have an airline and we're hopefully not going anywhere," said Helen.

"Ah, meeting somebody then?"

"Not exactly," said Geri. "We're hoping to stop somebody from leaving."

"Well what airline are they on then?" he groaned.

"We don't know," said Martha.

"You don't know? I don't think you ladies have thought this through very carefully have you?"

Reluctantly, Martha had to concede that the cabbie was correct. She had been caught up in all the excitement and urgency that she hadn't planned too far ahead. Hiding under a food trolley hadn't helped matters either.

"Well maybe you could help us," she said, thinking fast. "You seem to know your way about."

"A man of the world sweetheart, that's me," he said, going for another lap of the roundabouts.

"Our… friend—we think she'll be on a private charter."

"Oh, very posh, got a few quid this mate of yours?"

"More than a few," chimed Helen.

"Do you have any idea where that sort of thing would be?" asked Martha. "It's pretty important we get to her before she leaves."

"Hmmm," the cabbie scratched the bristles on his chin. "Needle in a haystack stuff there, I'm afraid. From what I know the private stuff normally lands and leaves from Luton or Farnborough. You sure this pal of yours is at Heathrow?"

"Definitely," said Martha. "We've got it from the source."

"Hmmm," he said again.

Geri kicked Martha in the leg. She winced and looked at her sister. Geri wore a strange expression. Her eyes were wide and she was nodding at the driver. Martha couldn't be sure, but she had always suspected some sort of telepathic bond with her sisters. A lot of old rubbish of course. The results, however, spoke for themselves.

"Roberta Steiner," she said to the cabbie. "We're trying to reach Roberta Steiner."

"Steiner?" the driver yelped. "You mean that lady that's been on the news all day. The one whose husband was bumped off or something."

"That's the one," said Martha. "She's a celebrity, does that help in pointing us in a direction?"

Martha held her breath. She wasn't sure if she had done the right thing. It felt like she was taking a risk, mentioning Roberta at all. Times were desperate and they were running out it.

"No," said the driver. "But that's never stopped me before. Hang on."

He cleared a load of empty crisp packets from the dashboard. Grabbing the radio, he twisted some dials and started barking into the mic.

"Evening all, Stan the Fish here, how we all doing this fine Saturday night?"

A host of voices, not entirely dissimilar to the cabbie came crackling out of the radio. Stan smiled.

"Good to hear you too. Listen, I'm in a bit of a jam here. I've got three birds in a fare, steady on, don't get too excited. We're at Heathrow looking to find out where a Roberta Steiner might be taking off from. Private charter, A-lister, anybody taken anybody recently, anybody got any ears on the ground?"

Another wave of voices—mostly whistles and put downs. Stan the cabbie laughed.

"Come on now, settle down, time's of the essence for these three lovely ladies," he said.

"Yeah I might have something mate," came a woman's voice from the set.

Martha sat forward, her stomach still lurching from side-to-side as they went around a roundabout for the fourth time.

"Just dropped a bloke off about twenty minutes ago, seemed quite edgy," said the woman. "I thought he was on something, had half a mind to chuck him out and let him walk, the flash bugger."

"Yeah? Go on," said Stan.

"Anyway, I do the usual routine, ask him where he's going and that. He blanks me. It's not until we get to the Saudi Embassy and he starts getting fidgety. Starts dropping names I've never heard of like I'm supposed to know who they are. One of them is Roberta Steiner. Doesn't mean a thing to me, I'm not clued up on my celebs these days, you know what I'm like. Still, a bit funny though, you coming on the radio asking and I've just had somebody in the back.

Martha looked at Helen and Geri. They were all equally confused.

"Okay, thanks pal," said Stan. "Where'd you drop him off?"

"Terminal Five," she said. "He hurried off inside and didn't even give me a tip, the stingy bugger."

"Terminal five it is then," said Stan, hurling the taxi back around and taking an exit. "Thank you for your help folks, owe you a pint."

The group signed off and the cabbie replaced the mic. He smiled warmly at the Parkers.

"There you go, best folk in the world taxi folk. You can have all the technology out there but it's the old taxi radio that gets the job done. You'll never beat that."

"Thank you, Stan," said Martha.

She sat back as they headed along the long roads that ran like veins across the airport campus.

"Who's the bloke?" asked Helen.

"I have no idea," said Martha. "Could be anyone I suppose. Police, journalist, anyone really."

"If it wasn't that long ago though, we might still be in with a chance," said Geri.

"Maybe," said Martha. "But we still have to get inside the bloody building first. This is an airport, they won't just let us swan in and walk around wherever we want. Unless…"

She trailed off, an idea forming in her mind. Helen and Geri sat with bated breath, waiting to find out what their sister had come up with.

"Well?" they both asked expectantly.

"It's another long shot. But you never know," she said. "We've had our fair share of luck with them this weekend. Why the hell don't we try to keep the streak going."

Her hands were shaking as she pulled out her phone and scrolled through the address book. She stopped when she found the name she was looking for. Hesitating for a brief moment, she decided that her plan was the only way they could catch Roberta. One last burst of courage and she pressed dial on the number. It started to ring.

Thirty-Six

THE PHONE WENT off, vibrating loudly on the hardwood of the bedside table. There was a grunt from somewhere in the darkness. Then a groan. Then a flurry of expletives that usually greeted a late night telephone call.

"Hello?"

Detective Sergeant Aileen Pope thought she'd managed the impossible—waking up and not descending into a coughing fit. No such luck. It started light, but then, before she knew it she could barely breathe. Sat bolt upright, heaving and whooping until her ribs ached.

The light went on from the other side of the bed. An inhaler appeared in front of Pope and she grabbed it. Sucking hard, she held her breath for ten seconds and then let it go.

"You okay?"

"Yes, fine love," said Pope.

She was bathed in sweat, her T-shirt stuck underneath her arms. Laura rubbed her back and stared at her, shaking her head.

"It's the heat," she said. "You're always worse in the heat."

"The hay fever doesn't help," said Pope. "Never has done. In fact I remember when I was eleven there was a particularly nasty summer where—"

"Hello? Hello? DS Pope?" the voice came from the phone.

"Bugger," said Pope, remembering why she was awake. "Hello? Who's this? I have a new phone, no numbers."

"It's Martha Parker."

Any lingering fatigue from the fit disappeared at the mention of that name. Her legs were out from under the covers and she was up, pacing around the bedroom before she knew it—Laura watching every step.

"Parker. Nosey Parker. What the hell time do you call this?" she said.

"I don't know what time of day it is, it's been a long one," said Martha.

"It's almost eleven at night, some of us have to be up before the sunrise, you know, to catch bad guys and do our jobs."

"I'm sorry," said Martha. "I wouldn't have called unless it was absolutely necessary."

Pope's mind was quickly cranking back into its usual paranoid gear. Unexpected phone calls were part and parcel of her life as a police officer. No self-respecting detective with lofty ambitions in a changing force should ever be caught unawares. And the job always, *always* came first. The look on Laura's face as she yawned and watched her wife move back and forth around their bedroom dictated that.

"Martha Parker," said Pope, holding a hand over the speaker. "Remember, from Christmas, the banker. She's the one with the sisters."

"I know who Martha Parker is Aileen," said Laura. "And her sisters. They've been making quite a name for themselves. Lovely of them to wake us up in the middle of the night though. We must put them on the Christmas card list."

Pope bit her bottom lip. She mouthed her apologies and skipped over to the door. Slinking out, she saw the light go out as she clicked the handle.

"You've got a bloody nerve Parker," she said, taking her anger out on Martha. "That's me in the doghouse now with the old ball and chain. I'll never hear the end of this."

"I'm sorry, truly I am," said Martha. "But this is important. And we weren't entirely sure of who to turn to."

Pope didn't like this. She didn't like this one bit. Since the Coulthard affair she'd been very cautious not to draw attention to herself. The department, the force even, didn't like celebrities. And they certainly didn't like amateur detectives. Above all else, they despised when part-time sleuths did their job better than they did—catching murderers and leading to lengthy, public apologies to the wrong suspect.

She had spent the better part of her recent career saying 'Yes, sir. No, sir. How high, sir? Can I flush that for you, sir?' The sound of Martha Parker's voice, its nervous tone, gave Detective Sergeant Pope heart palpitations.

"I don't like where this is going Parker," she said cautiously, heading into the kitchen. "In fact, I don't think I should continue this conversation. Like I said, it's late, I have a nice, comfy bed with an ever maddening spouse upstairs. Give me one good reason why I shouldn't just hang up."

"Roberta Steiner."

"Roberta Steiner?" asked Pope. "The millionaire TV mogul? What about her."

"She killed her husband last night."

"I beg your pardon."

"Look it's too long a story, and we really don't have any time," said Martha, sounding increasingly desperate. "Helen, Geri and myself are at Heathrow Airport. We're trying to stop Roberta from boarding her private plane back to California. If she gets away, we won't ever catch her and confront her about Murray Steiner's murder, and the police—the Met police—will just let her go. You have to help us."

Pope blinked.

"And how the hell do you suppose I'm going to do that?" she asked. "Even if I believed your crackpot theory, when the Met clearly don't. What do you expect me to do?"

There was a moment's pause. Pope could hear the roar of jet engines in the background, Helen and Geri Parker bickering too. Martha sighed.

"We need you to call the commanding officer—it's a Superintendent Henry Ghosh. He doesn't believe us, he's happy that Roberta's conference director is the killer."

"And why would I not agree with a leading officer of the Met?" she asked. "Why would I take your opinion over that of an experienced officer in one of the world's leading police forces?"

"Because it's not true," said Martha flatly. "Eleanor David isn't the killer, she's faked a confession to cover Roberta's tracks. She didn't know anything about the poisoning—Murray was poisoned by the way—when we confronted her at first. It's all a ruse. But we need you to get the cavalry down here to Terminal Five. It'll mean more coming from a fellow officer. Please."

"Parker, please tell me you're not going to do anything rash," said the cop. "You've got the sound of a woman right at the edge of reason."

"We have to stop Roberta," she said. "We're going to pull the fire alarm. That'll evacuate the terminal and hopefully delay any take-offs and such. It should flush Roberta out into the open long enough to grab her."

"You've lost your mind Parker," said Pope. "Are you serious? Do you have any idea how dangerous that is? I mean, if what you're saying is true, which I'm still not convinced it is—maybe you've been sniffing glue or something. What if you're wrong? Even if you're right, you'll have shut down a major terminal in one of the busiest airports in the world for nothing. You'll get five years, maybe more. And as for me, calling in the top brass over nothing. My feet wouldn't touch the floor. Quite rightly too."

"I know, I know, I know," said Martha. "Truly I do. And I only wish it didn't have to be you. You helped us out and I'm forever grateful for everything you've already done. But this is serious, deadly serious. If we don't stop her now then she'll literally get away with murder. She's a killer, Pope, she murdered her husband. We know it, we can prove it, we just have to get hold of her and get her to admit it."

Pope felt her jaw tightening, the tendons flexing in her cheeks. She caught sight of her reflection in the patio doors, the soft darkness of the summer night making her look like a ghost. This was insane. She couldn't really help them, could she? Call in an emergency, pull a string or two with some colleagues she knew in the Met.

"Look, I know we're not helping ourselves here," said Martha. "But you're going to have to trust me, trust us, on this. I'll be more than happy to explain and, should it come to it, take full responsibility for what happens. There isn't time now, there's no time at all."

"Do you know for certain that she's still at the airport?" asked the detective.

"No," said Martha.

"Then why are you even bothering?" she yelped. "For all you know, she could be halfway across the Atlantic by now, washing down to her lobster thermidor with a glass of bubbly?"

"She's here," said Martha firmly. "I know she's still here. It's a feeling. And somebody was looking for her, he was dropped off not long ago. We can still catch her, Pope, we really can. But we need your help."

Everything in Pope's mind screamed at her to hang up and forget all about it. She was a police officer, logic was supposed to be her best friend. Cold, hard facts were her business. Without them there was nothing.

Still, there was something about the desperation in Martha's voice that was enough to bring in that little bit of doubt. Just a hint, a smidgen of intrigue that appealed not only to her curiosity but to her gut instinct too. Police officers relied on the facts. But they also valued instinct. And that made Detective Sergeant Pope *very* nervous.

"Jesus and the Mary Chain," she said, rubbing her eyes. "I can't believe I'm about to say this Parker… but okay, you've hooked me."

"Are you sure?" asked Martha.

"Don't ask stupid questions, Parker, of course I'm not sure. You're skating on ice as thin as it can get. And this is a *terrible* idea, especially if it turns out to be completely bogus. But what do you need?"

"What did she say to it then?" came Geri Parker's voice from the background.

"Yes, she'll do it, now hush up," said Martha.

"Thank you, Popey," Geri shouted down the line.

"Yes, thank you Detective Sergeant," added Helen with a whoop.

Pope felt sick.

"What do you need, Parker?" she asked again. "Quickly, before I change my mind."

"We need you to call the guys at the Met and get them down to the terminal. I don't know what codes you guys have, I don't know anything of the sort. We just need the private planes to be grounded long enough to flush Steiner and her cronies out."

"You're right," said the detective.

"About what?"

"You don't know *anything* about how we work," she said.

"I'm sorry, I really am," said Martha. "I'm asking for the earth and giving you nothing back. I just hope that you'll trust me on this one, Pope. I just hope that I'm right."

"Me too," said Pope, with a growl. "Okay. You'll need to give me five minutes to put some calls in. Do what you need to do in the meantime, but don't set off any alarms. You're only going to get one shot at this. Do *not* waste it. Understand?"

"Loud and clear," she said. "Five minutes."

"Five minutes."

"Thank you," said Martha.

"I haven't done anything yet."

"No, I know. But you will. I have every faith in you."

She hung up. Pope placed the phone down on the kitchen worktop. Two beaming faces shone back at her through the gloom of the kitchen—Laura and her own on their wedding day. Minutes after that photo was taken Pope had gone off on one of her coughing fits. It was a nasty one too, the type that brought her out in big, red blotches around her eyes. Thankfully the photographer had left her well alone again until they had faded.

It had been a wonderful day for everyone, none more than Laura. Pope heard the floorboards creak above her head.

"What was that all about?" Laura shouted from the stairs outside the kitchen. "Are you having to go to the station?"

"No," said Pope, a little relieved that she wasn't telling any lies. "No I don't have to do that."

"Well then, what's the matter?"

"How do you know something's the matter?" she asked.

"Your voice. You sound like you're about to burst out crying."

It wasn't far from the truth. Pope was a woman driven by her career—she thrived on it, loved it, almost as much as her wife and family. The second was a blessing she never thought she'd have. And yet here she was, standing in the darkness, about to risk it all—for little more than a promise from a relative stranger.

That passion for the job still burned inside of her. That's why she was even contemplating doing what Martha Parker had asked of her. Instinct, gut feeling, a sixth sense. She only hoped that of all the times she had relied on it, this wouldn't prove to be fatal for her career, for her marriage, for everything.

Almost on cue, Pope felt the burning erupt in her lungs. She doubled over, gripping onto the worktop to steady herself. Laura came running down the stairs and ran her a glass of water. When the coughing steadied, Pope drank it down, and gasped for breath.

"Thank you, my darling," she said.

"Are you okay?" asked her wife.

"No," she said. "No I'm not. But that's nothing new."

"Then come to bed," said Laura. "You're up too early."

"Two seconds," said the detective. "I've got a very quick phone call to make."

Thirty-Seven

MARTHA HAD A terrible feeling in the pit of her stomach, like a bag full of antacids had been dropped in there and they were all fizzing away at once. It was dread. She knew that. Horrible, nail biting dread that wasn't going to go away.

From the side of the private concourse outside the terminal she could see people being hurried out. Staff with wooden pallets held up above their heads signalled them as Fire Marshalls—the ones charged with keeping this whole operation from turning into a panic. The air was singed with furious conversation, cursing and swearing as the business people, the rich and famous and their staff all drudged their way out of the terminal.

"This is ridiculous," said one random voice, hurrying past Martha.

"I bet it's a drill," said another.

"No doubt somebody burned their toast and set off a fire alarm," came a third.

Martha wished it was any one of those. Anything would have been better than the truth. She had caused this, a mass evacuation at a major air hub. She wanted to cry.

Only she couldn't do that. She had to stay sharp. Hawk-eyed. Every face needed to be scanned as it came out of the building. As soon as she spotted Roberta Steiner and her entourage it would be time to react. The risk was worth the reward if they could pull this off. She just had to keep her nerve.

"Do you see anything, Martha?" came Geri's voice down the line.

"No, nothing," she answered, phone pressed against her ear. "What about you?"

GERI WAS STATIONED at the northern entrance of the terminal. She regularly cursed how short she was. That was nothing new. She still refused to wear stilettos unless it was absolutely necessary. No extra inches in the world could force her into that particular world of pain any time soon.

Although she did resent having to stand on her tiptoes like this. People were too tall, she decided. When they congregated in groups like this, it was almost impossible for her to see anything. She tried though, making sure no face passed her by without being seen.

"I've got nothing," she answered, holding the mic of her earphones close to her mouth. "This is worse than trying to find a needle in a haystack. How can there be so many people here at this time of night?"

"It's an international airport Geri," said Martha. "This place is busy all the time."

"Yeah, and we've just flushed it out like a toilet."

The crowd seemed to swell as Geri spoke. Rearing up like a great wave, she felt herself being pushed and shoved backwards. Curses in several languages rained down on her and somebody jammed their suitcase into her shin.

"Oi! Watch it," she shouted, stumbling back.

The northern entrance wasn't as wide as the main one on the concourse. It was narrow and claustrophobic, a door at one end and a taxi rank at the other. People were already starting to get peeved as the open square quickly filled up.

"Ladies and gentlemen, if I could have your attention for a moment," proclaimed a voice from the front.

Geri hopped up on her tiptoes again. She could see a weedy looking man with a loudspeaker standing at the doors to the terminal. His nasally voice sounded particularly tinny as the loudspeaker hissed with every word.

"Thank you for your cooperation, we have identified a fire alarm that was set off in the private terminal," he said.

"Are you hearing this Martha?" asked Geri, holding up her phone.

"We will endeavour to have you all back in as soon as we can. Please be assured that *no* flight will leave until we have been given the all clear from the fire brigade and we can open the terminal once again."

A loud, collective groan went up from the gathered crowd. The man lowered his loudspeaker and retreated into the building with his staff, the doors firmly closed behind him. Geri spoke into her mic.

"That's it," she said. "Nobody else is coming out here. I've got everyone I'm going to get."

"Can you see her?" asked Martha.

"Hold on."

She spotted a large bin with an ashtray on the top. Hoisting herself up onto its lid, Geri had a birds 'eye view of the whole northern entranceway. She peered across the tops of the crowd's heads, checking everybody out. When she'd spun all the way around, she snapped her fingers.

"Damn," she said. "Nothing. She's not here. She must be with you or Helen at the south door."

"I've got nothing here," said Martha. "They've just closed the main doors and are giving me the same spiel as you. What do we do?"

"I think we head down to Helen," said Geri. "I swear I'll kill her one of these days. Who goes anywhere without their phone? She's an absolute nuisance that woman."

"Okay," said Martha. "Come down to me, I'll be at the taxi rank outside the main entranceway, I'll keep an eye out for you."

"Roger, roger," said Geri, climbing down from the bin.

HELEN DIDN'T LIKE crowds. She didn't particularly like people. And she rarely stayed quiet about it. The idea of being surrounded by a crowd of complete strangers made her skin crawl. That's why she was taking in the chaos from the safe distance across the road. There was plenty of air out here, nobody to push her, shout at her, or pinch her purse. She clapped the pocket of her long skirt in a panic.

"No purse," she said. "Now has it been pinched or did I leave it in the hotel room?"

She mulled this over for a moment. The south entrance was emptying like a bucket with a hole in the bottom. Travellers oozing out of the door and spreading across the forecourt. Helen let her worries about her purse ease. She settled down on her perch, doing her best to try and decipher the confusion.

"These bloody lights are too bright," she said.

The white glow from the street lights that lined the concourse gave everything a hard, bleached edge. Shadowing her eyes from the glare, she squinted and peered at the crowd.

"This is no use," she muttered. "I'm not going to see a thing from over here. I'll need to get in amongst it."

The thought made her shudder. Reluctantly, she got up, dusted off some grass from the knoll she'd been sitting on and hopped across the road that led away to the motorway.

"Here we go then," she said, taking a gulp of night air

Helen made her way into the growing crowd. She ducked and weaved, trying not to touch anybody. There were crying kids, adults tutting, people who looked completely lost and others that were dog-tired. The airport, she had always believed, was a wonderful mixing pot of society as a whole. The rich, the poor, the excited and the bored all came to the same place to get away from whatever it was they were leaving from. She thought there might be a thesis in there somewhere. Maybe she could make a note to check it out when she got home. The private terminal, however, was a little blander. Executives, millionaires, the other half.

"Concentrate," she said to herself.

"You what?" said a voice from beside her.

"I beg your pardon?" asked Helen.

"You talking to me or what?" said an old man in a Hawaiian shirt.

She scrunched up her face as he held onto his suitcase. His wife, equally flamboyant in a matching blouse, pulled the same expression when she spotted Helen.

"I wasn't talking to you," said Helen, sneering a little.

"Well it sounded like you was," said the old man.

"It sounded like you was," agreed his wife.

"Well I wasn't okay," said Helen. "And besides. It's not you was. It's you *were*."

"You what?" they both said, their faces almost folded in on themselves.

"Never mind," she sighed. "While I've got you. You haven't seen Roberta Steiner anywhere around here have you?"

"Who?" said the old couple, again in tandem.

Helen rolled her eyes. She threw her hands up into the air and walked away.

"Maddening," she said. "The public. They shouldn't be allowed out.

She meandered through some more of the gathered crowd, keeping her head low as she passed any members of airport staff. Before long she was back close to the street with nothing to show for her adventure.

"What a kick in the knickers this is turning out to be," she said, putting her hands on her hips.

Helen looked out across the crowd again, taking a long, steady arc from one side to the other. She was about to give up completely when something caught her eye.

She froze. Blinking to make sure she wasn't seeing things, she squinted again, wishing she hadn't been vain enough not to wear her glasses. A face shone through the crowd. She had it targeted, was concentrated on it, following it as it made its way in front and behind the others.

But it couldn't have been who she thought it was. It didn't make any sense. She blinked again then rubbed her eyes. Every time the face was the same. The face was one that she recognised immediately.

"No," she said. "It just can't be."

She wandered forward, almost in a trance. Someone bumped her shoulder and apologised. Helen didn't hear them. She stood on something that cracked and snapped, more children crying in her wake. She didn't hear them. Her eyes were fixed on the face wandering through the gathered crowd outside the southern entrance. When she thought she was close enough, she shouted.

"Tom! Tom! It's me, Helen. Tom!"

Tom Hopgood stopped for a moment. He looked back through the crowd, having heard his name. He wore a concerned look, his chiselled, tanned face taking on a sharper edge than before. Helen didn't mind. She was just glad to see the face at all.

"Tom! Tom! Tom! Tom! Tom!" Helen shouted again, forcing her way through the crowd. "Get out of my way. Tom! Tom! Tom! It's me, Helen."

The Australian private eye kept getting further from her. She struggled through the crowd, the numbers seeming to clog the entrance the closer she got.

"Get out of my way," said Helen, prizing gaps and spaces between the people in front of her.

She hopped and leapt over felled suitcases and trolleys. She slipped around and past those resigned to a long wait, stretched out across the forecourt. Helen stopped just short of vaulting on top of them all and crowd surfing her way towards Tom.

There was a break in the crowd, a small pocket of empty forecourt that gave Helen a chance to breathe. She tripped forward, gasping for breath. Clutching her knees she was bent double but kept her eyes firmly locked on Tom. He'd made his way towards the rear of the main building. As Helen steadied herself, she peered through the crowd. With every step and clap of her sandals, her blood grew colder and colder.

Between the bobbing, moving heads of the crowd still between them, Helen saw Tom come to a stop. He was smiling as he was handed a phone by someone close by. Guiding them into the little alcove where the main terminal met an outbuilding, a pair of smiling women stood and posed with a woman dressed all in black, wearing large, thick sunglasses. Two stern looking men in black suits, shirts and ties stood about her, faces mean and angry.

"No," said Helen. "No, no, no."

The two women kept smiling. They each made a peace sign as they stood on either side of the stern looking woman. Tom took the photograph and handed the camera back to them.

"No," said Helen again, her legs on autopilot, being dragged towards the other side of the clearing. "This isn't happening. I'm imagining things. I've finally lost it."

"Helen! Helen!" came Martha and Geri from behind her.

Helen kept walking, her jaw slack. The two women laughed and giggled, thanking Tom before disappearing into the crowd. The Australian gave another look back over his shoulder, his brow narrowed.

"Helen, where have you been?" asked Geri, appearing at her side.

"Have you seen anyone?" gasped Martha.

All Helen could muster was a point. She raised her quivering finger into the crowd and pointed towards Tom. The others followed her finger and the three Parker sisters stood perfectly still.

"Is that…" Geri trailed off.

"It is, you know," said Martha.

They watched, agog, as Tom turned back to Roberta Steiner and her bodyguards. Taking her face in his hands, he leaned in and kissed her passionately. When he pulled away, his head snapped around as if he'd heard the Parker sisters 'jaws hit the floor. Staring at the three of them, both Tom and Roberta's faces contorted.

"Oh shit," said Helen, feeling faint.

"Oh shit is right," agreed Martha.

Thirty-Eight

MARTHA WASN'T QUITE sure what to do. This had all seemed so far away only a short time ago. They had been running on fumes, living on instinct for so long now that reaching an end point had almost been secondary. When there was nothing else but hope, it was easy to forget that you could achieve anything. Now, here, in a forecourt outside Heathrow Airport, she found herself very much getting what she wanted.

A strange serenity seemed to sit over them all. There must have been fifty people, maybe more, between her, Tom and Roberta Steiner. Yet it felt like they were the only people in the world. The misplaced travellers and angry business people all stood frozen in time. It was as though only Tom and Roberta could see Martha and her sisters. They were in a little bubble separated from the rest of the world, from the place where logic and good sense prevailed.

The questions were back. If she could have cracked open her mind it would have overflowed with everything she wanted to ask. Tom Hopgood and Roberta Steiner. It didn't make sense. How did they know each other? Were they lovers? Had they *always* been in a relationship? What about Murray Steiner, had he known about it? Was this some sort of revenge on all of his unfaithful years? It was endless.

Most importantly, how did they fit into all of this? Helen had met Tom at breakfast that morning. The thought made Martha realise just how long ago that was. This had been the day from Hell and then some. And it seemed there were still a few surprises left up its sleeve before it was out.

Somewhere in the distance, Martha heard sirens. A flicker of blue in her periphery was enough to break the spell. The world and all of its reality came rushing back over her like a waterfall.

Her senses jump started and she was back in the world of the living.

A stream of police cars and fire engines barrelled down the motorway, heading for the terminal. Martha broke her gaze on Tom and Roberta for a split second to see the emergency services flowing like a loud, honking river.

When she looked back Tom and Roberta were on the move. They hurriedly collected their bags and were barking orders to Roberta's security guards.

"Stop," said Martha feebly, as if they could hear her.

"I don't think they heard you," said Geri. "Although I don't blame them for running. I wouldn't want somebody like me taking pictures either."

In a smooth, almost balletic motion, Geri aimed her phone and started snapping. Before Tom and Roberta could vanish into a small door in the outbuilding beside the terminal, she had twenty shots of them.

"Gotcha," she said.

"Come on, after them," said Martha.

She and Geri bolted. They were almost at the crowd again when they realised Helen wasn't with them. They both skidded to a halt.

"Helen," Geri shouted. "What are you waiting for?"

"They're getting away," said Martha.

Helen just stood there. Her head was bowed, her bottom lip trembling. She looked forlorn, defeated, a woman who had cracked. Martha hurried back over to her.

"I'm sorry Helen," she said. "I'm really sorry. But we don't have time to feel sorry for ourselves."

"Martha's right," said Geri, squeezing her sister's arm. "We can lament, bitch and berate later. We can't let them get away. We need to know what's going on."

"He's played me like a cheap fiddle, hasn't he?" said Helen. "How could I have been so bloody *stupid*. I'm not meant to be conned like this. I'm supposed to be a lot cleverer than that.

What a bloody idiot I've been. What a stupid bloody moron. Why would he think anything of me? Look at me."

"Hey," barked Geri. "That's enough, Hel. That's *more* than enough. Don't talk about yourself like that. You've done nothing wrong here. Do you hear me?"

"We don't know all the facts, Hel," said Martha. "But that's not going to stop us. Far from it. We're going to find out. I promise you that, right now. We're going to find out."

She pushed a clump of frizzy hair from Helen's face and tilted her chin towards her. Tears were making her sister's eyes glassy but they hadn't fallen yet.

"You're owed that much," said Martha.

Helen sniffed and nodded. A look of determination chased away the sadness. She shook out her arms and rolled her head, neck and shoulders.

"Right, let's do this," she said, leading the way.

The Parkers raced over to the door Tom and Roberta had disappeared into. Martha pulled it open and was met with a wall of heat and sound. They ducked inside and found the small outbuilding was full of generators, powering the main terminal. Huge, thick pipes and cables lined the roof, everything hidden behind cages, large boxes with flashing lights and important looking buttons the only light source. The pulsing sound made it impossible to hear anything. Only a flash of brightness from the far end of the building showed them where Tom and Roberta had gone.

"Over there!" Martha shouted but the others didn't respond.

She grabbed them and pointed across the generator room towards the light. They rounded the huge machinery and found another door. Barging through, it opened up to the other side of the high security fences. The terminal building loomed up behind them—long, skeletal arms stretching out from gates to waiting planes. A dry wind billowed across the huge, open space of the airfield.

"There they are!" said Helen.

Martha spotted four figures running away from them, dark smudges on the horizon. She started after them, Geri and Helen following. The roar of plane engines sounded out from somewhere overhead. The wind carried it into Martha's ears and she spotted a huge aircraft coming out of the night like a skyscraper with wings. If they hadn't been in hot pursuit she would have marvelled at being so close to the action.

Tom, Roberta and their security guards were heading for a small row of hangars towards the outer edge of the airport campus. This part of the airfield was empty and sparse. Only a few buildings were dotted about close to the perimeter fence. Cars and vans in official livery of the airport authority were parked lazily about, although their owners were nowhere to be seen.

Martha was panting and puffing but she kept going. They had come so close now, they'd ridden their luck enough to catch Roberta before she'd managed to skip town. They couldn't let her get away now.

More blue flashes cheered her. The snaking carriageway of the motorway weaved its way down the side of the airfield. More police cars and squad vans, coming to the rescue.

"She did it," said Martha to the others. "Pope, she called in the troops."

"We're almost there," said Geri.

The others disappeared through the huge doors of the nearest in a long row of hangars. Martha, Helen and Geri hurtled after them. Inside was a sleek, silver jet. Sitting like a trophy on a shelf, the aircraft seemed to ooze wealth, from the tip of its pointed, well-polished nose all the way back to the tailfin.

The steps were down at the front door, Tom wrestling a pilot in a short sleeved white shirt and cap up into the plane. Roberta was close behind him. She spotted Martha, Helen and Geri running towards them. Barking something to the two security guards, she sent them off to intercept the Parkers like wolves as she climbed onboard.

"That's far enough," said one of the guards, holding up a hand, sweat pouring down his forehead.

Martha, Helen and Geri slowly came to a stop. Out of breath, their joints burning, they kept their distance.

"What do we do now?" asked Geri.

The engines of the jet started up. The high-pitched squeal pierced their ears. It wasn't much but enough to distract the two man-mountains in black bearing down on them.

"Scatter," Martha shouted. "They can't catch us all. Make for the plane."

She shoved Helen off to her left as Geri darted to the right. The minders were distracted but it didn't take them long to work out what the plan was. They immediately took off after the sisters. Martha, the least able of the three, drew on every reserve she had. As one of the guards came lunging towards her, arms out wide like a grizzly bear, she ducked at the last minute. He let out a short grunt as he tripped over his own feet, crashing down face first onto the concrete.

Martha didn't look back. She sprinted—or as close to sprinting as she could still muster—towards the plane. The door was still open, a flurry of movement in the cockpit as figures moved back and forth preparing for take-off.

"Martha," called Helen, running towards her. "They're going to get away."

"Quick! Hurry!"

"Where's Geri?"

The plane's sleek fuselage loomed at them, its engines getting noisier by the second. Martha spotted Geri at the other end of the plane. She was cornered by the other guard towards the back of the hangar. He grabbed her, hands snatching at her jacket. He pulled her backwards with a short, sharp tug.

"Geri," Martha yelled.

"Go," Geri shouted back. "Get Roberta and that bugger, Tom."

Martha blinked. She had no time to think twice. Grabbing hold of Helen, she hurried them up the steps of the private jet.

Thirty-Nine

MARTHA TRIED NOT to let the opulence of the aircraft cloud her judgement, although it was very nice. From the floors to the fine wood that lined the walls, everything smelled of rich leather. It was stylish and classy, the perfect way to fly.

"Blimey," she let slip as they hurried into the cabin. "How the one percent live."

There was nobody about. The main cabin of the private jet stretched out, narrow and long, in front of them.

"Be careful," said Martha, stepping forward.

She took a few tentative steps, Helen hanging on her shoulder. Then there was a short gulp and she froze.

"Martha," Helen gargled.

She spun around. Tom had Helen by the throat, his tanned hand wrapped all the way round. He sneered at Martha and then nodded over her shoulder.

"Bravo, Ms Parker," came Roberta's voice, smooth as engine oil.

The media mogul emerged from a small alcove at the rear of the jet. She was still immaculately dressed, not a single hair out of place despite the pursuit. If someone could suit their surroundings more than Roberta Steiner in her luxury jet, Martha wasn't convinced. She exuded confidence, a confidence that she'd never seen before.

"Let her go Tom," said Martha, turning back towards the door. "I swear, if you hurt her, I'll break every bone in your body."

"Oh, I'm so scared," he laughed mockingly. "Trust me Martha, there's nothing you or this moron here is capable of that could hurt me. You lot couldn't hurt a fly even if you tried. And that's not a good thing by the way."

"Let her go," Martha repeated.

Tom stopped his sneering. He looked over to Roberta for instruction, then slowly released his grip on Helen. She fell forward, coughing and spluttering. Martha caught her before she tripped over.

"Close that goddamn door," said Roberta. "Tell the pilot to get us out of here."

"You can't do that," said Martha. "That's kidnap."

"Well done, very astute. You should be a private detective."

Tom laughed. He ducked out of the cabin and headed for the door. Roberta glided down the central aisle and took up one of the seats close to the Parkers. Straightening the cuffs of her blouse, she crossed her legs and flashed them a smile.

"You might as well settle in," she said. "It's seven hours to Chicago. We'll have a welcome party waiting for you when we get off."

"Chicago!" Helen blurted.

"Oh yes," said the mogul. "The police will be waiting for you two there. You'll be arrested of course, for breaking and entering onto private property. And what else, let me see, harassment, stalking, threatening behaviour, the list is endless. All less than a day after the death of my dear, departed husband. It's so very tragic. The media will eat it up."

Her words sent a cold chill through Martha. It must have passed to Helen who also shivered.

"So. Sit. Down," Roberta's instructions were clear.

Martha nodded to Helen and they both took up the chairs on the opposite side of the aisle. The plane was still trundling along slowly, the airfield wide and open ahead of them. There was still time, thought Martha. Still time to get out of this mess. She worried about Geri and where Superintendent Ghosh's forces were. She still had time to get the confession, she just had to keep Roberta talking.

"We were right then," she said, baiting the hook. "You *did* kill Murray."

"What an ugly thing to say Martha," Roberta feigned shock. "The idea that you would suggest I poisoned my husband, one of the most famous men in the world, is appalling. In fact, it's nothing short of preposterous, as you Brits like to say."

"Cute," said Helen. "We're right though. You did do it."

Roberta sat forward. She pulled open a drawer in the gilded table beside her seat. For a brief moment Martha held her breath, frightened she would produce a gun. Instead Roberta fetched a packet of cigarettes. Unpeeling the wrapper, she offered one to Martha and then Helen.

"Smoke?" she asked.

"No thank you," said Martha.

"I'd rather drink the toilet water," said Helen. "And it'd be better for me."

"That can be arranged." She lit the cigarette with a brushed gold lighter and took a long, hard drag. Blowing the smoke up into the filtered air of the cabin, she picked at her nails, cold eyes locked hard on the Parkers across from her.

"You three did me a favour," she said. "Well, you two didn't. Geri did, the little idiot. She fell right into Murray's lap, quite literally. The dirty old bastard could never resist a little bit of charm and adulation from a young woman. He was like a vampire, sucking the life force out of everyone and anyone who dared get too close."

"Including you," Helen challenged her. "Especially you, in fact."

"Spot on," Roberta winked at her. "I flew *far* too close to that light. Sure, it was attractive at first, charming even. He had a magnetism, something about him that made me think he was always going to be a star. Even when we used to shakedown perps in the early days, he did it with a sort of Hollywood glamour. He was destined to be a star. And, oh, didn't he know it."

She took another long drag of her cigarette. Martha had every sympathy for Roberta. She really did. She'd seen the woman's husband in altogether too close and too ugly a light the night before. A flash of blue whizzed past the window behind her. Then another and another after that. The police were close by but the jet was still moving.

"That doesn't warrant murdering him," she said. "There must have been other options. Nothing could ever justify killing somebody, taking another life Roberta. You've spent your whole life championing justice, enforcing the law, helping others when the odds were stacked against them. Why would you do this?"

"To be perfectly honest with you both," she said with a sad laugh. "It was quite by accident."

"Accident? How can you poison your husband by accident?"

"I never intended for him to die, not last night anyway," she said almost casually. "He was allergic to everything under the sun. And he wouldn't ever let me forget about it. But, as was always the case, it was up to me to make sure that Murray got what Murray wanted. That gave me unfiltered access to everything he put in his mouth. Well, not *everything* and I don't want to think about what I couldn't see or didn't know about. Every meal, morning, noon and night, I had final say. So who was going to know if something was slipped in there, eh? A little tablet, a potassium supplement mashed into his potato? A crumbled pill into his breakfast cereal. Nobody would suspect a thing because I was the loving wife, the darling other half of everyone's favourite scoundrel and lovable rogue.

"I got the idea from one of our cases. The irony. Some bored housewife in the Hollywood Hills had married an old oil baron retired to the California sunshine. You know the type, she's all flouncy hair and bikinis and he can barely raise a smile. She'd been hoping she wouldn't have to spend too long after their nuptials with this old geezer hanging around. What she didn't expect was his big, brash Texas genetics to keep him hanging in there for a decade.

Eventually, she gets bored, you see? Wants to start spending some of that hard earned inheritance. So she started slipping him rat poison in his dinner, then in his lunch too and finally his breakfast. We get called in to do a fly on the wall documentary with the LAPD. She gets caught, gets sent to jail and the family inherit the fortune. Watertight."

"And you did the same to Murray?"

"Potassium is a lot less suspicious when it shows up on a coroner's report sweetheart," said Roberta. "He wasn't exactly a clean living, upstanding member of our community, was he?"

"Very good," said Helen.

Roberta reached back into the drawer. She pulled out a little vial, two pills rattling about at the bottom.

"His dinner last night, when you three were there," she said. "Murray being the pig that he was, distracted by three new women to ogle at, ate it all up and didn't know the difference."

She finished her cigarette and crushed it out on the tabletop. Blowing away the last of the smoke, she reclined in her leather chair.

"Surely you must have known putting a large amount of that stuff would kill him," said Martha. "You couldn't possibly think you could get away with something as ridiculous as this?"

"Now that is something we agree on," she said. "Murray being Murray, his appetite only grew and grew the more he had. And the more of the stuff I kept putting into his meals the more resistant he became. So I kept upping the dose until…"

She ran an elegant finger across her throat. Martha swallowed, her mouth dry.

"So it was a mistake then? You didn't mean to kill him?"

"I always intended on killing him," said Roberta casually. "I just didn't think the dose I gave him last night would put him away. The timing was terrible. But you live and learn, don't you?"

"Don't you feel any remorse?" Martha blurted. "He was your husband. You said you *loved* him. Maybe not recently, but there was something there at one stage of your lives. Doesn't that count for something?"

"Hello?" said Roberta. "Where have you been for the last few hours Martha. Have you seen what's on the news? Have you read what people are talking about on social media? Murray Steiner, from coast to coast, all around the world. The world's media has been camped outside the hotel all day. And they're likely to be waiting for me when I touch down back in LA. This is publicity, sweetheart. The kind of publicity that *nobody* can buy, not even me. Subscriptions for next year's conference have gone through the roof. We literally can't print the tickets and release them fast enough for demand. I've made more money in the last twenty hours than I did in the last decade. And it's all down to a little pill."

"Eleanor David wouldn't agree," said Helen. "In fact she'll have plenty of time to be sitting stewing over what she'll do to you when she gets out of prison."

"I'm sorry, didn't you hear her confession?" asked Roberta. "She admitted to killing Murray. She's *more* than aware of what's ahead of her. And, more importantly, she's aware of the thirty million dollars waiting for her when she gets out, not to mention the healthcare for her family, the college tuition for her kids, the complete financial independence that she'll have gifted to her by a very generous anonymous donor when the conviction is confirmed."

"And she would do that for you?" asked Martha. "She would ruin her life just so you could get away with murder?"

"Honey, I don't know if you've had a bump on the head or something, you were a lot smarter this morning. Look around you—this jet cost a hundred million. It's mine, I paid for it in cash directly to the manufacturer. I'm Roberta Freakin' Steiner, one of the most famous and photographed women of *all* time. People would do *anything* for me if I asked them to."

"Not everyone," said Tom, stepping back into the cabin.

Roberta smiled at him. She reached out and took his hand. He leaned down and pecked her on the cheek before whispering in her ear.

"What!" Roberta roared.

She pushed herself up from her seat and stormed off towards the cockpit.

"What's the matter? Trouble in paradise?" Helen spat.

Tom laughed. He shook his head, scratching at the stubble on the side of his face.

"You know, I really should give you guys some credit," he said. "You genuinely are smarter than everyone thinks you are. Even Roberta."

"And what's that supposed to mean?" asked Helen.

"It means that even the big boss was surprised that you guys kept coming back and back and back. You should take that as a compliment."

"What's your angle in all of this anyway?" asked Helen, struggling to contain her anger. "Are you her toy boy or do you just like to sell out the people that trust you?"

"Bit of both actually," he blew out his cheeks and slid down into Roberta's seat. "We met about eighteen months ago. I went for a job as an intern at the Murray headquarters in LA. Mrs Steiner, as I knew her then, was very impressed with my assets. And it just went from there."

"You knew about this then," asked Martha. "You knew she was going to kill Murray?"

"I wouldn't be hanging around for very long if I thought she was happily married, would I?" Tom flashed that easy smile again. "I might be thirty years younger than her but I'm not stupid. Anybody who'd spent even five seconds in their company could tell she hated that arsehole through and through."

"So where do we fit in?" asked Helen. "Or can you just not help yourself when it comes to seducing women with your open shirt and your chest hair and your rugged good looks."

Tom kept smiling. Helen didn't. She was furious.

"I was the insurance policy," he said. "We hadn't counted on your sister Geri spending the night with him. But it was the perfect alibi. That was until you three went rogue. Roberta didn't trust you to keep your mouths shut. There's a reason you were the guests of honour at this year's event. It says a lot about your reputation I suppose. Then again, it's a convention for private eyes, we had to make sure nobody was going to be sticking their nose in where it didn't belong. That's where I came in. I was the mole, sent down to keep an eye on you three and make sure you were drip fed just enough information that would keep you interested."

"We were taken for chumps," said Martha. "Very clever though. Keep us in the loop just enough that the truth is out there, meaning we wouldn't get suspicious if there was simply nothing to see."

"What about Eleanor David?" asked Helen. "Are you sleeping with her too?"

"She's a fanatic, as you already know," said Tom with a mocking laugh. "There's nothing that woman wouldn't do for Roberta. And she was no fan of Murray's either, let me tell you that much. She didn't take much convincing when Roberta spoke to her. The big payoff helped too, I imagine."

"Life is cheap," said Martha with a snort. "Especially when you've got all the money in the world."

"But there's still something I don't understand," said Helen. "You told us what was wrong with Murray, you led us to the hospital and your contact, what was her name…"

"Daisy," said Tom with a smirk.

"Yeah, Daisy," Helen went on. "If you were the so called insurance policy, why did you lead us right to the answer? Surely you were meant to throw us off the scent or something like that. Or are you just as rubbish at that as you are at being a nice person?"

That made Tom laugh loudly. He relaxed and stretched out in the luxurious chair. Running a hand through his immaculate hair, he smiled at Helen and Martha.

"You two are adorable," he said. "I don't think I've ever met two women who are as clever as you two are, but who can't see the big picture."

"Enlighten us then," said Martha. "You've got nothing else to lose now. We might as well know."

"Despite what you might think of me, I know that there are rules that need to be adhered to," he said, sitting forward. "And one of those rules is that to kill somebody, anybody, you have to be clever. Why do you think there are so many people locked up in the pokey for murder? It's because they didn't think the whole thing through properly. See, that's where I'm different, that's where Roberta's different. She's clever, she can see things before they happen, anticipate other people's moves before they've even thought about it themselves. It's a talent I guess."

"A talent wasted on a murderer," said Helen coldly.

"Roberta knew she couldn't just bump Murray off and that be it. She needed a scheme, something that was watertight, like she said. Sure, she might not have planned on killing Murray here in London, but she's capitalised on it. She thinks so quickly, it's quite amazing to watch actually."

"You haven't answered my question," said Helen. "Why give us the keys to the castle? Why let us know that there was something fishy afoot? Why not try to steer us *away* from suspicion? It doesn't make sense."

"The closer you are to danger, the further you are from harm," said Martha.

"What?" asked her sister.

Tom gave her an acknowledging salute. Martha afforded herself a little smile as the pieces all fell into place.

"If you're guilty you can hide in plain sight," she said. "Tom is Roberta's insurance policy, he's here to keep us from discovering the truth. But that doesn't stop him and Roberta from letting us *think* we've discovered the truth. Murray was poisoned, there's no hiding that from a post mortem. It just falls to the guilty party, who would take the blame. Tom leads you, me and Geri to his contact at the hospital, a stooge I presume?"

"No, far from it," said Tom. "Daisy is a quite brilliant forensic scientist actually. She has no idea what I've been up to."

"Roberta gives us a hard time, although we made a rod for our own backs with all of that," Martha continued. "We start our own investigations and ultimately it leads to Eleanor's confession… because it was always going to lead to Eleanor."

"Roberta is one of the smartest women I've ever known," said Tom. "The way she orchestrated all of this at such speed was, quite frankly, breathtaking. I mean, I was tucked up in my bed at three o'clock this morning happily dreaming of our next encounter when I got the call. I was briefed, given a backstory, everything all within two hours. All I had to do was wait until you lot came down to breakfast and boom, boat that bass."

"So we were just a fishing expedition?" said Helen scornfully.

"Hey, just a figure of speech, Hel," he laughed. "But like I said, you guys should be honoured. Out of all the so called investigators that showed up to this convention, you lot were the only ones Roberta saw as a legitimate threat. And you proved her right in the end. You refused to give up, that's why you're here now."

"Thanks," said Martha. "We'll try to remain very proud of ourselves."

"Tom," Roberta called. "Get your ass in here. Now."

Like a scorned puppy, the Australian sprang into action. He hurried down the aisle and headed to the cockpit. Martha didn't hesitate. She lunged forward and grabbed the vial of potassium pills lying on the table. Holding them, she peered out of the window. The main terminal building was in the distance. A small army of police cars and vans were between it and the jet.

"What's going on out there?" asked Helen.

"We're going around and around in circles," said Martha.

"He won't take off," Roberta screamed from the front of the plane. "Get in there and make him get this goddamn bird in the air."

"He's the pilot, Roberta," Tom pleaded. "He knows what he's doing."

"Make him fly," she screamed again.

A sudden wave of panic came over Martha. She was very aware of what was going on now. They were hurtling around Heathrow Airport in a private jet, Roberta Steiner adamant that they should take off against the better judgement of the pilot. The police were outside the window trying to get them to stop. This could get very dangerous very quickly.

"Helen—" she said.

A mighty shunt came from behind. The whole aircraft started to spin, its tyres squealing on the tarmac. Martha was thrown against the table and landed in a heap on the floor. Dazed, she tried to get up, but another shunt sent her reeling. The whole plane started to lean to one side and she heard a scream from near the front.

Grabbing the underside of a nearby table, she pulled herself to her feet. She could see straight down the central aisle to the cockpit, the door rattling against the wall. The pilot was furiously wrestling with the controls as the plane pulled away from him. The runway disappeared beneath them, concrete turning to grass. There was a bump, then a jump, before the plane came to a sudden, dead stop, throwing everything and everyone forward.

Martha could taste blood. She touched a finger to her mouth and saw it turn scarlet, a heavy, throbbing pain in her stomach. As everything settled, she untangled herself and reached over to Helen, white as a sheet, clinging on to her seat for dear life.

"Are you alright?" she asked.

Before Helen could answer, a loud bang erupted from the front of the plane. There was shouting and flashing white lights, angry voices barking orders. Footsteps thudded down the aisle amid all the confusion. Martha and Helen were picked up by heavy, rough hands and dragged out of the aircraft. It all happened so suddenly that they didn't know what was going on. Only when they emerged onto the runway did they see the huge fire engine with a giant bash in its side where it had rammed the jet.

The Parkers were led away from the crash as a hundred different emergency service workers descended on them. Amongst the mayhem Martha heard a voice.

"Yoo-hoo!" it called.

She looked up. There, amid the flashing blue lights and chaos, was Geri. Flanked by cops, she waved at Martha and Helen.

"Did you miss me?" she asked.

"Get your hands off me." Martha spun around. Roberta emerged from the wreckage, looking as dishevelled as anyone had ever seen her. The immaculate hairdo was ripped and torn, her smart business suit just as tatty. A heel was broken on one of her expensive stilettos and she limped almost comically as the police guided her away from the plane.

Tom wasn't much better. Cuffed and struggling, he tried to wrestle his way free from the iron grip of the officers. He started swearing, all of his easy charm now firmly gone. They were both led into waiting police cars, the doors closing on them with a hard, sturdy finality.

And in that moment, Martha suddenly felt quite at ease. The weight of what had gone on was lifted. She could breathe again. The ordeal was over. For the briefest, most chaotic moments among the bedlam of the airfield, she could rest. She looked down at her hand and realised it was still clenched tightly shut. As she unfolded it, the little vial of pills came into view, intact, whole, two tablets still inside.

"Bloody hell," she said. "What a stroke of luck."

Forty

"PASS ME ANOTHER one of those digestives would you?" asked Helen.

She reached across Martha and Geri's laps and grabbed the plate. The drone of the porcelain on the tabletop filled the stale silence of the command centre. There was nobody else about, just the three of them, wrapped in blankets with their tea getting cold. Helen greedily scoffed two of the biscuits before offering the last one to the others.

"No thank you," said Martha, numb.

"You're a monster, Helen Parker," said Geri. "Come rain or shine, your stomach knows no end. It's a bottomless pit. Even in times of great crisis the beast must be fed."

"Suit yourself," said Helen, dribbling crumbs. "Being kidnapped by an international media mogul and surviving a plane crash must make me ravenous."

"Give me strength," said Geri, puffing out her cheeks.

Martha sat between her two sisters. She stared blankly ahead of her, not really paying attention. Something was wrong.

"Jesus, Mart, you look terrible," said Geri.

It was enough to snap her out of her trance. She sniffed and smiled weakly.

"I think I've finally hit the wall," she said. "I think after everything we've been through that my mind and my body have finally thrown their hands up and said that enough is enough. I don't even think I could stand up if I wanted to. I'm stuck."

"How's your… you know?" Helen tapped her own chest.

"Fine, I suppose," said Martha. "I mean I don't think I'm going to have a heart attack or anything. I genuinely don't think I've got the energy. This was supposed to be a relaxing weekend away, remember? A chance to let our hair down, be celebrated and bask in the reflected glory of the world's finest private investigators. Now look at us. It's nearly four in the morning, we haven't had any sleep, we've been all over London and back again and the world's most famous private detectives are either dead or in jail."

"Just another Parkers road trip," said Geri.

"You two are being far too dramatic as usual," said Helen, licking the chocolate from her fingers. "I don't know why I put up with you."

Both Martha and Geri turned to give their sister a dirty look.

"Drama queens, the pair of you," she said, draining her cup of tea. "Everything is one great, big drama. You should both just be grateful that we're here, we have our health and that's all there is to say about it."

"But you're just after saying—"

"Don't Geri," Martha quietened her youngest sister down.

"But she—"

"Don't," she shook her head. "It's not worth it."

The Parkers sat in silence for a little while longer. The command centre was still. They had been dropped off and told to wait. Being the good citizens they were, nobody had argued. It was peaceful and quiet, just what Martha had hoped for.

"Good evening ladies," said Superintendent Ghosh.

He appeared from behind them leading a team of officers. They proceeded to head to their computer terminals and within seconds the command centre was brought back into life. Martha stifled a sigh.

"Seems you three have had quite the evening," he said, removing his cap. "Can I get you anymore tea?"

"Oh that would—"

"We're fine," said Martha, cutting off Helen.

The senior cop smiled a little, his cheek twitching. He gave a quick look about the command centre to make sure his officers were at work before sitting down on the opposite side of the table. He reclined in the chair and let out a long groan before rubbing his eyes.

"You know, nights like this take me back to when my daughters were just born," he said. "Interrupted sleep and it feels like the sun is never going to come up. They're all grown up now of course but I still don't get a wink of sleep, even when I'm off duty. I guess you just get used to it. Do any of you three have kids?"

"Just me," said Martha. "One daughter, Margot."

"Ah, lucky you. Is she grown up?"

"She is," she said. "And, like her father, she usually doesn't want anything to do with my work."

"Then she would probably get on well with my daughters," smiled the Super. "Neither of them wanted to follow in their old dad's footsteps and join the Met. A shame really, I'm third generation. Although it was a blessing if you asked my wife. I don't think her nerves could have handled three police officers in the family."

"What do they do then?" asked Geri.

"One's a doctor," Ghosh beamed with pride. "Just graduated, she'll be heading up to Liverpool in August to take up her new post. And the other, the younger one, she's a plumber."

"Blimey," said Helen. "Quite a contrast there then."

"Not really," said Ghosh shrugging. "The medic is constantly skint whereas the plumber drives a Mercedes. Go figure."

Martha smiled at that. She liked Superintendent Ghosh. He had an approachable demeanour, a man who was comfortable in his own skin. His rank was inconsequential. He was somebody she could trust.

"As long as they're happy," she said. "That's all that matters. I tell these two the same."

"You're a strong family unit, I can tell," said Ghosh. "Families are important things. You don't get to choose them, like you do your friends or your partners, but they're always there for you, even when the proverbial hits the fan. As we've seen tonight. Although judging by the phone call my department received from the force up your neck of the woods, this isn't your first dabble with catching bad guys."

"No, it's not," said Martha. "And believe me, I wish that wasn't the case. I yearn for the days when the only problems we had to worry about were staking out blocks of flats waiting for cheating husbands to appear."

"Hey, that wasn't *that* long ago," said Helen.

"No, it wasn't," said Martha.

Ghosh laughed.

"You know your friend, DS Pope, spoke very highly of you," he said. "She said that she would be willing to put her entire reputation on you three being right about Roberta Steiner."

Martha felt a tinge of pride.

"Really?" asked Geri. "Old torn-face Pope said that about us."

"She did. And if I know police officers the way I think I do, coming out with that sort of chatter isn't done lightly."

"She's a very kind and generous woman," said Martha diplomatically. "We owe her a lot."

"And speaking of debts, it seems that I owe you three an apology." He leaned forward, clasping his hands together on the table. He was still smiling. "I'm a superintendent in the Metropolitan Police. We have some of the finest minds, most able officers and near endless resources when it comes to catching criminals. We have complete faith in the justice system and we're always, I repeat *always,* beyond reproach when it comes to our policing. I am, however, still human. And when I'm wrong or I haven't done something as thoroughly as I could have, I'm will admit that is the case. This, ladies, is one of those occasions."

"That's very kind of you Superintendent Ghosh," said Martha. "But really, this isn't about trying to pull the rug from under the feet of the Met. In fact, that was the last thing we wanted to do."

"There was a murderer on the loose," said Geri. "We knew who it was and we went after her. A simple equation really."

"Even if that meant breaking into a secure hospital unit? Even if that meant setting off a fire alarm at a major international airport terminal? Even if that meant endangering the lives, not only of yourselves, but of countless others with that private jet stunt?"

"Technically I wasn't on the jet," said Geri. "In fact, I was the one who flagged you guys down, so that should mean I should have one less blot on my record."

"Crawler," hissed Helen.

"Quiet you two," Martha hushed up the others.

Ghosh waited patiently. His look was still friendly, if a little more serious. He wanted answers.

"Superintendent, I'm sorry," she said. "I'm sorry we did what we did. We're passionate people, all three of us. We enjoy our work, most of the time. But most of all, we want the same thing as you. We want justice to be served. We all knew that Roberta Steiner was the killer, we just had to hear it from her."

"What about evidence? Did that cross your minds at all?" he asked. "The first rule of any investigation work is to secure the proof of what your accusations are."

"Yes, we know that," said Helen. "We were guests of honour at SteinerCon, you know."

Ghosh leaned back. He took a long breath in through his nose and then let it out again.

"The vial of pills," he said. "The ones you handed over to my officers at the airport."

"The potassium tablets, yes," said Martha. "I swiped them from Roberta's plane."

"They're covered in your prints," he said.

Martha panicked for a moment. She didn't like where this was going.

"Now what I'm about to tell you is strictly between us," he said, in a low voice. "But, with a little tidying up and a *lot* of hard work, my forensics teams are quite convinced they'll be able to find any other prints on that vial. Should, and I stress the *should* part, they be found to match the wife of the deceased, then there would be a very high chance, not absolute, but very high chance that Mrs Steiner could be linked to the poisoning of Mr Steiner."

"And that would mean that Eleanor David would be acquitted?" asked Helen.

"Not entirely," he said. "If what your statements say are true, which judging by the glowing reference DS Pope has provided they probably are, then she'll be charged as being an accessory. The same goes for Tom Hopgood."

Martha felt a flood of energy come surging back into her. It felt like she was waking up from a long sleep. Helen and Geri were much more ecstatic. They jumped for joy and celebrated, hugging each other and their older sister.

"Alright, settle down now," said the Super. "This is a police command centre not a kids 'birthday party."

"What about us?" asked Martha as the elation died down.

"I can't stress enough how disappointed the Met is with your behaviour. One of my officers is currently undergoing counselling for losing his hat."

Geri began to blush.

"But in all seriousness, this has been an ordeal for everyone involved," said Ghosh. "And while I can't thank you all enough for your commitment and actions going above and beyond the call of duty, I can't stress enough that this sort of thing should be left up to the professionals. We're the police ladies, this is what we do. We're trained in this sort of thing. Your help is very gratefully received. But you have to be much more careful in the future."

Superintendent Ghosh stood up. He picked up his hat and placed it smartly on his head.

"What's to happen to us now?" asked Helen.

"You're free to go," he said. "We have your details should we need to speak to you further as part of our investigations. But as far as I'm concerned, you've all done more than your fair share. I wish you a pleasant journey back up to bonnie Scotland."

The senior officer stood to one side. One of his team opened a door of the command centre and waited patiently for the Parkers to leave. Helen and Geri bid their goodbyes and Martha lingered a little behind.

"Thank you for this," she said. "It means a great deal to know that we're finished here."

"I know," he said quietly. "But I mean what I said, Martha. This is a dangerous world, these are dangerous people. We're the police, we see these things day in and day out. Take care of yourself and your sisters. Helen would eat us out of house and home if she could. And young Geri is sharp as a pin. They'll both go very far, just like our kids."

"I know they will," said Martha with a smile.

She shook Ghosh's hand and followed the others out of the command centre. The car park outside the hotel was quiet, all the journalists were off home or still lingering around the airport. Martha paused at the top of the stairs, as Helen and Geri walked off towards the hotel entrance.

The first rays of dawn were beginning to poke through the trees of Hyde Park. A new day at last. Martha hoped that it would be much better than the one she had just lived through. It wouldn't be hard. She closed her eyes and felt the cool morning air caress her face, her greasy, sweaty, unkempt hair bobbing gently against her neck. She was ridiculously tired, but also unimaginably grateful—for lots of things. But mostly, her freedom. She stepped down from the command centre and took a long, slow walk back towards the hotel. She was looking forward to going home.

Forty-One

MILK, BREAD, GRAPES, apples, cereal, juice, butter, yoghurts and toilet roll. Martha had committed that list to her memory. And it was going around and around in her head as she walked up and down the aisles.

She didn't want to look at the bit of paper in her hand. She wanted to see if she could properly remember it this time. If the adventure in London a month ago had taught her anything it was that she shouldn't be so hard on herself. But this was a matter of principle. She was determined, come hell or high water, to remember the shopping list.

"Milk, bread, grapes, apples, cereal, juice, butter, yoghurts and toilet roll," she said to herself, handling the trolley like a master. "Damn. I think I've forgotten something."

Life, thankfully, had taken a much quieter turn for Parkers Investigations. In fact, she hadn't opened the doors of the office in almost a fortnight. Giving her faithful employees some well-deserved time off, Martha had enjoyed some rest and recuperation. The London affair had taken its toll on all of them, emotionally and physically. She had absolutely no desire to venture much beyond the front door for the foreseeable future. The back garden would be *more* than sufficient stimulation for a good while yet.

Toby the tomcat didn't agree though. No open office meant no biscuits to steal. As a result he'd gone off to find a happier hunting ground. Martha still suspected he had another, if not more than one, family in the block who were feeding him. She thought that maybe some cat food had been the one that got away from her memory. Then she remembered she had a whole stack of tins hidden out of sight beneath the sink.

There was nothing else for it. She had to check. Unfurling the scrap bit of paper, she clicked her fingers.

"Corned beef for mum," she said.

Doing an about turn, she grabbed the trolley quickly, stopping it before it clattered into two old ladies walking behind her. The realisation that it was Rose and Pat did nothing for her confidence.

"Oh I'm sorry love," said Pat. "I didn't see you… oh, look who it is Rose."

"Who is it?" asked Rose.

"Ah, hello… again," said Martha awkwardly. "Look ladies, I would dearly love to stay and chat, but I'm actually running behind schedule and there are—

"Have you seen the news?" asked Rose.

"News? What news?" asked Martha.

"Get your newspaper out Pat," the pensioner said.

"Oh hold on, wait a minute, I've got it here," said Rose, reaching into her bag.

"You shouldn't put that in there if you haven't paid for it."

"I'll pay for it when we get to the checkout."

"You'll forget."

"I won't forget."

"You *will* forget Pat, you're *always* forgetting."

"My memory isn't as bad as *yours*."

"Ladies," said Martha, trying not to lose her patience. "Please. I really do have a lot to be getting on with."

"Here we are," said Pat, pulling out her paper.

She handed it to Martha. A picture of Roberta Steiner looked back at her. It wasn't glamorous or staged, anything but. The media mogul was in a drab jumper, no makeup, all her wrinkles on display for the world to see. Her hair was dishevelled, her eyes dead and empty. It was as ugly a mugshot as Martha had ever seen. And above it, the words 'I DID IT'.

"Roberta Steiner," said Rose. "She murdered her husband. Isn't that awful?"

"We thought you might want to know seeing as you're a private detective," added Pat. "She's the most famous private detective in the world."

"Well, her husband is… Was. I always liked Murray Steiner. He was such a lovely man."

"He used to be," said Pat. "He's dead now."

"Well of course he's dead Pat, she's just admitted to killing him."

"Who?" asked Pat.

"Roberta Steiner," said Rose.

Martha tried to ignore her geriatric fans. She scanned the front page article and then inside. Since they'd come home she had taken a break from the news. A lot of it was down to the fear of Roberta getting away. In those few seconds though, she caught up on what had been happening.

"She admitted it in court," she said aloud. "She said it was a crime of passion, according to this."

"How romantic," said Rose, then poked a finger down her throat. "I hope they lock her away for good. Murray Steiner was a lovely man."

"Bloody shame what happened to him," said Pat.

Martha had read enough. She folded up the paper and handed it back to the pensioners.

"Thank you ladies, thank you for thinking of me," she said. "One bit of advice though. Never meet your heroes."

"Eh?" Rose and Pat said in unison.

Martha pushed the trolley past them and carried on with her shopping. She afforded herself a little smile, knowing that Roberta Steiner was going to jail. But better still, nobody knew who had caught her. Martha liked it when that happened. It made the shopping so much easier.

ACKNOWLEDGEMENTS

I cannot, in good faith, NOT start the acknowledgements for this book without thanking my family. This is the first novel that I've written as a father. And the time, patience, effort and general awesomeness that my wife, my new baby son and my extended family have afforded me has meant the absolute world. At the time of writing, it's been a very odd, very challenging, but most of all bloody brilliant time in the Whitelaw household. Throwing an adventure with the Parker sisters into that mix has felt a bit like the icing on top of the cake. So it is with a million gestures of thanks that I bow down to my family and offer them my eternal gratitude.

And speaking of families, I'd also like to thank a much wider, more extended group who have fast become very much LIKE family. The writing community in general has been a great supporter of me throughout my career. Without everyone who is involved – writers, publishers, agents, bloggers, fans and of course, you, the reader – I highly doubt I would be the scribe that I am today. Yes, it's all YOUR fault. I jest of course. There are a few names I'd like to drop specifically though – Chris McDonald and Rob Parker – fellow Red Dog kennel mates, who have shown boundless enthusiasm towards any and every question I can throw at them. Marion Todd who continues to say such lovely things about my writing and is STILL faithfully waiting on her £5 bribe in the post. Both the Bay Tales and Honey and Stag teams, who dedicate so much time to helping writers do their thing. Steven Kedie, without whose constant music recommendations, I probably would still be listening to a load of rubbish.

And of course, the brilliant Red Dog team – Sean Coleman and Meggy Roussel – without w this book in your hands wouldn't exist and I would simply be another loudmouth on Twitter.

JW

Lightning Source UK Ltd.
Milton Keynes UK
UKHW010453080921
390192UK00004B/1188

9 781914 480287